C000133969

OUTCAST
SISTER

Noir detective fiction with a psychological edge

JAMES DAVIDSON

Published by The Book Folks

London, 2023

ISBN 978-1-80462-126-4

www.thebookfolks.com

For my parents

Prologue

The doctor woke screaming. He clawed himself out of the tangled, soaked sheets, and tumbled onto the floor. A freezing draught filtered through some hidden crack, offering a hint of relief. He tore off the damp shirt and underwear that stuck to his skin, and rolled on the ground. Tongue stuck out, he sought a taste of the cold, but it was no use. A skein of slime coated his skin and from deep in his bones he felt a wave of disgust and malice pulsate. He convulsed, writhing, trying to find purchase, something to cling onto while the fit possessed him.

Black vomit burst from his insides and sprayed into the unknown. He opened himself and let it unravel – bitter, sluicing, howling. The stream carried everything. When it was spent, he lay still and waited to die. But he didn't die. *Where am I?* His hands flung out in the dark and found a wall. He opened his eyes. Through a red fog, he found himself in a room with a bed, a door, and a closed window. He staggered to the door and tried the handle. Locked. He would have roared with loss, but he lacked the strength to make a sound. If he could call out, somebody might hear… but there no sound at all in this building, wherever it was. He crawled to the window, but it was slow progress, one inch at a time, crooked fingers hooking the floorboards, shifting his weightless corpse while the legs kicked uselessly.

At the foot of the window, he stopped to rest. A distant sound of cars on a highway reached him through the glass, and he might have wept. Life would not let him go, as much as he despised living. He tried but couldn't lift himself. His hands searched, experimentally, waving above his head, and tugged at the corner of a ledge. Above, the window was blocked with a metal grate. He was trapped. A hot tear broke the surface of his eye and rolled down his cheek, surprising him; there was still a source of moisture in his body.

He managed to lift himself and looked out through a gap in the grating. It was night outside. He was upstairs, looking out from a first-floor bedroom. He saw a row of shadowy houses picked out by a few lit windows. It seemed to be a housing estate, but there were no streetlights; the place was swallowed up in darkness. Something banged in the front yard just below. Stunned by the sound, he tottered, slipped, and hit his head on the floorboards. In a drowsy sprawl, he lay on the ground where he had landed and let himself splay. Outside, the banging sounded again. *What is that?* An unseen hand was hammering nails into wood. It sounded like a coffin being closed. As his consciousness wavered, he tried to remember anything. All he could think of was a name with a line drawn through it:

~~Eleanor~~

Thud, thud, thud, the nails bit and sank, sealing him inside as he slept.

1

Eleanor dreamt of home. Her cheeks were stained with dry tears when she woke with a gasp and couldn't remember where she was. The mobile phone under her pillow was vibrating, sending tremors through the mattress. Somebody groaned and stirred beside her in the bed. A man's hairy and sweaty arm brushed her side as he rolled in a dream. She almost screamed, but he didn't wake at the rumble of the phone. His thick breathing slowed and he sank back into sleep.

Eleanor tilted the screen to read the caller in the dark, but it was just a number. She pressed the phone to her ear and listened. Fuzz.

A voice said, 'We know who you are.'

The words made no sense, the voice even less.

'Who…?' She stopped as the sleeper beside her let out an arrhythmic snore.

'Run away, while you can,' the voice hissed.

'I'm going to hang up now. If you call again, I'll ring the police.'

'You *are* police. Think we don't know everything about you?' His cold voice was smug.

'What? Who are you…?'

The man beside her in the bed stirred; he seemed to wake up. She held her breath as he reached an arm around her and almost spoke, but it was just a drowsy mumble. His hot breath played on the skin of her neck as she cringed in his embrace.

Malicious laughter sounded in her ear, as if they were watching, as if they saw her confusion. 'You already know,' the voice said.

She focused, trying to pin the tone down, but it was quiet and distant in her ear. There was no trace of an accent, she couldn't even guess how old he was. She looked for a hint, anything she might recognize, but she was certain she'd never heard this voice before.

'What do you want?' she said.

'We want you to stop.'

'To stop what?'

'Don't play stupid. You forget, we know everything about you. There's no use pretending.'

'But—'

He laughed. 'And that man beside you, do you know who he is? Do you know his real name?'

They were watching her, somehow. Her eyes jumped around the room looking for a camera. Her heartbeat thumped through the bedframe. If the sleeper should wake…

'And so,' the voice in the phone sneered, 'you've finally grasped.'

'I'm going to hang up now.'

'Yes, hang up. Hang up right away. And run, Eleanor, run as fast as you can.'

* * *

Halfway down the street, she shivered and realized she'd run out leaving her coat behind. It was lost now; she'd never go back there. In the dark, early morning, the high street was empty. As she hurried along the pavement, she removed the sim card from her phone, threw the phone in a bin, chewed the card, and spat it into the next bin that she passed.

'Excuse me, missus.'

A voice from the shadows made her scream. She grabbed for a weapon and couldn't find one.

'Spare some change… It's freezing, I need a bed…'

She saw a homeless man bundled in the shadows against a wall by a cash machine. *He might be part of it. He might be one of them.*

'Missus, are you OK?'

She ran. Back at her apartment, she sprinted up the stairs and heard her feet too loud in the sleeping building. Would they be waiting here? Of course, they knew everything about her, they knew where she lived. It was dangerous to go back to the shitty little flat, but everything she owned was there. Through the front door with all its bolts and locks there was no sound inside, and nothing to see. It was all just the same as she'd left it, and yet the place felt different, like the walls were made of tissue. She threw a few clothes in a bag, stuffed her laptop in its case, and stopped.

What was she doing? This was crazy. Running out of her life, dropping everything, throwing away her sim card... for what? A prank phone call. She was losing it; she needed help, she'd known it for a while. She should speak to a psychiatrist or somebody, but she couldn't ask. There was nobody she could trust.

She dropped her bag on the floor and went into the kitchen to make a drink. While the kettle boiled, she tried to remember something good, or something true at least, but she found herself staring out of the window, through the tracks of rain, into the night, at the empty lot outside, terrified. There was nobody there among the bins and parked cars.

She made a drink and sipped it. That's what people say, have a cup of tea, you'll feel better. Maybe she did feel better. She could almost laugh. *Stop all of this, unpack your bag, retrace your steps and fish your mobile and sim card out of the bin.* She just needed to figure out how it all connected, then the creeping dread in her chest would stop. She'd been working on the gang for half a year now, observing them, mapping their operations. Someone involved must have identified her. They wanted to scare her away, but they wouldn't.

The phone in the hall started to ring. The sound echoed off the hard surfaces of the cramped flat. She almost choked on a mouthful of tea and spat it out. She ran into the hall and tore the phone cord from the wall and stood still with the lifeless, silent receiver in her hand.

2

The cold beginning of a new day came around, just like always. She hadn't run anywhere, and the threats of the unknown speaker on the phone hadn't materialised. In the dim, early morning, everything was normal, except she didn't have a phone, and she'd slept with her head on her arms on the kitchen table. She needed to get out of this claustrophobic flat. A bit of work at the office would clear her mind. She'd get to work on the gang, she'd shut them down.

It was still dark when she set off for the police station. The place was quiet when she arrived, an hour before the day shift started. The canteen and the staff room were empty, peaceful. She felt safe in here, among the blinking computers. The tension melted in her chest. She needed to speak to the boss, but he hadn't come in yet. Instead, she sat down at her desk and turned the computer on. As the screen came to life, she felt a void and realized she hadn't eaten since yesterday afternoon. *You're losing it, Eleanor.*

Scanning through her inbox, she stopped at an unopened message tagged "Oslo". She knew right away it was from Daniel.

Years had passed since his last message. For a while, after she first cut him off, along with her family and everyone else back home, he'd continued to send emails and messages to which she never replied, usually variations on the same theme: *Eleanor, I know you don't want to hear from me… I'm not asking for anything, not even an explanation… I don't know why you ran away, but I know it must have been my fault… if you ever wanted to come back…* and more of the same.

She wondered if he still had her name tattooed on his wrist. Perhaps he would have had it removed, but that wasn't like him. Daniel didn't go backwards. There were times she almost replied, if for no other reason than to make him stop, but maybe she didn't want him to stop. It had been years now since the last email. She assumed he'd moved on, met somebody new and settled down, but now, this message. "Oslo" was their special word. Nobody else knew about it.

She considered deleting the email without reading it, but with the night she'd spent, the dancing fears… she clicked and hunched over the screen, suddenly terrified of what it might say.

> *Eleanor,*
> *Can we talk? I'm in trouble. I'm scared. I've discovered something incredible. There's nobody I can trust.*
> *I don't care about the past anymore. I understand finally why you ran away: this place is stricken. Everything connects somehow. I think you know the answer. I can't talk about it here. I don't trust anyone on the police force. You're the only person I can talk to.*
> *Call me. Use the number below. Nobody else knows it.*

It didn't sound like Daniel; he was always a joker. The words were haunting, too close to her own fears. Did he know something about this knot around her throat, the phone call, the messages? Everything connected, somehow. It always had.

She looked for her mobile and remembered she'd thrown it away. How embarrassing; if her colleagues found out, they'd piss themselves. She picked up the receiver on her desk phone and entered the number Daniel had sent. At the sound of ringing in her ear, she knew she couldn't speak to him. Too raw, the memories, his red hair dusted with snow, his blue eyes in the cold. Oslo. *This isn't real, it can't be.* So why was she pressing the phone into her ear so tightly it hurt? She was about to hang up when the ringing stopped, somebody answered. She heard hoarse breathing.

'Daniel…?' she said.

The person on the other end laughed. It sounded like a girl, fluting and playful, but the laugh was vulgar.

'Who is that?' Eleanor said. 'Is Daniel there?'

The phone cut out. She listened to the disconnect tone, her mind blank. She opened the top drawer of her desk to find her notebook. The drawer was empty apart from a slip of paper. She lifted it out and read:

RUN, ELEANOR, RUN AS FAST AS YOU CAN

Her throat closed over like she was choking. She staggered out of the chair, knocking a tub of pens onto the floor. There was nobody else in the room. One of her colleagues must be part of it, maybe more than one of them. They must be involved with the gang. The corruption spread; it was worse than she'd thought. She'd run away from corrupt police before, but it had followed her here. The fine hairs of her neck felt somebody watching. She jumped up and scanned for a camera, a phone; all the blank screens of the office looked back at her. She ran out of the door.

She was hurrying down the corridor towards the entrance, when the boss came in and stopped, seeing her.

'Eleanor. You were supposed to…'

Could she trust him? Was he a part of it?

'Change of plan,' she said.

'Where are you going?'

'I think… I think I need some time off.'

'You look ill.' He stepped towards her, causing her to flinch. 'Are you alright?'

'I don't know. Stress, I guess. This operation, it's getting to me. I need a break.'

'But now? We're so close to a breakthrough.' He frowned, trying to understand, or perhaps he already did.

Could she trust him? "I don't trust anyone on the police force," Daniel had written in his email.

'I just need some time off,' she said. 'Maybe you should find somebody else for the job.'

'But I don't understand. You already did so much work.' The morning sky was brightening through the glass door behind his back. She longed for it. If only she could get outside…

'I'll brief my replacement,' she said. 'I'll hand over all the files.' She tried to edge around him. The exit was so close.

He blocked her path. 'Is there something you're not telling me?'

'What?'

Their eyes held, wondering what the other knew.

'No,' she said.

'Have you been compromised? Are they onto you?'

'Not at all. Really, I just need a short break, a day off to clear my mind.'

'Take two days. After that, we'll need to talk.'

She tried to speak but couldn't. She gave a weak smile and ran out of the door.

'Eleanor!' he called after her as she raced into the wind.

3

The train left London slowly; it felt like the capital would never end. She sat in a corner seat and glanced around, but nobody was watching her. She wore a dark tracksuit and kept the brim of a cap over her eyes. She was sure nobody had followed her, and yet, she wasn't sure of anything. The landscape opened out into brown, autumnal fields as the train picked up pace. Finally, she could breathe. When was the last time she'd been home? Back to Liverpool, where she was born, and raged, and never wanted to leave, and left.

Five years ago, it must have been, when everything fell apart. Five years ago since she last saw Daniel. In truth, there was little in Liverpool to go back to. Her parents were dead. There was her stepfather, but they'd never been close. Friends? They'd all moved away over the years and lost contact. As the train raced through a vanishing landscape, new memories arose, things she'd tried to forget.

There was one other person she'd left behind, her half-sister, who had a different surname, a different father. Beth Krush was a year younger, but she had always outshone her elder sister. A top pupil at school, and later a star on the Merseyside Police. Everyone was surprised when Beth joined the force. With her academic record, she could have done anything, but she chose to copy Eleanor's career choice. It had irritated her, now it just made her feel sad.

They hadn't spoken in years. If their mother had been alive, she'd be devastated at the distance between the sisters. Lucky she was dead then. Beth was nothing like Daniel; after Eleanor abandoned them, Beth never sent a message or an email. After a year of silence, she had almost contacted her sister herself, but she couldn't. She would listen to those sad voicemails from Daniel in the hope he might mention Beth. The three of them had been inseparable, once. Come to think of it, their trio was even a little weird, the loved-up couple with the tag-along little sister. It was far too late for them to talk about what happened, and besides, there was nothing to say.

Beth Krush, the star detective, never quite a sister, what would she be doing now?

4

Detective Beth Krush preferred to work alone. As soon as she drove through the barren, leaf-strewn passage into the housing estate, she knew this wouldn't be that kind of job. Several squad cars and a van were already parked in the street, and a crowd of people huddled around the edges of the crime scene tape. Ugly, gawking, jostling each other with their phones.

'Get out of the way.' Krush pushed through and ducked under the tape.

'They're waiting for you inside,' an officer said.

'Clear the area. Get these people out of here.'

She moved around a burnt-out car and approached the house – a two-storey building, cheaply made. A quick glance around showed all the houses in the estate were the same. Half of them appeared to be abandoned. In the doorway, an officer she didn't recognize came to meet her.

'Scott,' he said and offered his hand. 'This is my beat. I know the estate. They said I should assist you.'

'I work alone.'

She entered the house and found Elliot, the forensics chief, in the hall.

'How does it look?' she asked him.

Elliot shook his head. 'Never seen anything like it. I needed to come out and get some air.'

'There'll be time for that later. Come on.'

'Should I…?' In the doorway, Scott made a move to follow.

'Wait out there,' she said. 'Keep the locals at bay.'

It was dark in the hall. An officer was dusting the light switch for fingerprints. She looked up at the light bulb that was turned off.

'Fuse box is blown,' Elliot said.

'Somebody did it on purpose?'

'Don't know yet. Could be an accident. The wiring in these places is shite. They cut corners putting up the estate; dodgy electrics, leaking pipes. The doors don't fit in the frames.'

'Alright, we're not estate agents.'

She followed the sound of quiet voices to a living room at the end of the hall. Three junior officers stopped talking when she entered. They didn't like her, she knew. On the chintzy wallpaper above the mantelpiece, somebody had painted a pair of eyes in red. Underneath, childish letters were daubed.

DON'T LOOK

She moved up close and sniffed the red shapes. 'Blood?'

'Fresh,' Elliot said. 'Can't have been there more than eight hours. Must have been painted late last night.'

'And the victim?'

Nobody replied, but the junior officers stood back to reveal a form in the corner of the room. The furniture had been pulled away to make space. Krush put on crime scene gloves.

'Can you all get out of the room? Everyone except Elliot.'

She knelt, sinking into a dense stench of blood. She shone her torch over a naked figure that was curled against the corner where the walls met, as if seeking shelter there. At first the body seemed small, like a pre-pubescent, but it was an adult who had drawn up on herself, knees tucked in under her head, arms wrapped around her, hands covering her face as if she were too afraid, or too ashamed, to look. She was red, soaked all over with congealed blood.

'What the fuck?'

'It's a woman,' Elliot said. 'Neighbours said a Mrs Bennett.' He checked his notepad. 'Margaret Bennett. Fifty-one. Lived here with her husband. He's outside in the back of the van. State of shock. Can hardly speak.'

'He's the one who called 999?'

'Yeah.'

'Any kids?'

'Not here. There's one grown-up son, he lives in London.'

'He's been tracked down?'

'Not yet.'

'Cause of death?'

'Not determined, but she's lost a huge amount of blood, as you see. Could fill a bath with it.'

'Anybody moved the body?'

'We waited for you. But she's so wrapped up, with the rigor mortis, she's stuck like that. It'll be hard to straighten her out now.'

'Doesn't look like she wanted to straighten.'

Elliot shone his torch over the dead woman's face. 'Her hands over her eyes like that, it's creepy. Was she trying to hide?'

'Let's take a look.' Krush knelt, took hold of the woman's left hand, and tried to move it. 'Christ, it's stuck.'

She pulled harder. The forearm creaked like a piece of old wood, but it didn't move.

'Careful,' Elliot said. 'You'll tear the skin.'

'Is it the rigor mortis?'

'Let me try.' He squatted down beside her and tried to pull the hand away, but it didn't budge. 'It's stuck to the face.'

'Stuck, how? Like glue?'

He shrugged. 'I have no idea. Let's try the other hand. Hold her steady.' He reached around for the woman's right arm, while Krush gripped her shoulders. 'Nah, it's stuck just the same. We'll have to take her back to the lab like this.'

'Alright, I'd better talk to the neighbours. Anything else to see in here?'

'Check the bathroom upstairs.'

She was glad to get away from that woman's crouched body. She glanced back once at the set of eyes painted on the wall.

DON'T LOOK

They seemed to move, following her gaze as she retreated, hypnotizing. She turned her back and went up the stairs. It might have been a relief to move upwards, out of the stink of that room, but the smell of blood continued. She followed the scent over the landing into a small bathroom. Red footprints on the tiles. A few towels were smeared with gore. In the sink, a kitchen knife lay in a puddle of water and blood.

'Jesus.' She pulled back the stained shower curtain and found the bathtub pooled with dark red liquid.

'What do you make of it?' Elliot said, behind her.

'The killer must have been coated with blood,' she said. 'First, they tried to wash the murder weapon, then they jumped in the shower. But it was too much. Maybe they were in a rush, maybe they were interrupted. There wasn't time to clean it all up. Bag the knife. It's the murder weapon. Might still find a print on it.'

'Why would the killer take a shower in the victim's home? Wouldn't they try to get away from here as quickly as possible?'

'Because he lives here,' Krush said. 'It was the husband.'

5

The dead woman's husband, Leonard Bennett, was seated in the back of the van with a blanket over his shoulders, holding an empty coffee cup in both hands. He looked up when Krush climbed inside, but his eyes were glazed.

'Give me that.' She took the empty cup and threw it out of the door of the vehicle.

'What are you doing?'

'Let me see.' She pulled his hands out. 'There's blood here.'

'It's… it's hers.'

'You touched her?'

'I must have. I don't remember.' His daze seemed genuine, like he was in a trance.

'Show me.' Krush rolled up his sleeves and found spots of dried blood on his wrists and forearm.

Elliot called through the open door of the van. 'Krush, slow down.'

She ignored him. 'You took a shower, didn't you? To get the blood off. But there was too much.'

Bennett stared at his hands, transfixed by the stains. 'Did I?'

'And you washed the knife.'

'What knife?'

'The one that killed your woman.'

'Krush.' Elliot touched her on the shoulder. 'Not here. If you want to interrogate him, it has to be at the station. Have to do things by the book.'

'This isn't an interrogation; I'm just having a chat with our friend here.' She turned to Bennett. 'First you took a shower. How long after that did you wait before you called the police?'

He stared back. 'I rang the police?'

'Alright, drop the act. Answer me.'

Elliot touched her shoulder again, stronger this time. 'Krush, Jesus, let's talk outside a minute.'

She scowled and followed him out of the van.

A few yards away, he whispered, 'That guy's in shock. He doesn't know what's going on. If you push him, his lawyers will claim harassment.'

'I know, I know, it's just… I keep seeing those eyes.'

'Eyes?'

'From the wall.' She shook her head. 'I'll talk to him at the station. He's guilty, I'm certain.'

'Whatever you say.' Elliot started to walk away. 'I'll call you when the post-mortem's starting.'

'I guess I'd better look around this shithole estate and talk to some people. See what we can find out.'

'There's the local officer, he knows the estate well, apparently.' He pointed at Scott, who was standing outside the front door of the house, staring into space.

'He looks like a creep.'

'Go with him, Beth. They don't like police around here. You'll need all the help you can get.'

6

The murder took place in number 14. Number 12 was derelict. Nobody was home at number 16. At number 18, an elderly lady peeped out through the side of the door. She had a mass of frizzy white hair.

'What do you want?' she said. 'I already told them, I'm not leaving here. They'll have to carry me out dead.'

'We just want to talk.' Scott put his foot in the door before she could close it.

'Talk to someone else.'

'Nobody is asking you to leave,' Krush said. 'You stay right where you are.'

The old lady scrutinised her. 'Who are you? Some bitch in a suit they sent to butter me up. Well, it won't work. I won't leave here. It's my house. You can't make a person give up their own house. Ten years I've been living here. People think, because I'm old—'

'There's been a murder,' Krush shouted over her monologue. 'I don't care if you stay in there forever. I just want to talk about the murder.'

The woman's mouth fell open.

'It's alright, Mrs Willis,' Scott said. 'Don't be scared. We'd just like your help.'

Krush glanced at him. Scott wasn't what she might have expected for the local officer on a beat like this. He spoke softly and slowly. He was pale and skinny, unthreatening. No wonder the place was lawless.

Mrs Willis stared. 'What murder?'

'At number 14,' Krush said. 'Sometime last night. Did you hear anything? Did you see anything?'

'Why would I hear anything? I was lying in bed asleep like a decent person. There are decent people on this estate, you know. We're not all animals. It's those kids, running around, and the police do nothing. Your friend here is worthless.' She gestured at Scott. 'Useless. Those kids laugh in his face.'

'Mrs Willis…' Scott said.

'In my day, they weren't afraid to discipline children. If kids went wild, they took them aside and showed them something that would terrify the bad out of them.'

'It's not like that anymore,' Scott said.

'Of course it's not. Look around you.' She nodded at the burnt-out car in the road in front of her house.

'Mrs Willis, please,' Krush said. 'We just need to talk to you about the murder, that's all.'

'What are you wasting time talking to me for? Ask someone who knows. Ask those kids for a start. If old man Bennett got himself killed, it's probably because he tried to stop them running wild. If the police won't do it, someone has to try.'

'It wasn't the man who died,' Krush said. 'It was his wife.'

'His wife?' She stalled, her monologue broken. For the first time, she came out in her slippers from behind the front door and looked across at number 14. 'Well, that's just wrong. I didn't mind her, Mrs Bennett, but she was… I don't know. She didn't fit in.'

'What do you mean, "didn't fit in"?' Krush made a note on her pad.

'She–'

Scott interrupted, 'We don't need your opinion of her personality. We're looking for witnesses. Anyone who might have heard or seen something.'

'Well, I can't help you. I didn't leave the house all day.'

'Did you look out of the window?' Scott said.

'No.'

'Did you hear anything outside?'

'No.'

'Did you–'

'Shut up a minute.' Krush turned to the old lady. 'Mrs Bennett "didn't fit in". What did you mean by that?'

'Well, you know, she wasn't from here,' the woman said.

'Where was she from?'

The old lady looked at the grey sky where vast cloud formations furled. 'I couldn't tell you. Just not from here.'

'Where was she from, the murder victim?' Krush asked Scott.

'Dunno,' he said.

'You're supposed to be the local expert.'

'Hah!' Mrs Willis retreated further inside. 'He doesn't know a thing. And neither do you.'

Her door slammed shut.

'You see what it's like here?' Scott touched the shut door. 'They're all the same. They don't cooperate. They don't realize we're trying to help them. They won't tell us anything.'

'She did tell us something.' Krush set off back down the driveway. 'Come on, we'll try the next house. Let me talk this time. You keep quiet unless I ask you a question.'

* * *

They checked the next three houses, but nobody answered. The owners must have been at work, or else hiding inside. Krush crossed the middle of the estate, a large roundabout covered in overgrown grass and dead trees.

'What's this?' She gestured at an empty plinth covered in graffiti.

'That was the sundial,' Scott said. 'Somebody stole it.'

'What sundial?'

He shrugged. From this central vantage point, Krush gazed around the dilapidated buildings.

'What went wrong here?' she said.

Scott smiled weakly. 'The estate was built twenty years ago, but it's never been finished. The construction firm went bust. They built the houses in time, but they never installed the streetlights or the kerbs.'

'What about the local council?'

'The land is unadopted. It's up to residents to take care of things.'

'Still, in two decades, something could've been done.'

'There are discussions and promises but nothing ever happens. Who cares about a place like this, tucked out of the way? Tourists would never guess it exists. The middle classes don't come out here. The rest of the city ignores it. People have their own problems.'

They skirted around the ashes of a giant bonfire that had fizzled out leaving charred pieces of old furniture and all kinds of junk in a black patch of ash.

'There are thirty-six houses in the estate,' Scott said. 'Only about half are occupied, as far as we can tell.'

'And who lives here?'

'Honestly, these are good people, most of them. Families, workers. They don't trust police though. They won't talk.'

'They'll talk to me. Don't worry.'

'Be careful, Detective. There's a gang that runs the estate, and wild kids. Out of control. Nobody can do anything about them. The courts aren't interested. Central police turn a blind eye. So long as they stay out here in the middle of nowhere, and don't cause trouble in the city centre, they let them do whatever they want. Don't park your car in the estate, is my advice. It'll be ruined. Park outside and walk in.'

'What's that?' She stopped.

'What?'

'There, don't you see it?' She set off towards a derelict building where somebody had spraypainted a pair of eyes in red along the front wall.

'Oh. The kids, they graffiti everything. It's one of the reasons houses here aren't worth a damn.'

'It's the same as the crime scene.'

'The same?'

'Shut up a minute.' She felt dizzy as she approached. The eyes seemed to move, watching her, seeing inside her. She resisted the feeling; she'd never been squeamish, and she was proud of it. Murder, corpses, mutilation, she'd seen it all and never thrown up, unlike some of her colleagues. When she came up close, the spell was broken, the graffiti didn't even look like eyes anymore, just crude red markings on brick. She rubbed at the surface and her finger came away with a stain.

'Do you think…?' Scott's voice in her ear startled her.

'Whose house is this?'

'This one's derelict. Nobody's lived in there for years.'

She could believe it. The blackened window frames showed fire damage. The place stank of ash and urine.

'And next door? Maybe they saw something.'

7

The doctor woke up on the floor and lay motionless. *This locked room…* He remembered waking, but he couldn't remember how he came to be there, who he was, why he had to exist and couldn't stop. All he held onto was the vague sense he was a doctor. Voices nearby carried on the wind. Somebody banged on an outer door. They must have woken him. Otherwise, he might have died in his sleep. Why did they do that? Did they hate him? *Who are they?* He strained to hear the distant voices.

'It's abandoned,' a man outside said. 'The door's boarded over.'

'Doesn't mean nobody's in,' a woman said.

The voices were just on the other side of the blocked window, but they came from below; his prison must be on the first floor.

A front door downstairs rattled. The woman banged on it. 'Anybody home?' she called.

The doctor tried to lift his head to call to her, but he was too weak.

Boots moved dully through whatever wasteland was outside.

'Is there another way in?' the woman said.

'What's the point? This place is deserted.'

'Just a minute.' Her boots moved below his window.

The doctor made a vain attempt to sit up. He drew breath and tried to make a sound, but only a guttural sigh came out.

'We're wasting our time,' the man said. 'There's another twenty houses in the estate to check.'

'We've got all day, haven't we? Shut up a minute.'

The doctor twisted his neck to look at the blocked window as she knocked on a boarded-up surface below. If he could raise his hand…

'Anyone in there?' she called. 'There's a smell. Something chemical. Something like sick.'

The doctor sucked up the poisoned emptiness in his belly and tried to make a noise, just any kind of sound at all. Amazingly, something came out; a choked glug, almost a retch. Was it loud enough?

'That door doesn't even open,' the man outside said.

'Maybe you're right,' the woman said. 'I'll make a note about this place. We could come back with crowbars if we need to.'

'Yeah, well.' The man's voice was distant, moving away. 'You won't find anything.'

The doctor made a last effort to lift his fist. Perhaps if he could knock on something, she might hear outside. But his hand was paralysed, and her boots were walking away. Their voices faded from earshot. She was already gone. He forced himself to think. *Why am I here?* As his brain throbbed and groaned, he dug into its meat for a memory. All that came back was a name in black ink with a line through it. The line was in red.

~~Eleanor~~

8

It had been five years since she last set foot in the Merseyside Police HQ in Liverpool. As soon as Eleanor stepped out of the wind and into that ugly building, a mass of blocky panels and square windows, she felt the last five years contract, as if she'd only been away a single day. She'd tried to escape, but everything came around in a circle. The corruption didn't end, no matter how far she ran. Now she was home.

A young officer she didn't recognize was seated at the front desk. She was glad he was new; she wasn't ready to see anyone from the old days.

'Can I help you?' he said.

She showed her police ID. 'I'm looking for Daniel Reynolds. Does he still work here?'

'You could've rung,' the officer said. He was young, with a downy moustache.

'I was passing through. I used to work in this place.' She looked around. The building hadn't changed, it even smelled the same – the same air freshener.

'Daniel's not been around. He's working on some special operation. I don't know what.'

'But he's still in Liverpool?'

The youth looked at her like she was weird. 'Of course.'

She remembered then that in Liverpool, people didn't leave if they didn't have to. There's nowhere else to go, they reasoned, when you already live in the greatest city in the world.

'Can you give me his address, or a phone number?'

'I guess.'

While he checked his computer, she heard herself say, 'How about Beth Krush, is she here?'

'Oh, they split up.'

The words amazed her, impossible in this kid's bored, careless voice. 'They… with Daniel?' she stammered. 'I never knew they were together.'

The kid shrugged. He didn't care, and why should he? The last time she saw Beth was in this building, two floors above, in her office. Somehow in her imagination, her sister had never left that room. The thought frightened her. She needed to get out of the building.

'Who are you exactly?' The youth looked at her as if beginning to recognize her face. 'What do you want with Daniel?'

'Are you going to give me his details or not?'

'I think... I think I need to check with the boss.'

'Don't bother.'

She turned and was about to leave when a deep voice called from the shadow at the bottom of the stairs, 'Look who came back from the big city!'

She swung around, startled. Carmichael, her old boss, came out of the dark.

'Never thought I'd see you again,' he said. 'What, you got bored of the fine life? Decided to come back and visit us barbarians in the North?'

'You know that's not how it is.'

'Were the streets not paved with gold down there?' Carmichael was joking, but he didn't smile.

She noticed the youth at the desk smirking as he ducked behind his screen.

'I'm looking for Daniel.'

'You'd better come up to my office, if it's not too humble for you.'

* * *

Upstairs in Carmichael's "humble" office, Eleanor sat down on the other side of his desk, and it was all the same: the giant gold plaque with his name; the kitsch photographs of his wife and kids done in soft focus; the oversized, chipped mug that said "BOSS"; an empty pot-noodle container next to it. Nothing here had changed since she ran out five years ago.

'I hope you're not looking for a job,' he said. 'People around here didn't like it, the way you left. No warning, no goodbyes. I stuck up for you, of course, but, well, you know what people are like.'

She studied his red, pock-marked face. Could he be trusted? No. Carmichael was in charge; Daniel would have gone to him first, instead of Eleanor, if he thought the boss was honest.

'I'm just passing through,' she said. 'I wanted to catch up with Daniel.'

'The one that got away. Were the men down south not what you hoped for?'

Eleanor knew from experience that Carmichael considered this kind of talk "banter", an essential part of staff morale, but he'd never seemed to grasp that banter was supposed to be playful, not aggressive. The only way to deal with him, she'd learned, was directness.

'I've unfinished business with Daniel,' she said.

'Are you sure that's a good idea? Things are strange with him, they always were. He left Beth. I'm pretty sure he's drinking. You turning up now, it could tip him over the edge.'

'I just want to talk to him.'

Carmichael cocked an eyebrow. 'What about?' He picked up a circular keyring and twiddled it.

Eleanor remembered how he used to fidget with things like that. He always needed to control. The more she remembered about this place, the more she felt the old need to escape.

'Will you tell me where he is, or not?' she said.

Carmichael grinned, showing yellow teeth. 'Are you sure he wants to speak to you again? After everything that happened?'

'Five years is a long time.'

'He's working on something at the moment. Drug ring. Hasn't been around. Between me and you, I think he's struggling. When a man's treading water, it shows in his face. A man who's about to go under starts gasping for air. Maybe you could help him. Find out what's up. If he's back on the drink, you let me know.'

'Where can I find him?'

'I have no idea. He was living with Beth, but since he left her, he's gone off the rails. Could be anywhere. He was working undercover, doing his own thing. Nobody's seen him in a while. You could speak to Hughes, that's his partner on this drugs op. I'll give you Hughes' number.'

'Thank you.' She stood up.

'But, Eleanor, be careful with Beth, she'll kill you. I'm not joking. She's never been the same since you walked out. And she didn't take it well when Daniel left her.'

9

A homeless man was sitting in the drizzle against the wall outside a burnt-out house at the far end of the estate. He waved a plastic cup in their direction.

'Spare any change, love?'

Krush walked over. 'Do you live here?'

'What?'

'That's just Mac,' Scott said. 'He's homeless. He sits there every day.'

'In the estate?' Krush said. 'An odd spot. Why not in the city centre? Don't homeless people usually sit outside cash machines or shops?'

Mac gazed up at her through the rain. 'What do you care?'

As she came closer, she saw he was wearing strange clothes: a polka-dot bow tie, a red waistcoat over multicoloured shirt and trousers, and long red shoes. The waistcoat was torn and stained, the trousers ragged. A small pair of headphones on twisted wires were looped around his neck, attached to an old cassette Walkman.

Noticing the confusion on her face, Scott said, 'Oh, Mac works as a clown. He does tricks in the city for money. Not so much recently. Been drinking a bit too much, haven't you, Mac?'

The clown looked up at Krush. 'I used to know some jokes.'

'We're investigating a crime,' Scott said. 'Here.' He fished some coins out of his pocket and dropped them in the plastic cup.

'What are you doing?' Krush said.

Mac waved the cup at her. 'Go on, be kind.'

She knelt closer and was hit by a wave of vodka on his breath. 'Do you always sit out here?'

'I don't snitch.' He waved the cup again.

'I'm a police detective. You have to answer my questions.'

'No, I don't. Just coz I don't have a house, I'm not stupid, and I'm not a grass.'

Scott knelt beside her. 'Give him a coin, if you want him to talk.'

'For God's sake.' She looked in her purse but could only find a ten-pound note. 'I don't have any change.'

'Here.' Scott slipped a fifty-pence piece into her hand.

'This is ridiculous.' She dropped it into the cup. 'Answer my question or we'll take you down the station and ask you there. Do you always sit out here?'

'Sure,' Mac. 'Where else? I'm not invited to fancy parties.'

'Did you see anything last night?'

'What kind of thing?'

'A crime was committed at number 14. Did you see anything? Did you hear anything?'

'A crime?' He sat up straight against the wall.

'We can't disclose any details yet,' Krush said. 'The investigation is still in process.'

'Well, what do you want me to say then?'

She took a breath. 'Alright. Was there anybody in the estate last night whom you haven't seen here before?'

'No.'

'Did you see anything unusual?'

'On this estate, what's usual?'

'Do you have a view of number 14 from here?' She squatted down next to him and peered with a hand over her eyes to shield them from the rain.

'Sure. I see it all from here.'

'And last night, you didn't spot anything in that direction? People shouting? Somebody running away?'

'Nothing I wouldn't normally see.'

'What time were you sitting out here till?'

He shook his head. 'I don't have a watch, love. It was dark. The place was quiet when I left, I can tell you that.'

'And where did you go after you left here?'

'I wandered over to the all-night garage and bought a bottle. I drank under the highway bridge until I fell asleep.'

'How did you pay for that?'

He shrugged. 'People are generous. But you wouldn't understand.'

'Why wouldn't I understand?'

'You're police, aren't you? You hate us.'

'I don't hate anybody. I...' She stopped. 'This is a waste of time. If you remember anything, if you think of anything you might have seen—'

'I'll be sure to send you a fax.'

She nodded towards the Walkman. 'What do you listen to?'

'Clown music.'

10

Daniel's partner, Sergeant Colin Hughes, sat behind the wheel of a black Audi. He had long hair tied in a knot, and he wore sunglasses even though it was cloudy outside.

'The famous Eleanor,' he said.

When she hesitated in the open door, he beckoned. 'Get in, come on. Don't stand out there in the rain.'

She climbed into the passenger seat and the thick smell of his aftershave. 'You work with Daniel?'

'Drugs. We've been profiling a gang, major player in the city. But it's a slow business. Daniel gets bored. He's been off doing his own stuff. Said it was private. Well, you know what he's like.'

'Did he tell you anything about it?'

'Like bollocks. Secretive bastard. Touchy. I leave him in peace. That's why he likes me. He told me to cover for him with the bosses, and I did, like a divvy. Now I can't find him anywhere. No one's seen him in weeks.'

'Is there any place he might have gone?'

'Nowhere. Now you turn up. What's that all about? He used to talk about you when he was drunk. The rest of us told him you were a crazy cow who ran away. No offence. A man's got to get on with his life, no point feeling sorry for himself. You know he never got that tattoo removed? I found a place where they do laser removal. A guy owed me a favour, said he'd do it for free. Instead, Daniel got a line put through it, he couldn't let it go. You really messed him up.'

'I had my reasons to leave.'

'Hey, I'm not criticising. Do what you want. Life's complicated. I know that. I don't judge. I just want to know where the sad bastard's disappeared to. Now that you turn up out of nowhere, I'm thinking, are the two things related?'

'Why would they be?'

'Listen, love, everyone knew; you were never coming back to Liverpool. You even left your sister behind. I get it, something must have happened. A falling-out, whatever. Like I said, I don't judge. But for you to come back here, now, out of the blue, and he's disappeared. There's a connection. What's going on?'

She wanted to trust him. As Daniel's partner, he'd be closer to him than anyone else on the force, but Hughes' eyes were invisible behind the sunglasses, she couldn't read him. She longed to tell him about Daniel's email and the phone call, just to share the fright with somebody else, but she couldn't. If Daniel had trusted this guy, he would've shared with him.

'Nothing's going on,' she said.

Hughes lit a cigarette. 'You can trust me. I'm a prick. Everyone at the station will tell you that. Know the good thing about pricks? They don't care about other people's bullshit. I don't care about Daniel's broken heart or your guilt, or any of that. I just want to find him.'

'So do I.'

'Well then, let's help each other.'

'I can't help you. I don't know anything. I just came back home from London and the only place I've been is the station and then here. I haven't seen anyone. Not even Beth.'

Hughes nodded, but his smile showed cynicism. 'And what brought about this change of heart? Why come back after so long?'

Could she trust him? Her knotted stomach said no. "I don't trust anyone on the police force," Daniel had written.

'I heard he left Beth,' she said. 'Do you know where he's living now?'

'He moved into his parents' old house. He inherited it after his mum died last year. It's—'

'I know where it is.'

'Well then, you can look there. It's a mess. Daniel let himself go, it's more like he's camping than living there. But I've been knocking on the door and ringing every day. He's not home. He's gone somewhere else. All we can do is wait for him to come back.'

'And what if...' She struggled to put the idea into words. 'What if something's happened to him?'

'Something bad, you mean?' Hughes took off his sunglasses and his whole face was changed. His eyes were smaller, paler than she'd imagined, and surrounded by dark bags like he hadn't slept in days.

No, she didn't trust him.

'Is there anyone else I could ask?' she said.

'Shit.' He rubbed his eyes. 'I really shouldn't tell you this, it's secret. But you're Eleanor, I guess you must be special to Daniel or he wouldn't still have your name on his wrist. There's one guy. Hunter. He's an informant. His identity is secret, even on the force. He's connected to the gang we're tracking. Him and Daniel got close, I've no idea why. I found out they were meeting up without me. Maybe they stopped trusting me, maybe Daniel is losing his mind. As far as I know, Hunter is the last person who saw Daniel. They had a meeting last week. I've tried to call him, but he doesn't answer. You can try.'

He reached across to the glove compartment, brushing her knee, and took out a calling card and a pen. 'I'll give you his number.'

'Thanks.'

'But, Eleanor, truth be told, I'm not sure Daniel wants to see you. He takes women to heart too much. I told him that, but he doesn't listen. I–' He stopped as his phone on the dashboard buzzed.

They both looked at the device, but he didn't pick it up.

'Listen,' Hughes said. 'I've got to go somewhere. Are you alright?'

'I'm fine.' Suddenly she was desperate to get out of the car. She opened the door and climbed out hurriedly while the phone vibrated on the dashboard.

'And, Eleanor – be careful.'

'What do you mean?'

'If Daniel's in trouble…'

'Don't worry about me.'

She slammed the door shut.

11

'This house looks different to the others,' Krush said.

They stopped outside number 19. Structurally, it was identical to the rest of the buildings on the estate – the same shape and dimensions, the same brick and cream-colour stucco – but number 19 was bright and clean, the front yard was tidy, the blue door had been freshly painted.

'It's like brand new.' She walked up the driveway and didn't see any dirt or rubbish.

Scott stuck to her heels. 'Some rich guy lives here. He pays a caretaker to look after it.'

'A rich guy on the estate? Doesn't seem likely.' She came up to the blue front door. It was so immaculate she leaned forwards and sniffed it. 'It's been painted recently, smells fresh.'

'Yeah, like I say, rich. He doesn't live here. He's down south somewhere.'

She went over to the living-room window, which wasn't boarded over but clean and bright like a mirror. The curtains were closed inside.

'You're telling me some rich guy bought the place, pays to keep it clean and tidy, but doesn't use it?'

'He's never even looked at it. He's got property all over the country, supposedly. He's a kind of speculator. He buys places over the phone and waits for the value to go up. He sells them without ever setting foot inside.'

'I don't understand. If the place is empty, why hasn't it been looted like the other houses? Why haven't the kids smashed the windows?'

'I dunno. They're scared of him, maybe.'

She knocked on the door, but nobody answered.

* * *

Approaching number 21, a blare of music drowned out the sound of cars on the highway.

'Who lives in there?' Krush said.

'Oh, that's the Andersons. They like to party.'

She skirted around a pile of wet bin bags and went up the driveway. 'Is it always this loud?'

'What?'

She raised her voice. 'The music. Is it always this loud?'

'They're into karaoke.'

'Karaoke? What the hell…' She rang the doorbell.

'They probably won't hear that,' Scott said.

She rang the bell again, several times. The music didn't subside, an unrecognizable song was being screamed over a microphone by three women at the same time.

'What song is that?'

'*A Hard Day's Night,*' Scott said. 'The Beatles.'

'Is that what it is?'

'I'm a big fan.'

'Right.' Krush went over to the living room window, where the curtains were closed. Through a gap, she saw a room full of people, nine at least, of different ages, some men, some women. The ones who weren't singing were on their feet, swaying.

She banged on the glass and shouted, 'Hey! Police! Police!'

The curtains opened and a man looked out; his face was red, he seemed angry. 'What?' he mouthed. Behind his back, the others looked out in confusion. The three women sharing the microphone carried on singing.

Krush held her police badge up to the glass. 'Police!' she shouted. 'Turn that racket off, now!'

The music stopped. In the abrupt silence, rain pattered on the window and into her face. A room full of faces stared at her. The three women held onto the microphone.

'Open the door.'

Nobody moved inside. She ran back to the front door and rang the bell. The music started up again. Somebody must have adjusted the volume; it was quieter now.

'For Christ's sake.' She was about to go back to the window when she saw somebody through the frosted glass of the front door. It opened, and the red-faced man looked out. He wore a cowboy hat and had a tinsel boa wrapped around his neck.

'Sorry, Officers,' he said. 'Was it too loud? I've turned it down now.'

Scott patted him on the shoulder. 'That's alright, Davey. It's better now. Nice hat.'

'It's not better,' Krush said. 'It's way too loud. What about the neighbours?'

'The neighbours are in here. Do you want to speak to them? They're about to sing *Eleanor Rigby*. That's our favourite.'

'It's OK,' Scott said. 'Just—'

'It's not OK,' she said. 'Turn it off now. I need to talk to you.'

'Talk to me?' Davey said.

'To you and to everyone else who's inside.'

'But that's not fair!' he shouted. His face contorted, showing wolflike incisors beneath his gums. 'It's just a party. Everyone on the estate's invited. We do it all the time, nobody complains. They like it.'

'Calm down, please, sir,' Krush said. 'It's not about the party. There's been a murder on the estate, I need to ask you a few questions, that's all.'

He gaped. 'A murder?'

'That's right.'

Davey bellowed down the hall, 'Turn the fucking music off!'

'Thank you.' She pushed past him and went inside.

The front room stank of cigarette smoke and sweat. There were twelve people in all, four of whom seemed to be at least in their seventies; two young men in their twenties; a girl who looked about fifteen years old; and five middle-aged people, including Davey and the woman he introduced as his wife, Melinda. They were all sweaty, with bags under their eyes.

'How long has this party been going on?' Krush said.

'It doesn't stop,' Melinda said. 'It's just… sometimes the people change, or the house.'

'Are you all related?'

'It feels like it,' Melinda said. 'Sometimes I can't remember where I met any of them.'

Krush raised her voice over the hubbub. 'I'd like to chat to each of you, one at a time, about number 14, the Bennetts. Don't worry, you're not in trouble.'

Several people shouted at once, proclaiming their innocence. 'We never did nothing!'

Krush raised her hands. 'Please, calm down, everyone. There's no need for alarm, I just want to ask a few questions. Then you can go back to your party.'

'We can start the music again?' Davey said.

'After we're done,' Krush said. 'But keep the volume down. Where can we talk? Not in here, it stinks. How about the kitchen?' She turned to Scott. 'Stay by the front door, don't let anybody leave until I've had a chance to speak to them.'

She set off through the house, with Davey following, and passed a room that was painted entirely in red. 'What goes on in there?' she said.

'What? Oh. That's the back living room. We never finished redecorating. Ran out of paint.'

The kitchen was a mess, the sink full of dirty dishes, empty bottles piled up, and bin bags and dirty footprints on the tiles. Davey opened a window to let some air inside.

'Sorry about the state of the place.' He sat down at a table covered in bottles, pizza boxes, and leftovers. 'If I'd known you were coming…'

Krush noticed a patch of white powder. 'What's this?'

'What?'

She dabbed her finger in the powder and licked it. 'Cocaine. What kind of party is this, Davey?'

'Honestly, I have no idea where that came from.'

'It's your kitchen table.'

'Sometimes people turn up, strangers, new people from the estate. They hear the party going on, they knock on the door, we invite them inside. Everyone's welcome. I don't know what they all get up to. Anybody might have brought that.'

'I think it's yours,' Krush said. 'That would explain how you and your grandparents are able to keep the party going for so long without falling asleep.'

'Detective, you know, it's just a bit of beak.'

'If you keep this up, Davey, it'll kill you. At your age, too much coke will give you a heart attack.'

'Honestly, I... it's not what you think. It's just a bit of beak...' He stuttered and repeated himself. He seemed to have run out of things to say.

'Whatever. We're wasting time. This is a murder investigation, it's not about petty drug use.' She took out her notepad. 'How well did you know the people in number 14?'

'Number 14?' He took off the cowboy hat to scratch his bald head. 'Who lives there again?'

'The Bennetts.'

'Bennetts, Bennetts... short guy, wears glasses? Sure, I've seen him around, but I never spoke to him. He's a quiet type.'

'You never invited him to one of your karaoke parties?'

'He could've come if he wanted, most people just turn up. They don't wait for an invite. But he wasn't the kind. Too shy. So, he's dead now, is he?'

She stared at his face for a sign of deception, but his eyes were hollow, expressionless.

'It was the wife who died,' she said.

'Oh.'

She let the silence settle, but the news brought no reaction from him.

'Did you see anything last night?' she said. 'Anything unusual on the estate?'

'I didn't go outside, Detective, I was in here doing karaoke. Can I go now? The others will be wondering what's going on.'

She sighed. 'Alright. If you think of anything, or if you hear any rumours, anything, you call me. Here's my number.'

He took the card without looking at it.

'Send the next person,' she called after him as he hurried out of the room.

Scott stuck his head in the kitchen. 'Sorry, some people left. I tried to stop them.'

'What do you mean, they left? How did they get out?'

'They just… they just walked out.'

'Alright, never mind. Who's left? Send the next one.'

She spoke to Davey's parents, as well as his mother-in-law, and someone who might have been his second cousin but wasn't sure. They were all the same – sweaty, with bags under their eyes. They looked around the corners of the kitchen with twitching faces and couldn't tell her anything. It seemed that nobody on the estate knew the Bennetts, even though they'd lived here for years. They never socialised with them, never spoke to them, never saw them. Davey's dad, who might have been eighty, claimed to have never even heard of them.

'Bennetts?' he repeated.

'Yes. In number 14.'

'But it's the Lamberts in number 14.'

She checked her notes again. 'No, it's definitely the Bennetts. You must be mixing it up with another house.'

'I'm telling you, it's the Lamberts who live in number 14. Just because I'm old, doesn't mean I'm stupid. I can still see, with my glasses. I've still got my memory.'

Back along the corridor, another Beatles song started playing on the karaoke machine. One of the men broke out with a toneless rendition of *Eleanor Rigby*.

'Alright.' She turned a page in her notepad. 'Tell me about the Lamberts then. Who are they? What do they do?'

'They…' He stared vacantly. 'I can't remember. There was a man and a woman. They must have been married. Did they have children? Maybe. He was a builder or something like that.'

'Do you remember their first names?'

'Oh no, we weren't close. And they're dead, are they? Mrs Lambert was murdered?'

'No. Mrs Bennett was murdered. That's why I called you all in here. I need to find out if anybody knows anything.'

'Mrs Bennett? Never heard of her.'

She closed her notepad. 'Fine. Did you see anything last night on the estate? Any strangers? Anything out of place?'

'I was in here all night. Didn't go outside once.'

'Of course.'

'Can I go now? I'm singing next.'

'Sure.' She stood up. 'What are you singing?'

'I can't remember.'

12

Eleanor bought a cheap disposable phone from a store in the city centre. It had changed – new shops, new streets – Liverpool never stopped growing. She found a quiet place on a verge overlooking the docks, and entered the number Hughes had given her for Hunter, Daniel's informant. She still felt jittery using a phone, but it was safe here, in public, in an open space, in the late afternoon, and this was a brand-new phone; nobody knew her number. Hunter answered at the third attempt.

'Hello.' His voice was quiet, almost a whisper, as if he were hiding in a corner.

'Are you Hunter?'

'Who are you?' He sounded frightened.

She felt exposed giving her name over the phone, but she had no choice. 'I'm Eleanor. I'm looking for Daniel. I–'

'Shit. You're *the* Eleanor?'

'I guess so, yeah. It's about…'

'What's the code word?'

'Code word? I don't know.'

'Daniel told me, if you ever rang, to ask you for the word. Otherwise, I can't talk to you.'

'You do know Daniel, then,' she said. 'I need to find him.'

To hear his name spoken aloud, Daniel felt alive for the first time. She watched the dark, melodramatic clouds that swirled over the docks. She had forgotten the skies of Liverpool.

'What's the word?' Hunter hissed through the phone.

'The word…'

'Daniel said you had a secret word, just the two of you.'

'You mean, "Oslo"?'

'Alright.' He let out a sigh so loud she heard it through the speaker. 'You came back. He said you might, but I didn't believe it.'

'What's this about?'

'I can't talk here, meet me.'

'Where?'

'I'll text you the address.' He hung up.

13

Carmichael was waiting at the bottom of the stairs in the morgue. He twiddled a circular keyring in his fingers. Krush tried to repress her hatred.

'Is the body ready?' She pushed past him and went through the main door.

'Met an old friend of yours today.'

'The morgue isn't the place for banter.' She hurried ahead, hoping he wouldn't follow, but he kept pace.

'This isn't banter.'

'Krush!' Elliot called from the slab where the dead woman lay in a bundle beneath the lamps. 'Come see.'

They put on facemasks as they approached. Bodies down here were usually laid out flat on their backs, as if sleeping, but the woman from the estate was curled into a foetal position, knees tucked tight beneath her chin, arms wrapped around them, hands covering her face.

'God, she's rigid.' One of the assistants tugged at the leg. 'Have to break the bones.'

'Did you manage to see under her hands?' Krush said.

'Not yet. We need to shift the legs first.' Elliot set an electric saw against the dead woman's shin, and tested the edge. 'Stand back.' He put on a pair of goggles.

Krush watched, entranced, as the team of three technicians sawed and hammered through the frozen sinews. Carmichael sidled up close beside her.

He grinned. 'That's what you called "scared stiff", hey?'

'Did you want something?'

They jumped back as the dust of sawed skin and bone sprayed out from the table.

'Sorry,' Elliot said.

Carmichael raised his voice over the buzzing tools. 'I told you, your old friend is back in town.'

'I don't have any friends.'

'No, I guess you don't.'

The first leg came free. It was disgusting and yet oddly satisfying to watch the neatness of their work. The leg was removed from the body in three sections, which were set aside on the slab. It was like watching a doll being deconstructed.

'It was your sister,' Carmichael said.

'What?'

'Came back from London.'

'Eleanor?'

Carmichael smiled, and she realized she had given herself away.

'Why should I care?'

'She was looking for Daniel.'

'What did she want with him?'

'Wouldn't say.'

Eleanor. Eleanor Rose. Krush had been jealous of her half-sister's pretty surname, and always hated her own. Last time she saw her... Jesus, the look on her face, that sad smile of hers that all the boys fell in love with. Not long after that, Krush's dreams started, the dreams of grinding that pretty face with glass.

'Maybe you should talk to her,' Carmichael said. 'Find out what she's up to.'

'Ask someone else. I'm busy.'

'And Daniel? When did you last see him? I heard...'

'That's none of your business.'

'It's really over then, between you two? Shame. I thought you were a good match.'

'Police officers shouldn't date each other.'

'Maybe that's what brought Eleanor back. She heard you split up.'

The sound of sawing stopped. Elliot took off his goggles. 'We'll try and get to the face now. Want to observe?'

'Yeah.' Krush moved away from Carmichael and was glad he didn't follow. She refused to look back but heard his feet moving away. Her shoulders only released at the sound of the door closing. He was gone, with his leering, obscene face, his twiddling fingers and his jokes that weren't funny.

The corpse was just a legless, armless stump. The hands were still stuck to the face. Elliot took a scalpel and started to cut beneath the fingers, while his colleagues held the body still. Krush knelt to look closer.

'Goddamn thing.' He pulled at the forefinger as he dug under with his scalpel.

'What's it stuck with?' Krush said.

The finger came loose from the woman's face with a string of congealed blood.

Elliot peered underneath. 'It's just flesh.'

'What?'

He stood straight and wiped his brow. 'Looks like the skin was removed from the face and the inside surface of the hands. Then the raw flesh on both was pressed together. As the blood clotted, they bonded, and the hands stuck to the face.'

'Shit.' She knelt to look. 'Why would anyone do that?'

'We'll get a better idea when the whole thing comes off.'

The technicians bent back to the work.

'Careful now,' Elliot said. 'Don't damage her.'

Fifteen minutes later, both hands had been prised away. The dead woman's face was a mask of exposed flesh. The eyeballs were missing.

Elliot tilted her empty gaze to the light. 'Whoever did it was in a rush. It's a rough job, bits of skin here and there. They didn't bother to finish the nose. Over here, see – in the cheek – they cut too deep, gouged a hole.'

'We found a kitchen knife,' Krush said. 'Reckon that could have done it?'

'Doubtful. More like a paring knife. Something precise. But the kitchen knife killed her. There's a stab wound in the heart, another in the neck.'

'Shit. We need to do a full search of the house, see if the skin and eyeballs are hidden somewhere.'

'It's already been checked top to bottom,' Elliot said.

'We'll check again,' she said. 'The toilet bowl… what if they flushed the eyeballs?'

'Could be.'

'I'll have the toilet taken apart.'

'Her eyes will be in the sewer by now, if he flushed them,' Elliot said.

'He?' Krush echoed.

'The husband. He's your suspect, isn't he?'

'Could he have done this?' She gestured to the faceless woman. 'Wouldn't you need experience? I don't know, like a butcher, or a surgeon?'

'A butcher maybe. A surgeon would have done it neatly. What's his job, the husband?'

'Something to do with numbers. Guess I'd better ask him.'

14

Thirty minutes after Hunter hung up, he texted through an address and directions to Eleanor's mobile. Some old warehouse in the Baltic Triangle. She abandoned a half-finished pastry and a coffee that she'd sat down to in a café, and ran out into the rain. As she walked headlong into a powerful wind – a taste of bright salt and concrete, freezing cold – she knew she really had come home; this wasn't just a fantasy. Hanging seagulls screamed in the gale. Eleanor held onto her cap with one hand as she pushed forwards.

She walked between immense polygons of red brick. There was an imposing geometry in these structures that had been left to die but were too strong, too solidly built to fall down. Fossils of the city's lost maritime splendour. Weeds grew in the broken gutters, pigeons looked out from crevices in the brickwork.

Eleanor found Hunter waiting for her in a doorway at the bottom of a dead end. From his fearful, whispered voice over the phone, she had expected a ghostly man, but he was tall and broad with a bald head. He wore a high-vis jacket.

'What's the word?' he said.

'I already told you, it's Oslo. Can I–'

'Follow me.'

He locked the door behind them and led her through a short passageway into a storeroom filled with shelves.

'Make this quick,' Hunter said.

'I just… I'm looking for Daniel. He emailed me to say…' She glanced at Hunter, and he averted his face as if he were shy.

Could she trust him? She felt that Daniel must have; he'd shared the code word with him.

'Daniel said he was in trouble,' she said, 'and he was afraid. He wanted me to come back. He gave me his number, but when I tried to ring…' Her voice failed at the memory; it was unspeakable.

Hunter looked around fearfully, but there was nobody in the room. The building was silent.

'Daniel dug something up,' he said. 'Something big. The police are mixed up with it. He doesn't trust anyone, not even his partner, Hughes. He thought maybe you… because you've been away so long… maybe you're not contaminated. He thought, maybe, that was why you ran away in the first place. You discovered the corruption before anyone else. He said, if I saw you, to give you this.'

He reached in his pocket and pulled out a keyring with three keys.

'What for?' She grabbed the keys and held them to the light. One was a standard front-door key, one appeared to be a car key, and the other... she couldn't tell. 'What does he want me to do?'

'I have no idea,' Hunter said, 'and I don't care. I'm out. I told him last week, I quit. I'm not police, this isn't my job. Jesus Christ, I'll end up shot and left in a skip for some tramp to find.'

'So...'

'You'll have to find him yourself.'

'But... I've looked,' she said. 'Nobody knows where he is.'

'He was living in his mum's old house. She died. You could try there.'

'Alright, thanks.'

'One more thing, there's a housing estate. Sundial Court, it's called. Daniel found something there. I don't know what. He was obsessed with it.'

'A housing estate?'

'Don't go there. Whatever happens, don't go to that estate.'

'Why not?'

'You'll see. I'm leaving now. Don't call me again.' He went to the door and unlocked it. 'Do me a favour. Delete my number from your phone, and the text message.'

15

From the other side of the two-way mirror, Krush studied the suspect. Mr Bennett was seated alone in the interview room. He stared at the wall in front of him and didn't glance at the mirror.

'He doesn't move,' Carmichael said. 'I left him to stew with his thoughts, but he doesn't seem to have any.'

'How long has he been in there?' she asked.

'Half an hour now.'

'Anybody been in to offer him a drink?'

'He doesn't want anything.' Carmichael pressed his nose to the glass, watching. 'It's eerie. He's like a statue in there.'

'He's waiting, that's all.'

'He must be guilty. An innocent man would be looking around the room, checking his watch, wondering what's going on.'

'So would a guilty man.'

'Not if the murder was premeditated; if he had it all figured out. That guy in there knows what's going on. There's no doubt in him at all. He's got it under control. Cold-blooded like a snake.'

Krush shook her head. 'He left the knife half-washed in a sink full of blood. He's not cold-blooded. He's so shaken by everything, his brain has shut down. I've seen it before.'

'He refused to call a lawyer. He doesn't want one.'

'He's in shock,' Krush said. 'He needs a shrink, not a lawyer.'

'Bet you fifty quid he's guilty.'

'Fifty whole pounds?' She stared through the glass. Was he guilty? He had to be, she'd felt certain before, but now... the post-mortem must have shaken her. She was getting soft.

'Keep your money,' she said. 'You just want this to be a quick solve, so you can play golf at the weekend. I'm going in.'

As she moved towards the door, Carmichael said, 'Want any help?'

'No. Stay out. Keep the others out. I'll deal with this guy by myself.'

He chuckled. 'Why do you hate the world, Krush?'

When she entered the interview room, the suspect didn't look up. She closed the door behind her and pulled out the chair opposite him. She laid her briefcase to one side, letting him wonder what it might contain.

'Mr Bennett, I need you to talk to me.'

His eyes were cloudy, they showed no recognition. 'What about?'

'We found your fingerprints on the knife.' For effect, she opened the briefcase and took out a photograph of the knife.

'Oh, the knife. I must've picked it up.' Bennett gazed blandly at the photograph that she set in front of him.

'Why did you wash it?'

'The blood… so much. Blood everywhere. Who'll clean it up? Where would they begin?'

'There were no other fingerprints, only yours. You need to talk to me.'

Bennett slumped in his seat, so quiet and still, he didn't appear to breathe. A few moments stretched into half a minute, and she realized that he didn't intend to respond. She couldn't help but glance at the mirror where Carmichael would be grinning to himself.

'Mr Bennett, understand, you're currently the prime and only suspect in this case. If you have anything to say in your defence, you need to let me know. You have an alibi?'

His eyes wandered into the distance behind her, as if he saw an expanse of sky and not the dull brick wall.

'Do you understand?' Krush said.

'Did I really kill her?' His eyes were so wide, she felt there really was just endless sky behind her back.

'That's what the evidence suggests. Do you have an alibi for last night?'

'Oh Christ. Why did I do that? I don't… it doesn't make sense. We were chatting over dinner, she seemed happy. We were making plans. We thought we might leave the estate. My wife has family down south. Maybe we could relocate, try something new.'

'You don't have an alibi? You were at home the whole night and the morning?'

'Where else would I be at night?'

'Do you have any friends?'

'No.'

'Any family?'

'Not since we moved into the estate.'

Krush leaned forward across the table. She tried to hold eye contact, but his pupils were distant, scanning faraway cloud formations.

'Mr Bennett, did you kill your wife?'

He blinked. 'Is that what they say I did? Maybe they know something. You should ask them. I'm lost.'

'Do you remember killing her?'

'I… I only remember taking a shower. I was in the shower and, I looked down, the water was red around my feet. I looked at my hands, they were covered in blood.'

'What time was that?'

'Dunno.'

'Alright, let's try and piece things together. What do you remember from last night? Let's start with the dinner, the chat you had with your wife. What time did you eat?'

Bennett's left eyelid began to flutter. His hand came up and touched his temple. He lolled in his seat.

He tried to say something. 'D… d… d…'

'Mr Bennett, are you alright?'

'D… d… d…' His eyelid trembled like a butterfly.

'Mr Bennett?'

The door burst open, and Carmichael ran into the room. 'He's having a stroke, the son of a bitch. For God's sake. I'll hold him. Call for help.'

16

Eleanor left the city centre behind and entered the suburbs. She felt another layer of the past peel back as she crossed wide boulevards, tall, overhanging trees, and spacious parks. She didn't need a map to find the old house that Daniel's parents had owned – a dilapidated three-storey tenement down a curving side road, not far from Sefton Park. In the drizzle, green tinges of leaves and grass were released, hinting at memories of a happy childhood she'd never had. Along pavements warped by overgrown tree roots, she followed the path to this old house that had always been falling apart, even while its owners were still alive.

Eleanor used to feel happier there, freer, than in her own mum's place. Daniel was one of those men who kept living at his parents' house long after he should have flown the nest. She used to think that was because he was lazy, but now, in the rich smell of the rotting leaves and the thick grass, she realized it was because he loved it here.

Nothing had changed, not even the rain, this soft drizzle that smelled green and left a delicate film over the skin. By the looks of things, no work or maintenance had been done on the old house. The front garden was overgrown and the paint on the front door was peeling. Ivy covered the front wall, creeping around the upstairs windows. Two enormous sycamore trees towered over the house, blocking out the sunlight.

She tried the doorbell but it was broken. She knocked on the cracked glass and peered through. The floor inside was littered with mail. Nobody was home. She took out the keyring Hunter had given her and tried the first key. It slid in and turned easily. She pushed the door open through a wedge of unread mail and stepped into a musty atmosphere of old carpets and furniture, accumulated dust, and spiderwebs. She tried the light switch, but nothing happened.

In the shadowy hall, she stopped to get her bearings. This huge building was a leftover from a different world where upstairs and downstairs were divided between classes: in the nineteenth century, a rich family occupied the top floors, from where they rang down to their servants who lived on the bottom floor. The wires for the bells were still in place along the walls, but they no longer made a sound.

She wandered the rooms and couldn't believe how unchanged it all was, and how dusty. Their past had been left to its own devices. During the five years she was away, the world back home had turned inwards. The kitchen stank. The oven was thick with dust and seemed to have been unused for years. The worktops were crammed with the remains of takeaway dinners and crushed beer cans. She tried the fridge, but it was turned off and smelled awful.

The back living room was filled with empty wine bottles. A sleeping bag lay discarded on the couch. On an impulse, she picked it up and smelled the interior: Daniel, unmistakable. In all the years since she ran out on him, she still knew his scent more intimately than any other. She felt dizzy. The sleeping bag dropped from her hand. She stumbled out of the living room and crossed the hall. At the foot of the staircase, she stared up through the banisters.

'Daniel?' she called into the heart of the building.

Dust swirled around her. She set off up the stairs into a deeper layer of must and spiderweb. The bedrooms were abandoned, thick with dust, but not empty. They'd been left just how they were: Daniel's room from adolescence still had his posters on the wall, his old clothes in the wardrobe. It was creepy in there. She crossed the landing and found his parents' room. The bed was still made, with the duvet cover drawn back, as if his mother had only just climbed out of bed, only it was pale with dust. Eleanor almost choked on the thick air. She ran out and back down the stairs.

She was ready to burst out of the front door into the cool rain outside but she stopped dead in the vestibule. Somebody was coming up the driveway. She peered through the glass and saw her half-sister. Her stomach sang with distress and yearning. Beth was looking down at her phone, she didn't notice the face in the vestibule window. Her sister had changed. Her blonde hair was tied back, her face sharper, sadder. She'd put on weight. Almost a different person, and yet she recognized her right away, somehow still the younger sibling who was the star at school.

Eleanor ducked down and curled into a ball against the bottom of the door. The wooden panel rattled against her spine as Beth banged on it. She banged again while Eleanor held her breath. Through the letter box she heard that familiar voice, slightly shrill, call, 'Daniel!' Another bang on the door, and then, 'For Christ's sake.'

Beth was so close, she could hear her breathing. All Eleanor had to do was pull herself up and open the door. Beth's feet moved away. She banged on the window of the living room, and shouted, 'Daniel!'

Still Eleanor couldn't move. She lay paralysed as her sister retreated, muttering to herself, back down the front driveway. She wasn't ready for the meeting yet, it had been too long, the emotions were too complex. She waited until the sound of her parting was erased. Silence.

She lay there quietly, among the pile of mail, until her ears tuned into the birdsong and the hiss of wind that breathed through the wet sycamores over the driveway. She wasn't the only one looking for Daniel. He said in his email that he didn't trust anybody, could that include Beth? These past five years, Eleanor had thought of those two as co-conspirators, neck and neck in sin. *If he no longer trusts Beth…*

17

The lights were all turned off at her dad's house, which was unusual as he rarely went out in the evening now that he lived alone and had arthritis in his knees. Krush looked through the living room window and saw him slumped on the couch watching television. She withdrew, not wanting to startle him, but his gaze was sleepy, lost in whatever was on the box. She knocked on the front door and opened it with her key.

'It's only me,' she called.

'Oh.'

'Why are you sitting in the dark?' She went into the living room.

'What?' He didn't look up from what he was watching, some kind of musical talent show.

She laid down the bag of groceries she'd brought. 'I said, why are you sitting in the dark?' She turned the light on.

Neil Krush blinked and seemed to surface from the television. 'I didn't realize it had got dark.'

'Night falls early this time of year.'

He lowered the volume on the remote control. 'What are you doing here?'

'I brought you some stuff.'

'You look funny. Not sad, are you?'

'Sad?' She glanced at the mirror on the side wall, but she couldn't detect any emotion in her own face, only the lines of fading youth.

'You spend too much time around here, Beth. You should be out with people your own age, not a half-dead old bastard like me.'

'Dad, come on…'

'What's in that bag?' He pointed with the remote control at the shopping she'd set down. 'Not more of that bloody low-fat crap, I hope.'

'The doctor said you have to lose weight.'

'Yeah, well, you're too late. I already ate.' He gestured to a greasy plate of bones on the couch next to him.

'Dad, you shouldn't–'

'Jeez, Beth. Leave me in peace. Why are you here bothering me? What happened to Daniel? I thought that was going well.'

'He… we're taking a break.'

'Ah come on, Beth, what did you do to upset him?'

'You're supposed to take my side.'

'It's you. I knew you'd chase him away. You're not right. Ever since your sister left–'

'My *half*-sister…'

'She's still your sister.'

'It's not my fault she left. She left Daniel as well – she left you. She left everybody.'

'Yeah well, the rest of us got on with our lives. You're still stewing. Let her go. She's not coming back.'

'She…'

'It's been five years. We all thought she'd come home, but we were wrong. She doesn't want to see us. We've tried. Me as well. She doesn't want to come back. So, her let go. The rest of us have.'

'I moved on, years ago.'

'You got engaged to her ex. That's not letting go, it's the opposite. It's weird. It's like trying to take her place.'

'What…? I can't listen to this.'

'Because you know it's true.'

'I'm going.'

'Good.' He pointed the remote at the TV and put the volume up. 'And take that low-fat junk with you. I'm not eating it.'

She grabbed the shopping bag. 'I don't know why I bother trying to help you.'

'I don't know either. Try helping yourself instead. Find some friends your own age. Get a new boyfriend, one who never heard of Eleanor…'

He stopped. They looked at each other over the tinny din of the TV show playing in the background. Eleanor's name was never spoken aloud by either of them. Neil always said, "your sister", and Krush always said, "my *half-*sister". Spoken aloud after such long disuse, it was like the name of a stranger – some word from a foreign language she'd never heard.

His eyes returned to the TV screen. 'Go on, get out. You can leave the food. I'll think about eating it.'

18

In the dream, they judged him. What was this place? An endless city, far from home; he'd never find his way. A gang of dirty children followed him. They pointed and sang, chanting his guilt. And yet, he hadn't done anything. He only wanted to help.

'I'm a doctor,' he tried to say, but no words came out.

He couldn't bear their eyes on him. The world accused him, he was judged and found wicked. He ran. The streets expanded, subdivided, forming new cities; peripheries without centres, dead ends lined with junkshops and dark, sinister doorways. He ran without moving, screamed without making a sound. Beneath it all, the rising knowledge of some buried evil. What had been done? Who did that thing? A crowd pursued him, thickening with more and more faces that hunted him. They'd punish him. Somebody had to be sacrificed to appease the gods of this place – the crossroads of highways, the tower blocks and the black sky. Somebody had to die.

He ran down an alleyway, found a door, pushed inside.

'It's you,' a woman said. Her limbs were all broken. She'd fallen from somewhere high up, the top of one of these never-ending towers.

'No, no.'

He was back in the shelter. Somebody pushed him down on a bunk. A group of homeless people loomed over him. The smell was so unbearable he drowned in it; they wouldn't let him breathe.

'You're the doctor?' they said.

But he wasn't the doctor, he never had been. He was just a patient. It wasn't his fault. They didn't understand that; they didn't understand anything. They only felt this chemical compulsion, biological knowledge: somebody had to die.

A clattering sound woke him with a groan. He was still in the locked room, his skin coated in a freezing film of dried slime. He'd never escape this place. The reek of his own sick was like a bed that sucked him down. He'd smelled it even through the dream.

'Shush!' Somebody laughed in the dark.

The doctor flinched and tried to see, but when he focused his eyes, red blobs danced in front of him, his head span. He let his head fall back.

'There's someone in there,' a man said.

'Shut up!' a young woman shouted and laughed. 'I'm too high. I need to lie down. What did you give me?'

'Shush,' the man said. 'Listen.'

The voices came from the other side of the locked door. The doctor raised his head and tried to speak.

'Fuck,' the woman said. 'What's that smell? It's like somebody died.'

Their accents were a guttural version of Scouse, stronger than the one he'd grown up with. He must be back in Liverpool. Christ, how did he get here?

'Keep your voice down,' the man said. 'There's someone in there, I'm telling you.'

'No, there isn't. This place is abandoned. Nobody's lived here in years. It's disgusting, it stinks. Who could bear it?' Her voice changed, she sounded bored. 'Let's go back. I feel sick. I think I'm going to throw up...'

'Help me,' the doctor called out. He tried to control his voice, but the words came out in a warped crow's caw.

The woman screamed.

'Shit!' the man yelled.

The doctor tried to call again but it was too late, he heard their feet sprinting down the stairs. They laughed hysterically as they ran.

19

Where could she stay? Eleanor had nobody to turn to in Liverpool. Her parents and grandparents were dead. She found herself standing in the road outside her stepfather Neil's house. A scruffy terrace that opened directly onto the street, the place hadn't changed – even the scrappy green paint was still the same. The house was dark apart from a glow behind the living room window. Somebody was watching television. Would Neil be happy to see her? They'd never been close. He was Beth's dad; after she cut off Beth, she had to cut him off too. He'd never tried to reach out to her.

In a way, she pitied him. It can't have been easy taking on somebody else's daughter. Her "new dad" was a dour man, unimaginative, uninterested in his kids; there'd never been any kind of bond between them. The closest she ever felt was when she saw him cry at her mother's funeral. And yet, there was a sense of safety in his dourness. In his lack of imagination, there was no room for wild fears and nightmares. A phone could ring in his house and just be a phone, a regular phone.

She almost knocked on his door, but it was too late. No, she couldn't go to her stepfather. She hurried away from his little house before he might look out of the window and catch her there.

She considered a hotel, but the thought of being alone in a sterile, empty box was unbearable. Or perhaps it was nothing to do with that; in truth, she just wanted to stay in Daniel's old house. If she waited there, he might come back. Surrounded by threads that almost connected but didn't quite meet, the dusty house, with its old service bells, felt like the only sanctuary. She found a corner shop at the end of the road and bought a toothbrush, toothpaste, and other essentials that she hadn't stopped to pick up in London. There were spare blankets and pillows in Daniel's parents' room, although she could barely stand to be in there.

She passed from room to room, looking for a place to make a bed, but as the darkness set in outside, the place felt grisly, she didn't want to stay in any of them. She found herself back in the lounge where Daniel had left his sleeping bag. It was the only room that had any sense of life. She laid out some blankets on the couch and tried to sleep. Night fell. In the darkness, the house around her felt different, it shivered and moaned through its warped beams. She kept Daniel's torch close by under the blanket.

This was impossible. She'd never fall asleep. In the morning, she'd have to find a hotel. But as the streets fell into a trance of silence outside, she did begin to feel drowsy. She was fading into the edges of dream when a telephone sounded in the hall. She sat up straight. The ringing vibrated through the floorboards. She grabbed the torch like a weapon. The ringing phone was hypnotic and she found herself out of bed, tiptoeing in the cold towards it. She turned on the torch and flashed it around the room that felt completely other at night – the ceiling was too high, the wallpaper peeling, the corners filled with junk.

Clouds of dust shifted in the beam of light. The phone didn't stop ringing.

She went out into the hall and saw it positioned on a small table against the wall. It rang and rang. She stepped closer. Could she pick it up? She tried to tell herself there was no way they were calling for her. Nobody knew she was there. There was no reason to look for her in this antiquated house. But she felt certain, somehow, that if she picked up the phone, it would be the same voice that had taunted her in London – smug, cold, and vicious. It couldn't be, and yet, who else would phone here in the middle of the night?

She should confront them, show them she wasn't afraid. She tried to imagine picking up the receiver and shouting into it, "Leave me in peace!" but she couldn't. In the dark, it was too much. In the morning, in daylight, she'd be ready, but not like this, disoriented, dragged from the verges of sleep. She was caught in the cold, afraid to go forwards all the way and answer the phone, but incapable of going back into the living room to try and sleep. The floorboards were chilly and uneven beneath her feet. Still the phone rang; they would never relent. Who could it be, if not the voice?

Or… could it be Daniel? At that thought, everything changed. Suddenly she was terrified to miss the call. She sprang forward before the phone could stop ringing, but in the dark, she missed her footing, tripped on the edge of a thick rug and flew forwards. The torch dropped from her hand and rolled away. Still lit, it cast a shaft of light along the floor.

'Shit.'

She pulled herself upright. The phone stopped ringing. The echoes repeated in her mind before it adjusted to the silence. Torn between relief that the temptation to answer was passed, and loss that she'd never know if it was Daniel, she lay on the floor and looked into the beam of torchlight. Part of the rug was folded over where her foot had caught against it. The torch showed the end of the floorboards. There was something else there under the rug.

She reached and pulled the corner free to reveal a trapdoor set into the floor. Made of the same wood as the boards, it was smooth and flat, undetectable beneath the rug. There was a ring in the centre, set into a circular hollow. She grabbed hold of this handle and pulled. The trapdoor shifted.

It was awkward and heavy; she needed both hands to wrestle it loose. A freezing draught came issuing out of the ground. The square space revealed was just wide enough for one person to climb into. She grabbed the torch and shone it over the edge. A ladder was set into a wall of brick that was coated with old spiderwebs and dust. It led down some six feet into the shadow. She coughed on the air of powdered stone that danced in the beam. It was silent down there. She wanted to call Daniel's name, but she didn't dare make a noise.

20

Krush lived in a flat overlooking the river mouth that poured into the Irish Sea. It was all glass and chrome inside, like herself. Bleak sky filled the floor-to-ceiling windows. She was alone. Not even her father wanted to spend time with her. It was true, what he'd said; she pushed people away. First her half-sister had left, and now Daniel. If she couldn't figure out how to make human beings hang around, she'd be alone forever.

There wasn't even a dog or a cat in the flat to keep her company. She hated pets. It was one of the things that irritated her about other people, the way they constantly talked about their animals as if they were real people and not just expensive creatures that parasitized their so-called "owners". Maybe she could get a spider or a snake, something that wouldn't pretend to love her in return for pet food. Or maybe she should take up drinking, like Daniel. That's what lonely police officers were supposed to do.

She looked in the fridge and cupboards but there was nothing left of Daniel's. When he'd moved out, he'd taken everything that belonged to him. It was shocking to discover how little remained of her own. This place was bare. She liked it that way, it suited her, but tonight she only felt alone. Perhaps Daniel would come back. He'd been busy recently with some secret operation. He'd changed. He was distant. No, he wouldn't come back. He'd never really loved her anyway; it was only because of her half-sister. After Eleanor left, he'd almost lost his mind. Perhaps she had manipulated that to gain a hold over him. Or perhaps he was the one who used her. Neither of them ever found what they were looking for, and Eleanor had never come back. That goddamn tattoo on his wrist. She'd begged him to get rid of it, but he only put a red line through the name, which somehow made it even worse.

She went into the living room. It was a wide, empty cube containing an uncomfortable sofa and a television that she never turned on. The floor-to-ceiling windows looked over the city centre. Brilliant light flickered against a mass of shadow, the dark impressions of the twin cathedrals. She closed the blinds and turned on the television. A panel show filled the screen, a bunch of people arguing about politics.

'Why are you so angry?' she asked them. 'Why…?' She stopped. Talking to yourself is a symptom of too much time alone.

The people on the screen kept shouting at each other. She wondered how they could get so emotional about it all. One woman on the panel, a politician apparently, looked as if she was about to cry. Krush wondered how a politician would cope if she had to pull the hands away from a corpse's face. Probably, things would feel different. She turned the TV off.

Most nights, she worked. She didn't need entertainment or friends, she only needed her job. She was good at it. She overheard others at the station ask how she got promoted so fast while the rest of them just stayed where they were. They'd never understand; they were ordinary folks who went home to their stupid pets and their annoying children, and watched TV so they could forget about work. Krush never stopped working. Even while she was asleep, she kept on investigating. That's why they made her chief detective, she was the one who chased the killers at night while everyone else slept. The solitary one.

She found herself sitting in the dark. Loneliness has a feeling all of its own, something akin to sadness, but airier, softer. It was good to be alone, she told herself, she could do whatever she wanted. The wind shook the panes of glass. Pale gulls drifted on the currents of gale. Up here on the fifth floor of the tower, the elements blew raw.

She put on her coat and left the flat. The elevator descended slowly through a silent building. Mirrored on all sides, she saw herself reflected in a loop of empty space. Her face was sharp. She never wore make-up. At the station, she overheard them say she never smiled. She tried now and saw the cold twist of her lips repeat in the mirrored surfaces. The isolation was spreading through her limbs like drowsiness, if she let it fill her body completely, she'd end up bunched in a corner with her hands over her face. She shook the feeling away.

'I'll sell this flat,' she said. 'I'll move somewhere nice.'

Talking to herself again. She didn't bother to try and stop this time.

'I could move somewhere with people. A community. I could get a dog.'

It was like listening to a stranger. Whoever this person talking was, she must be crazy, she thought. Outside, a freezing wind of sleet swept through the car park. She savoured it. Fresh, metallic. She climbed into her car and turned the radio on. Human voices. Music. She skimmed through the stations to find the shipping news. It was calming, a tender boredom. She pulled out of the car park and moved quickly through deserted night-time streets. It was beautiful to drive. Control. Movement. The whirr of wheels over the tarmac.

* * *

At night, the estate was different. Without streetlights, the drizzle was saturated with darkness; all around, the houses sank into a pool of absence. Rain poured down through the beams of her headlights. Nobody was outside, not even the homeless clown, Mac. A few lit windows showed between the patches of shadow formed by the abandoned buildings. Although it was a compact, self-enclosed space, the estate was confusing in the dark. She felt disoriented and slowed the car to a crawl as she stared out of the window, trying to get her bearings. All the houses looked the same.

She parked in the driveway of a burnt-out building and climbed out of the car. With her hood up, her torch flashing through the rain, she crossed the street. Something moved in the bins behind her. She spun around. Holding her breath, she listened through the thrash of the downpour. Nothing moved. There was a trace of ash in the air. She went up the driveway of a derelict house, stopping to listen after every few steps. Her torch beam swept through the damp remains of a bonfire.

'Is anyone there?' Her voice was snatched away by the wind.

She went around the side of the house and found a broken fence. The gate had been pulled down. She looked through the gap into the rear yard; it was filled with bin bags. Raindrops pattered on the plastic. Her torch beam crossed the side wall, over a blocked-out window, and stopped at some graffiti on the stucco. A rough pair of eyes were spraypainted in red. They transfixed her through the beam until she lowered her torch. She stepped closer and rubbed the paint with her fingers. Still fresh. A metal bin clanged in the backyard.

She whirled around, the torch spinning madly, and caught a glimpse of a cat running away.

'For fuck's sake.' She dropped down and wiped a layer of rain from her face. 'What am I doing out here?'

She kept moving. The lights were on at number 21. She heard the din of karaoke from halfway down the street. She turned the torch off as she approached the house. It was some pop song they were singing; she didn't recognize the tune. Several people were bawling down the microphone, mouthing different words. They laughed too loud, hysterical, frightening.

Krush crept up the driveway and looked through the frosted glass of the front door. Somebody was in the hall; a grey, misshapen form. They walked away towards the kitchen at the back of the house. The curtains were closed over the living room, but she found a crack of light in the corner where the interior showed.

She knelt and looked inside. It was crowded. Even more people than she'd seen last time. Some of them were the same. She recognized a few other people from around the estate. There was even a dog, a squat bulldog sitting between the legs of the singers. Davey and Melinda oversaw their party from the back of the room. Their blank faces were red and sweaty. Others in the room were laughing and shouting. To one side, she recognized Davey's father-in-law as he leaned over a coffee table to snort a line of cocaine.

She was so absorbed by the scene, she'd stopped thinking about the rain. A leak came down from a gutter over the other side of the front window. She realized abruptly that her face was soaked. She pulled back from the window to wipe it. She checked her watch: 01.33 a.m. It was true, the party here never ended. Could she go inside? Davey had said everyone was welcome. She could just knock on the door. She wasn't wearing a uniform. She had her tracksuit on; she was just like anyone else on the estate.

Go inside, eat some pizza, snort a line, sing a song on the karaoke, join in with everybody else instead of being alone.

The song ended. It was too quiet. She felt guilty standing out there, spying. If somebody caught her... A new song started up on the machine. She recognized the intro, it was something by The Beatles. Was that the only band on the machine? A man started to sing. She leaned again to look through the window. It was Scott, the local police officer. He wore a vest and shorts, a green party hat perched sideways on his head. He sang in his bland voice and the words were garbled, more like humming. The others laughed. Somebody slapped him on the back. A woman put one arm around him and grabbed hold of the microphone to sing as well, but it sounded like a different song. She screamed over the top of Scott so that he was barely audible. Somebody glanced over at the window.

Krush jumped back. Had they seen her? It felt as if they'd made eye contact, but that was impossible, she was in the dark, the interior was lit, they wouldn't be able to see outside. So why was she running? She hurried away through the puddles and stopped to look back. Nothing moved at the house. The front door didn't open. The music carried on. She ran back to her car and drove away. Despite the solitude that ate at her, it was better to be alone; she didn't belong with anyone.

21

Eleanor put the torch and a kitchen knife in her bag and climbed down the ladder slowly, testing each rung as she descended into a pocket of icy cold.

At the bottom of the shaft, her torch showed a low door set into the wall. It was a rough panel of wood with no hinges, more an obstacle to block the way than a door.

She pulled it back and shone her torch along a tunnel dug into the brickwork. How long had this been down here? Had there always been a secret tunnel under the house, even when they were young, playing upstairs in Daniel's room? She remembered Daniel's parents had talked from time to time about an old WWII bunker, but she hadn't imagined it still existed.

The passage was low; she had to crawl. She cringed as powdered brick caught in her hair. There was hardly room to move her limbs. The roof of the tunnel grazed her back and she could only pull herself forwards, stopping now and then to shine the torch around. The tunnel didn't feel stable, it could collapse on her head. She stopped to listen. A gentle rain of dust. The murmur of a car driving along the street outside sending vibrations underground. She would have called for Daniel, but she feared bringing the ceiling crashing down on her head. She crawled forwards.

At the end of the tunnel, she reached another panel of wood. Panic caught at her throat. If this place was sealed, she might never get out; it was too narrow to turn around. She shoved the panel, and it gave way, falling backwards and clattering to the ground with a cloud of dust. With her face averted, she crawled out of the tunnel into a small brick room. The ceiling was just high enough for her to stand up.

She shone her torch across a table that was covered in documents – old newspapers, files, and scribbled notes. On the far wall, a map had been stuck up, surrounded by Post-it Notes. She tried to take it all in but there were too many details, it was overwhelming. There was no other door; Daniel was not down here, but he must have spent time in this claustrophobic chamber. These had to be his notes.

She found a candle and a box of matches. Her hand shook as she lit one, starving for light. In the candlelight, the map was illuminated. It didn't show anywhere she recognized, it didn't seem like a real place, none of this was real. She scanned the notes that were stuck up haphazardly around the wall. One jumped out at her:

Eleanor

Her own name had become terrifying. She pulled the note down and put it in her pocket with the prickling sense that she was being watched. But there were no windows down here, she was in the one place where nobody could spy.

She focussed on the map. It showed a suburb of a city. Looking closer, she realized it was Liverpool, as some familiar roads appeared at the edges of the page – some out-of-the-way periphery she'd never been to, or only passed through. In the middle of the map, Daniel had drawn circles and arrows, and added words that were illegible in his crooked handwriting. All these marks were in the same area, a cluster of buildings surrounded by a criss-cross of highways. She peered closer. *Sundial Court.* She'd heard of it before. It was one of those dangerous places, the no-go zones that nobody bothered to fix. Daniel's comments in tiny letters were inserted between the streets. One of the houses was circled.

Hunter had said something about an estate. *Don't go there,* he'd warned. She folded the map and put it in her bag.

Next, she skimmed through the newspaper cuttings. There were too many to read in detail but after scanning the headlines, she found several that pertained to a doctor. A doctor of psychiatry. The papers were old, some dating more than ten years ago. The doctor in the pictures wore glasses and a suit; he had a dark beard, and was exactly like she'd imagine a psychiatrist to look. She didn't recognize him.

The news stories were too dense in the candlelight; she put them down and moved to a pile of photographs. These had been taken on a police camera, they had to be Daniel's work.

Flicking through, she saw the buildings and inhabitants of an estate, passers-by going about their business unaware their picture was taken. Most of the images were prosaic, just people and houses. Some of them were marked with notes; one showed a police officer in the estate, gazing into the distance. Daniel had written "Police involvement?" in one corner of the photo, and "How far does it go?" beneath.

Several pictures showed kids running around, and one showed a girl sitting in a corner somewhere with her knees pulled up under her chin, and her hands over her eyes as if she were crying, or perhaps as if she was afraid to look. It was a disturbing image. The walls of the room were painted red, the girl huddled there, back pressed into the corner, as if it were the last place of safety.

She was still studying this picture with disturbed fascination when a phone started to ring in the hall above her head. It rang and rang. For a moment she just listened. They would never leave her alone. They pursued her, they laughed at her. The photograph dropped to the floor. She was about to move when the phone stopped. Suddenly, it became unbearable in the bunker, airless, too narrow. What if somebody was to close the trapdoor and seal her down here…? She stuffed the pictures, the map, and the notes in her bag, and crawled out through the tunnel.

22

In the morning light, her anxieties seemed absurd. The phone in the hall was an antique with a rotary dial, she could hardly believe it still worked. Eleanor laid Daniel's map out on the kitchen table, and it was just a housing estate, brick and cement depicted in ink – there was nothing to fear. She gathered the map and called a taxi.

The driver stared at her in the rear-view mirror. 'Sundial Court? I can't take you there, love.'

'Why not?' The windscreen wipers turned, but the car didn't move.

'You're not from Liverpool, I guess.'

'Actually, I…'

'My insurance doesn't cover it. That's the most dangerous estate in the country.' His voice betrayed a certain pride.

She looked up from the map. 'Is it that bad?'

'I can park nearby, and you can walk.'

'Fine.'

'But I don't understand, why do you want to go there?'

'My boyfriend.' She hoped this would end the conversation.

He gave her a strange look, sighed, and turned the key in the ignition. The car pulled out from the kerb. Eleanor kept her eyes on the rain that trickled down the window. She hoped to discourage questions, but the driver said, 'Where are you from, love? What are you, a tourist or something?'

'I'm from Liverpool. Grew up here. Spent most of my life here.'

'Don't sound like it. What happened to your accent?'

'My accent?' The question took her by surprise. 'I was in London the last five years. I guess I must have lost it.'

'London? What did you want to go down there for?'

'Err… work.'

'A good job, was it? Must have been.'

'The same job I had here. I'm a police detective.'

His eyes swivelled in the rear-view mirror. Perhaps she had found the right way to end the conversation.

'You don't look like a police detective,' he said.

'I'm in disguise.'

'Well, welcome home, I guess.'

* * *

The taxi parked on an empty stretch of highway.

'It's through there.' The driver pointed through the rain at the intersection up ahead. 'Follow the smell of bonfires and dead dogs. Can't miss it.'

'Thanks.'

'Be careful though, hey.'

'I'm police.'

'Don't tell them that.'

He closed the door before she could respond, and quickly drove away.

By the side of the highway, she took out the map and followed the driver's directions. There really was a smell of bonfires. She took the turn and came to a sign that might once have said "Sundial Court", but it was completely covered in graffiti. For the first time, she felt afraid. Could it really be so dangerous? She was a police officer, but she was dressed in a tracksuit with a cap, and had no weapon. She entered the estate.

The main driveway leading inwards curved around a long, tattered, wooden fence. Broken in places, it showed the backs of a row of houses, all the same: two-storey, semi-detached, brick, with sloping roofs. The nearest buildings seemed to have been burned out. The smashed windows were set into black smudges. There was nobody around. She felt there was something missing; a detail wasn't right, but what was it? At the end of the drive, she came to a roundabout. From here, four other streets branched like spokes, showing the sides and fronts of houses, many of them blocked with piled rubbish.

Across the other end of the estate, one of the houses was fenced off by police tape that fluttered in the wind. For a moment it was just like being at work. She set off towards the black-and-yellow tape with curiosity. Coming closer, she saw a police officer stationed outside the front door of a house that otherwise appeared normal. But she wasn't here as a police officer, and besides, Beth might be in that house. She moved away, perhaps a little too quickly, a little suspicious. She realized what was missing, the subtle detail: there were no streetlights.

She checked the map and put it away. Daniel had circled number 35, in the opposite corner of the estate to the house with the crime scene tape. She headed in that direction, keeping her head down and clutching her bag. She heard a door slam nearby and glanced around, but there was nobody to see, just the flicker of a curtain closing.

She passed the remains of a bonfire turning to ashy mush in the rain. Bits of old furniture stuck out of the pile beside a bent shopping trolley. She stopped to look, but it was just rubbish. Footsteps splashed in the puddles behind her back, and she swung around to see three teenage boys in tracksuits running away. The rain intensified. She pulled her hood up and kept walking.

Number 35 appeared to be derelict. The door was boarded shut and the windows were sealed behind metal grates. She felt weary and depressed as she went up to the door. This was a dead end. Daniel had dragged her all the way out here, the middle of nowhere, a wilderness, for nothing. But he had circled it on the map. Why? She looked closer. The boards over the door were new; the heads of the nails were still shiny; the wood wasn't warped from wind and rain. They might have been stuck up just in the last few days. If she had a crowbar, it would open easily, but she didn't have a crowbar; she didn't have any tools. She tried the living room window, but it was blocked behind a metal panel.

Somebody stepped in a puddle behind her. She choked a scream and jumped back, spinning around, her hands balled into fists. A girl stood in the rain, watching.

'You startled me,' Eleanor said. She felt the fright subside and almost laughed at herself.

The girl watched, one eye showing through her black hair that was plastered across her wet face. She wore a tracksuit and dirty trainers. She didn't react when Eleanor stepped towards her and said, 'You're soaking. What are you doing out here? You should be in school.'

How old is she? At first, she'd taken her for a child, she was so small and scrawny, but looking closer, her face was marked with acne, her eyes were red like an insomniac's. The girl held out her hand, palm upwards, as if asking for something.

'What do you want?' Eleanor said.

The little hand, flecked with dirt and what might have been ink, hung open in the rain, demanding.

'I don't have anything to give you, I'm sorry.'

The hand dropped down to her side, but she didn't speak.

Eleanor knelt. 'Hey, do you live in this estate?'

With a swish of greasy hair, the girl whirled around and set off sprinting away through the puddles.

'Wait…' She took a step to follow, but it was pointless. She watched the kid disappear between the fences of the houses across the right-hand side of the roundabout. 'Suit yourself.'

She turned back to number 35. To one side, a wooden gate, spraypainted with "RIP", led to the backyard. It was locked, of course. She grabbed the top of the gate and pulled herself up, feet flailing against the slick boards. At the top, she glanced around, feeling herself watched, but there was nobody out there. Her hands gripped the rough wooden ends of the boards, her shoulders tense, she pulled one leg up and onto the top of the gate, and swung herself over, tumbling down on the other side.

The backyard was concrete, strewn with old leaves and bin bags that let off a ripe smell like compost. A bike with no wheels rusted in the rain. A long rear window was sealed behind a metal panel. The back door was boarded over, but the boarding seemed older than out front, with soft wood and dirty nails. A clear space in the form of an arc showed in the dirt where the door, opening outwards, had brushed the old leaves aside; it must have been opened recently.

She tried the handle and felt it give. She pulled, and the door came free. The boarding was just for show, it wasn't attached to the frame. A horrible smell issued out when she opened the door wider, the heady smell of blood that she knew from her work, and something else, an acrid, burning trace. What was that? She looked back once and listened, but there was nobody to see. The estate beyond was silent, just a shimmer of rain in puddles. She covered her nose and went inside.

23

'Good news,' Carmichael said. 'Bennett is alive. We got him to hospital fast enough. They managed to stabilise him. Bad news, he suffered brain damage during the stroke. Too soon to tell if he'll be able to walk again or speak.'

'Thank God,' Krush said. 'Almost had a fatality in police custody on our hands.'

She was seated across the other side of the desk in Carmichael's office. Next to her, Scott stared out of the window. She hadn't expected the officer from the estate to be there. It was typical of the tricks Carmichael liked to play in order to keep his underlings on edge. She had dreamed in the early hours of the dead woman's eyeless face. What had she seen?

'Still,' Carmichael said, 'he had a stroke during an interview. Lawyers could use that against us. Media will kick up a fuss. Don't talk to anyone outside the station about that, let me deal with it. It's my goddamn headache.'

'What do we know about Bennett?' Krush said. 'Is he guilty or not? Scott?' She glanced at Scott, who said nothing, seemingly embarrassed. Here in the station, he was even more waifish and withdrawn; even less of a police officer.

Carmichael took out two sticks of nicotine gum and put both in his mouth at the same time. 'He's guilty, of course. That was the most convenient stroke I ever heard of.'

'It'll be harder to prove now. We won't be able to get a confession.' She looked again at Scott, who offered no opinion.

'Don't be so sure.' Carmichael threw a third stick of gum into the mix. 'The state he's going to be in, we can probably get him to sign anything.'

'I thought you wanted to avoid the lawyers and journalists.'

'Got any better ideas?'

'Scott.' She turned to face him. 'Tell us about the suspect. You're the one who knows the estate. Who was he? Could he have killed his wife?'

'Oh.' Scott seemed to wake from a trance. 'Bennett didn't attend the local residents' meetings, never signed his name on the petitions. Never heard him complain once. That's unusual on the estate. I've been working there a decade, I attend most of the meetings, but I've barely spoken with him.'

'A loner,' Carmichael said. 'Fits the profile of a killer.'

'I'm a loner,' Krush said.

Carmichael stood up heavily. 'Let's not waste time here. Bennett is the killer. We just need a motive, or any kind of explanation. If we could prove that he had psychological problems, I could sell it to a judge. You two go to Bennett's office, speak to his colleagues. Dig something up.'

Krush glanced at Scott who was looking at the floor.

'It's fine,' she said. 'I can do this alone. Let Scott go back to the estate, he can keep an eye on things.'

'No.' Carmichael grinned. He was enjoying this, the bastard. He could tell she didn't like Scott; he had a talent for sniffing these things out. 'You two work together on this case. Scott will come in useful, you'll see. You're a shady one, aren't you, Scott?'

Carmichael came around the table and slapped him on the back, but the beat officer said nothing.

24

It was dark in the derelict house. Eleanor took the torch out of her bag and sent a white beam around the contours of what might have been a kitchen, except the units had all been torn out. A pale outline in the filthy wall showed where a fridge used to stand. She stepped carefully through broken glass, wincing at every sound.

The kitchen door was closed. She put her ear to it and listened to the hall... what was that? A quiet, persistent background noise like humming, perhaps from an electrical device that had been left on, but it seemed unlikely; everything of the slightest value had been looted. She listened again, but the sound was too quiet to pin down. She thought about calling out, but she was afraid. She pushed the door open.

The darkness of the hall was washed by thin, dirty light through the frosted glass of the front door. The torchlight sent a sliver of brightness over bare floorboards and shreds of carpet. Something smelled bad in this house. The humming sound was closer, but still indistinct. She caught her foot on a bent nail sticking out of the floorboards and dropped the torch. In the near darkness, her heart thudding violently against her ribs, she squatted down and picked it up.

Somebody was outside in the driveway. Still on her haunches, she panicked and for a moment couldn't find the switch to turn off the torch as a hand rattled the front door.

Muffled through the wood, she heard a man outside say, 'Doesn't look like anyone's been in.' His Scouse accent was thick and throaty.

Another voice replied, 'It was a woman, they said. Snooping around. Trying to see through the window.'

'Probably nothing.'

Hunched on the ground, she listened as their feet moved away from the door. The sounds of the outside came through clearly, there must be so many gaps in the walls of this building – broken windows, cracked frames. She smelled blood on the floor, a strong, sudden whiff that made her gag. The panel over the living room window shook.

'Nobody's been through this way,' the voice said, more distant now.

'And the back?'

A hand rattled the gate. Eleanor was paralysed on the floor. Had she closed the back door?

'It's locked.' The voices had moved further away, almost out of earshot.

'Could she have climbed over?'

'Why would she? This woman, whoever she was. She must have got lost.'

'We could check?'

'Leave it. She's gone.'

Their feet splashed away through the puddles. Eleanor waited for her breath to return. The torch shook in her hand. She didn't dare to turn it on. When the sound of their receding feet had faded away, the humming noise returned. She crept to the end of the hall, crouched down to keep her shadow from the frosted glass in the door. Peering out through the letter box, there was no sign of the two strangers. The smell of blood down here was rich.

She flashed her torch and found a dark red trail spattered across the wall and the skirting boards.

She reached into her pocket for her crime scene gloves and notepad, but she hadn't brought any. She wasn't here as police, she was dressed like a scruffy, nameless member of the public. She barely knew who she was without the paraphernalia of the job, but she could still investigate.

Crawling on all fours, she followed the trail of blood. It was smeared and dull in places, as if somebody had hurriedly tried to wipe it away. She followed the blood back along the hall until it disappeared by the kitchen door. She searched all over for another spot but couldn't find any.

Back in the hall, she went to the foot of the stairs and looked up into the shadow. There was no banister and no carpet, just bare boards with nails poking out. The humming sound seemed to have stopped, but it must have come from up there somewhere. She turned back from the stairs, there were still rooms to explore on the ground floor: a living room, a small back room, and a bathroom.

The back room was bare, having no carpet, no wallpaper, no furniture, and a window without glass that had been covered over. The bathroom was empty, even the toilet and sink had been pulled out. What tiles remained were cracked and dusty. She began to give up hope of finding anything in this house.

At first view, the front living room was just like the back, no carpet and no wallpaper, no furniture, but there was one thing: a stool lay on its side by the window, where a couple of torn curtains were closed over a metal panel. Trying not to give way to desperation, she picked up the stool. It must have been set just there, by the window. She sat down on it and looked around. There was a gap in the curtains and the panel directly in front of the stool. Somebody might have been sitting in this spot to spy out of the window. She closed her eyes. Could it be Daniel? Could he have been seated here, looking out at the estate?

It was a perfect vantage point. She sat forward on the stool and stared through the gap. Yes, everything could be seen from here, the whole of the central roundabout and all the houses stretching away. She strained, but there was nothing to see except rain. What did Daniel see? As her eyes studied the view, more details grew out of the background grey – a trace of red. Opposite, across the front of the burnt-out shell of a building, a gigantic pair of red eyes had been painted. They stared back at her as if they had been placed there to look directly through the crack in the window.

She jumped up and ran into the hall. At the front door, she tried the handle and felt it give beneath the boards. She longed to run out of this place, but she couldn't leave yet. She had to go further. The humming sound had ceased, and perhaps she'd only imagined it. Peering up through the stumps where the banisters had been removed, she saw the floor above receded into shadow. With nowhere else to go, she climbed the stairs.

25

Krush drove over to the office block where the suspect, Leonard Bennett, worked. It was a new building that overlooked the river. Scott didn't speak during the journey, and she was glad. In the parking lot of the block there was a little shack with a sign saying, "Bacon Butties". A few staff members in their suits were queuing under umbrellas outside.

She saw Scott gazing at the sign. 'Hungry?'

'I haven't eaten.'

'Why don't you go and queue up there, get a sandwich and a drink? I'll talk to Bennett's boss. It'll only take a minute.'

'Don't you need my help?'

'I work better alone.'

She walked away before he could argue. In the foyer, she took the lift to the top floor. There was a window up there that surveyed the parking lot and the skyline of office blocks. She saw Scott standing in the queue below, the only person waiting who didn't have an umbrella. Hopefully he'd catch a cold, and then she wouldn't have to work with him anymore, she thought. Feeling slightly guilty at this wish, she entered the office.

The supervisor spoke to her in his cubicle. 'Oh, yeah. Bennett. Leonard, that's his name, right? Quiet type. Like a mouse. Never comes on a work night out. Never joins in when in the staff room. He works from home when he gets the chance. I feel embarrassed to say it, as his supervisor, but I hardly know a thing about him.'

'How long has he worked here?'

'Years, I guess. You'd have to check with the secretary. He was here before I started.'

'And how long have you been here?'

'Couple of years.'

'You didn't get to know Mr Bennett at all during that time?'

He looked away, rueful. 'It sounds bad, doesn't it? Don't get the wrong idea, it's not like I don't care. If you ask anyone here, they'll tell you, I get on with everyone, even the cleaners. The thing is, some people, they want to be left in peace. You can tell. They keep their heads down, never join in with the banter.'

'Mr Bennett is one of those people?'

'Sure. Leave him alone, that's what he wants. I sensed that. I knew to leave him in peace.'

'What does his job involve, exactly?'

'It's accounting. Mostly statistics.'

'Mr Bennett is good at spreadsheets?'

'He's fine, I guess. Not outstanding. Does his job. Goes home to his wife. What's this about, Detective? Did something happen to, err, Mr Bennett?'

'Did he ever speak about his wife?'

'He never spoke about anything.'

It was peaceful in the office, with the clacking of keyboards, the drone of the air conditioning, the workers at their screens.

'Did Bennett have any problems?' Krush said. 'Difficulties, money woes... I don't know, issues of any kind?'

'No.'

'This quietness of his, do you think it could have been linked to depression?'

The supervisor shrugged. 'I'm not a psychologist. If he was suffering from depression, it never affected his work.'

'Alright, thanks.'

Krush spoke to everyone in the office, but they all said the same thing: Bennett liked to keep to himself. None of them had ever socialised with him outside of work. None of them ever heard him talk about his home life. For four years he'd worked there like a ghost. As she wandered between the desks, her eyes strayed over their work: files, numbers, complex spreadsheets. There was something soothing about the order of it all – the numbers, pure abstraction, an absence of violence – this was an alien space to the world where she worked. If she ever quit the police force, perhaps she could become an accountant.

She was about to leave when the supervisor called her.

'Just a moment,' he said.

'What is it?'

'Detective, is there anything I should know, in terms of the job, I mean. Is he coming back to work?'

'You'd better hire a new spreadsheets guy. Try and talk to the next one, get to know them a bit.' She walked out.

26

The smell hit her on the upstairs landing, something acidic, almost sweet. Eleanor covered her nose as she inched forwards. The bare floor was hazardous with exposed pins and nails. In the dark, her hands found the back of a closed door. In the dim light, she made out a handle. She put her ear to the door but couldn't hear anything over the quiet patter of rain that played over all the outside surfaces of the house. There might have been a tremor of movement, but it was gone before she could be sure it was real and not some aural hallucination. She tried the door, but it was locked.

'Goddammit.'

She was about to go back, when she remembered the keyring Daniel had sent to her via Hunter. *Surely not...* She tried the narrow key, and felt it bite in the lock. She turned it, slowly, carefully, easing it around, trying not to make a sound, but the click was like a thud as it released. She felt the hinges give and listened again. Nothing responded inside. This must be what Daniel wanted... She opened the door.

Trapped air leaked out, sweet and rancid. She covered her nose with both hands and looked into a dark bedroom, lit by gaps in the covered windows. A bed was pushed against the side wall. It was vomit she smelled, all over the floor, up the walls, even on the ceiling as she flashed her torch. No choice, she'd have to go in there.

With her jacket pulled up over her face, and one hand covering it, she flashed the torch around the corners of the room. There was somebody in the bed. She stifled a scream. The sleeper flinched. They might have felt the electric light brush their skin, but they didn't wake. It was a man, lying on his back with his limbs splayed, completely naked.

'Oh Christ.' She stepped closer, probing with the light.

The man was like a skeleton, his limbs skinny, his ribs poking through his chest. The curly hairs that covered his skin were white. Could it be Daniel? She longed for anything else. In a narrow circle of torchlight, the man's head lay as if dead, its eyes closed, the mouth slack beneath a scraggly white beard. That humming sound she'd heard was his snoring. His skin was weathered, creased, ugly. It wasn't Daniel.

She felt relief for a moment, followed by acid futility. All this was a dead end. The naked man in the bed must be homeless, he'd broken through the back of the house to sleep. Whatever she'd hoped to find in this place was a phantom. She was going crazy; she'd thrown her phone in the bin, she'd ran out of her flat, her job, London, and taken a train up here for no reason.

A groan. The man in the bed convulsed, his body spasmed, spine arching, limbs flexed. A spatter of blood shot out of his mouth as he sat upright and screamed. Paralysed, Eleanor kept the torch beam on him. With the blood on his lips and the redness of his eyes, he looked like a predator gone senile. She stared too long. The man lurched, screaming something that was almost language but dissolved into animal cry. He tumbled off the end of the bed and fell to the floor with a bang. The torch dropped from Eleanor's hand, and she left it where it lay. She backed out of the room as he crawled towards her. She was about to run down the stairs when she caught a word he growled: 'Please.'

She stopped at the stairwell and looked back. Half hidden in the shadow, the man dragged himself along the floor, and groaned.

'Please,' he said.

'Stay back!' She went one step down the stairs, not taking her eyes away from the doorway opposite. 'Don't come any closer!'

He muttered something too quiet, too distorted to hear.

'What did you say?' Despite herself, she leaned forwards, straining to pick up the thread of his mournful whispering.

'Help me…'

'I said, stay back.' She descended another step on the staircase. 'That's close enough. Who are you?'

'Help me.' He tried to pull himself closer, panting with exertion, but he was so weak he slumped on the floor.

He couldn't be dangerous; he was so malnourished, he could hardly move, and wouldn't be able to hurt a trained police officer.

She came back up the stairs, covering her face with one hand. 'What happened to you?'

He rolled on his back, breathing heavily through his nose that had been broken more than once. His eyes closed, his limbs fell to the side, he seemed on the verge of passing out. She kept out of reach of his horrible, stick-like arms. He coughed and mumbled to himself like a dreamer.

'Are you alright?' she said.

His head lolled back on his neck. She should leave him there. This wasn't any of her business; he was just some homeless drug addict who had wandered into a derelict building. His breathing slowed, he sank away. She had done enough and could leave him like that. When she was safely out of the estate, she could make an anonymous phone call and get somebody to help him.

She retreated to the top of the stairs and looked back at the sleeping figure. If Daniel had been here, there was just the chance that this man might know something. He might have seen or heard… what? Nothing, perhaps the tiniest clue.

'Wait there.'

She hurried down the stairs and felt better to be in motion, but the feeling didn't last. In the kitchen she poked about in the detritus and found a chipped mug, dirty with spiderweb. She looked for somewhere to clean it, but the sink had been torn out. She crept out of the back door, keeping below the level of the fence, and found a tap for a hosepipe in the wall at the side of the garden. It was bright outside after the darkness. She blinked and rubbed her eyes. The tap was stiff, she needed two hands to twist it open. Water came gushing out, spraying over her shoes. Had anybody heard? There was no sound in the estate above the rain, the background roar of cars on the highway, and a police siren somewhere.

On an impulse, she crouched and drank from the tap, a clean, cold water that didn't quite manage to wash away the clinging disgust. She rinsed the old mug and filled it to the brim. It wasn't much. There was a hairline crack in the mug where the water dripped out; she'd have to hurry. Cradling it, she ran back inside and up the stairs. The man lay where she'd left him, he looked dead. She knelt beside him – God, what a stench – and tipped the water gently into his open lips. Just a little, but it was too much. He coughed and spat, then tried to raise his head.

'Stay down there,' she said. 'Drink. Drink some water. You'll feel better.'

He didn't respond, didn't open his eyes, but lay still and let the water flow through his chapped, stained lips. He swallowed painfully and let out a sigh that almost sounded like pleasure.

'That's good, good. Drink some more.' She tipped the cup again and watched him swallow. The more she tipped, the more avidly he drank.

'It's all gone.' She put the cup down. 'Can you talk now? Can you sit up?'

He muttered something. She moved her ear closer to catch the words. His hand shot up and grabbed her arm.

'Hey!' She tried to pull away as his second hand grasped her shoulder and dragged her down. 'Get off me!'

His arms shook as he held on. She felt his desperation. His body writhed on the ground and his lips curled with effort. He wouldn't let go. His eyes opened, raw, red eyeballs with agonised pupils. She had come home in search of Daniel, beautiful, yearning, and young in her memory; now she was confronted with the spectre of grisly decay, horror, and life gone wrong.

He was too weak to pull her down, but he held on tightly so she couldn't break away. He lifted his head from the ground, all the muscles of his neck straining through his translucent skin, and his breath was foul as he exhaled into her averted face, and said, 'Kill me.'

'Let go! Get off me!'

His voice was weakening, but he managed to growl again. 'Kill me.' It must have taken all the life he had left, as he dropped back against the floor, his hands released and fell to his sides, and his eyes closed. He breathed heavily.

'Jesus.' Eleanor jumped back. 'Who the hell are you? What are you doing in here?'

'Please,' he whispered. 'Please.'

She backed away and stopped at the top of the stairs. She took one step down and felt the crooked staircase wobble. The urge to run out of this building was unbearable, but all she had done was run. She'd run five years ago away from Liverpool, from her lover, from her sister, and now she'd run back from London, from her flat, her career, her whole life. At some point, she had to stop running.

'I can't help you,' she called from the stairs. 'I'm leaving now, but I'll ring the police. They'll send someone to help you.'

'No!' he shouted. He lifted a shaking hand to stop her. 'No police. Please.'

Now she really should just run, but she was curious. The word "police" seemed to have woken him. She watched as he raised his head, looking for her, and she pulled back into the shadow.

'Why not?' she said. 'You some kind of criminal?'

'No.'

'Why then?'

His hoarse breathing deepened as he gathered his words. 'Please, not the police.'

'Do you want me to help you?'

A pause. Every word seemed to cost energy he didn't have. 'Yes.'

'You have to talk to me,' Eleanor said. 'Tell the truth, who are you?'

'I'm… the doctor.'

'What doctor?'

'I… he wanted me to… I just wanted to help… but I didn't know…'

'Alright, stop blubbering. What are you doing in this place? Do you live here?'

For a moment she thought he'd lost consciousness, but his voice broke out, weaker, almost a whisper. 'He brought me.'

'He?'

Another pause, longer this time; he was drifting. 'Eleanor,' he said.

'What?'

Dread caught her by the throat. In her mind she was sprinting, clattering down the stairs, but she couldn't move, her hands pressed the bare wall as if stuck there. It had followed her, the laughing voice in the phone, all the way up here, and it would follow her forever. It knew her name, everything about her. Running was pointless, it only fed the laughter. Her old escape route, the way she'd dealt with every problem in life, by dropping it all and leaving, was closed off like a sealed door. This looted house was her life now.

'Eleanor…' he whispered.

She saw Daniel, clearly, more clearly than he'd appeared in memory for years. He was seated across the table from her in some old wine bar down Lark Lane. They held hands across the table. He'd never looked so bashful, this impossible human being. He wore a white shirt, with the sleeves rolled up to the elbows, and there was the tattoo on his wrist: *Eleanor.* She'd always hated it.

She took a few steps closer to the man. 'Where did you hear that name?'

No reply. She leaned over him, cautiously, braced for his hand to shoot out and grab her, but his form was lifeless. He might have been dead, but there was still a faint rattle of breath in his throat.

'Where did you hear that name?' she said. 'Answer me. Was it a tattoo you saw?'

She kneeled and almost touched his face.

'Alright, alright. Sleep there a moment. I'll find some food, some clothes. I don't know, some medicine. But don't go anywhere, and don't die, please.'

She ran down the stairs and no longer knew why. She burst out of the backdoor without stopping to check first. Outside, free, she didn't slow down to taste the clean rain. She just ran.

27

After finding out nothing useful at Bennett's workplace, Krush drove over to Sundial Court. In the passenger seat beside her, Scott stared out of the window. He hummed to himself absently as if she wasn't there. It was unnerving. She had to speak to break the silence.

'I hope this murder gets resolved soon,' she said. 'I don't want to have to spend another minute in this estate.'

'Do you think it will?' Scott said. 'Get resolved, I mean.'

'The husband must be guilty. His prints were on the knife. He has no alibi. There are no other suspects. It must be him, but… I don't know. Why would he kill her? If we could find a motive…'

'I don't think he's guilty,' Scott said.

She looked across at him. 'Why?'

'It's just hard to imagine.'

'I thought you hardly knew him.'

'I don't know him, but it's his face. He doesn't look like a killer.'

'Faces don't mean anything,' Krush said. 'I've seen all kinds of faces in this business. Pretty faces, ugly ones, ones that look the same as everyone else; it makes no difference.'

'But your face looks like a detective's,' Scott said.

Despite herself, she checked her eyes in the mirror. A detective? No. She only saw the eyes of some solitary seabird that rides the high air currents and crosses oceans without touching down to rest.

* * *

George Watkins lived at number 4 on the estate. He was the leader of the local community group.

'He won't talk to you,' Scott said as they walked up the driveway. 'George hates police. He thinks it's part of his job.'

'He'll talk to me,' Krush said. 'I know that type. You just keep quiet and let me deal with him.'

The doorbell sounded a pleasant, welcoming chime. A light turned on in the hall. The man who opened was short, wore a tracksuit and glasses, and had a wart on his chin. He looked her up and down.

'You'll be wanting to talk about the murder,' he said. 'Well, I don't know nothing.'

'Mr Watkins? I'm Detective Krush. I just want to ask a few questions. They say you're in charge of the residents' group. You must know the estate better than most.'

'The residents' group never meets. It's just me. I arrange everything. The others don't show up. They complain to anyone who'll listen, but they won't do anything about it.'

'But you do know the estate.'

'Of course I do.'

'So you can help us.'

He grimaced. 'Why should I?'

'Mr Watkins, there's been a murder.'

'I don't see how I can help with that. I didn't see nothing. I didn't hear nothing…'

'You knew the victim and her husband. The Bennetts. You know their neighbours. You know everyone around. Anything that you can tell us–'

'I don't see why I should. The police never lifted a finger to help us. People like him…' He pointed at Scott.

'It's not my fault,' Scott said.

'That's what you always say.'

'Guys, please,' Krush said.

Watkins kept pointing. His face was red, his eyes furious. 'He's part of it. He's one of them.'

'No, I'm not,' Scott said.

'Shut up a minute.' She turned to Watkins. 'A part of what? One of what?'

'I'm not part of anything,' Scott shouted.

Watkins folded his arms. 'I'm not talking to him.'

'Alright.' She spun around to Scott. 'Go and wait in the car. I'll talk to Mr Watkins alone.'

'What?' he said. 'You can't.'

'I can. Go on, go back to the car.'

They watched him trudge away slowly, his shoulders slumped.

'I'm from central HQ,' Krush said. 'I've got nothing to do with Scott or the local branch. You can trust me.'

Watkins laughed. 'No chance.'

'Can we talk inside, out of the rain?'

'Whatever. It's your time you're wasting.' He went through the hall and Krush followed him into a living room decorated with Everton FC memorabilia. A giant blue banner bearing the club's crest hung on the side wall, and the mantlepiece was covered with old match-day programmes and signed photographs of players. She inspected the pictures, noticing Watkins posed alongside one of his heroes.

'Are you a Blue?' he asked.

Everyone in Liverpool was either a Blue or a Red. She had been asked this question countless times in her life. Carmichael always said she should play along, to win their trust. Sometimes she did. Today she was feeling irritable. Truth was, neither colour appealed to her; she liked grey.

'I don't watch sport,' Krush said. 'It's irrational.'

'Yeah, that's what's beautiful about it.'

'In my job, the irrational isn't beautiful.' She sensed herself slipping; she needed this man's cooperation, and here she was, alienating him. 'I play poker,' she offered. 'Not for the money. I like to count the cards.'

He shrugged. 'At least you're not a Red. Sit down. Do you want tea?'

Krush perched on the sofa. 'You said Scott was "one of them". What did you mean by that?'

'Not very well informed about the estate, are you?'

'It's Scott's job to inform me.'

'Well, there's your problem. Did he tell you about Solar Construction?'

'I know Solar Construction. They've put up half the buildings in Liverpool.'

'Then you should know that they have a plan to redevelop this estate. The council already gave the green light. Problem is, they want to bulldoze it first, start from scratch. To do that, they have to buy up all the property. They own more than half of it now, mostly the empty buildings, but they need all of them. The other residents won't sell. There's a stand-off.'

'And Scott…?'

'Solar Construction are running us into the ground. By leaving their properties empty, the value of the whole estate drops. They've let it all fall apart. They think they can force us to sell. They're the only buyers now that our houses are worthless. We try to fight back, but the local police are part of it. Including your man, Scott. He's in their pay.'

'Do you have proof?'

Watkins scoffed. 'Proof? The whole system is corrupt.'

'Alright, well, I don't know anything about this. I'll see what I can find out. If Scott is corrupt, I'll report him. You have my word. And I'll check about Solar Construction. If they're not above board, I'll see what I can do.'

Watkins chuckled. 'Sure you will.'

'I need your help,' Krush said. 'You know this estate. Who might have killed Mrs Bennett? Did she have enemies? Any feuds going on around here?'

'If you ask me, the construction firm had something to do with it. They're desperate to get us out. The last homeowners won't sell. Not to them. It's war now.'

'You're not suggesting they would have somebody killed?'

'I'm suggesting nothing. All I'm saying is, that murder is pretty handy for them. Folks will be scared. Some might take the bait and sell up. There'll be nobody left.'

'Nobody but you, I'm guessing.'

'You got that right. I'll never leave. Don't care if they offer me a million. They'll have to kill me first.'

* * *

Back at the car, Scott gazed with dead eyes through the windscreen. He didn't notice as Krush approached and walked around the vehicle, but he flinched when she knocked on the window.

'Tell me the truth,' she said.

'What did you say?' He shook his head, disoriented, as if he'd just woken up.

'Are you corrupt?'

'What?'

'Watkins says you're in league with the construction firm.'

Scott laughed. 'That's what he always says. He's obsessed. He thinks Solar Construction runs the whole world. He probably thinks they killed Kennedy.'

'Maybe.' She tried to hold the gaze of his weak grey eyes, but they drifted away from her. 'You never mentioned Solar Construction before. You were supposed to be filling me in about the estate.'

'There's nothing to say. They're just a company that wants to buy the place. I don't know them. But I'll tell you this, they've offered these people double what their houses are worth.'

'I'm going to do some digging, Scott. If there's anything dodgy about you, I'll find out.'

'Do what you want.' He sounded bored.

Krush climbed into the driver's seat. 'Alright, I'm headed back to the station. Do you want me to drop you somewhere?'

'I'll stay here. My car's parked on the highway. I'll keep an eye on things. Got nothing better to do.'

Krush drove away. When she looked back, he was still standing in the rain.

28

Eleanor hurried across the estate with her head down, keeping an eye out for police cars. She could still smell that bedroom in number 35; she'd got it on her hands. She was close to the exit when she heard feet running in the puddles behind her. She didn't dare to look back. With her head down, she kept moving towards the sound of cars on the highway outside the estate.

'Hey!' a lad called from behind. 'Who are you?'

He wasn't alone. Two or three others called, 'Hey, come here. We want to talk.'

She kept walking, kept her head down. Her feet wanted to run, but that would only provoke them to chase.

'Hey! Are you deaf?' They gained on her quickly.

By the time she realized she should run, they had circled around and blocked her path. Four young men in tracksuits with hoods pulled up over their heads in the rain. They smoked rolled cigarettes that smelled of weed.

'Never seen you before, love. You must be new here.'

She didn't reply. Avoiding eye contact, she tried to push through them, but they jumped around, filling the spaces, laughing at her unease. When she turned to walk back the way she'd come, they pulled at her arm and tugged her back.

'Hey, love, stop a minute. Where are you going? Don't run off like that. We're talking to you.'

There was no way out. 'Let me go. I'm busy.'

They laughed. 'Listen to her. Where's that accent from? Are you from London?'

'Is she posh?'

'Where'd she come from?'

She folded her arms, feigning control that she didn't feel. 'I'm from here, alright? Let me pass, I'm busy.'

'Busy doing what? You don't live here, do you?'

'How did you end up here, love? You don't seem like the type.'

'I'm police,' she said.

They laughed at that as well. 'Didn't know policewomen could be sexy. I never saw one like that before.'

'What are you doing here, love? Is it about the murder?'

She almost said, "what murder?" but only stared at the distant crime scene tape, a dot of yellow at the far end of the estate. Surely, she couldn't be in danger here, with police officers not far away.

'It's about the murder,' she said. 'Do you know anything about it?'

They glanced at each other, grinning. It seemed that everything was funny to them.

'We're good lads. We don't get involved in that kind of business.'

'Let me go then,' she said.

'Oh, we couldn't do that.'

'Why not?'

'You'd miss all the fun. There's a party. Don't you want to go?'

'No.'

'You do, you just don't know it yet, because you haven't seen it. Wait till you see it. Tell her, lads.'

His mate beside him grinned. 'You've never been to a party like this one. It never stops, and it never gets boring. You'll be laughing your head off. You'll never want to leave.'

'I don't like parties.' She tried again to push through them, but they blocked her in.

'Just try it, you'll see.'

The first lad grabbed hold of her arm, and the others copied him. She felt herself being manhandled back in the direction she'd come from.

'Let me go!'

They were strong; she tried to dig her feet into the pavement, but she was brushed along easily. She screamed, which set them off laughing again.

'Don't be like that. You're going to love it. You're going to have the time of your life.'

She screamed again. Over their heads her eyes jumped around the surrounding windows. Couldn't anybody see what was happening? Didn't anybody care? The curtains were closed in every house. A car drove past. She tried to call out, to wave her arms above the bodies around her, but the car drove on and disappeared around the bend. She revolved in the grip that kept pulling and pushing her backwards – the background a blur of houses, the same blankness repeating, until her gaze found the red eyes painted on a building opposite. They fixated on her. She gave up struggling.

An engine roared over the sound of laughing. The men looked around. Instantly, they released her. A police car pulled up at the side of the kerb. Eleanor ran towards it and tugged at the door handle. It was locked.

'Don't go,' the voices behind her said.

The window of the car lowered, and an officer looked out. 'What's happening here?'

'These men…' She gestured.

'They're bothering you?'

'Yes.'

The officer called to one of them. 'Hey, Lee, are you bothering her?'

Lee laughed. 'We just wanted to take her to a party. She'd enjoy it if she could let herself go, but she's some frigid bitch.'

'She doesn't want to go to the party, Lee.' The officer opened the passenger seat, and Eleanor jumped in.

'Thank you.' She pulled the door shut and locked it.

'Ignore them,' the officer said.

Lee poked his head through the open window. She got a whiff of his breath: weed, vodka, sleeplessness.

'If you change your mind,' he told her.

'I won't.'

'Get your head out of my window,' the officer said.

Lee grinned. His cuboid, bald head seemed to fill the frame. 'You're just sad you're not invited, Scott.'

'I've told you before, Lee, you're out of control. You'll end badly.'

Lee pulled his head out of the window to relight his joint.

'Can we just leave?' Eleanor asked Scott.

He didn't seem to hear, but continued gazing out of the window as Lee blew in a mouthful of smoke. 'You go too far,' he said.

'You should leave,' Lee said. 'You have no power here. We only put up with you because we're nice. Get out before we change our minds.'

Scott stared through the smoke as if confused.

'Drive,' Eleanor said.

Through the window, she saw the lads grabbing bricks and rubbish from the abandoned house by the pavement. Something heavy hit the roof of the car, and Scott jumped in his seat. He still didn't drive away as a full bin bag crashed on the windscreen and burst, spilling rotten food waste across the car. The lads jeered and laughed.

'Drive!' Eleanor shouted.

Scott shook his head, chasing some thought away. He pulled out from the kerb as bricks and old junk rattled on the roof of the car above their heads. She watched in the mirror as the lads chased them down the road, throwing stones, whatever came to hand, but the car quickly picked up speed. They rounded the driveway and left the estate.

'Thank you,' she said.

Scott leaned forward, squinting to see through the rain that lashed the windscreen. She felt for a moment that she recognized him, but no, she was certain she had not known him before, when she worked in Liverpool.

'You could turn the wipers on.' She fastened her seat belt as the car picked up speed.

'What?'

'The windscreen wipers.'

'Oh.' He flicked them on.

'It's OK, you can drop me here. I'm fine now.'

The car didn't slow. They filtered onto a dual carriageway.

'What were you doing in the estate?' Scott said.

'Where are you driving us? To the station? I can get out here, this is fine, thanks.'

'On the dual carriageway?'

'Really, it's fine.' She wondered if she should tell him she was a police officer. There was no way to tell how far Daniel's fears extended, or if they were even real, who could be trusted, who could not. 'Actually, I'm…'

'You're not from here, are you? Your accent is strange.'

'I came up from London yesterday. I lost my way, but I'm alright now. I'll get out here, thanks.'

'I can't let you out on the dual carriageway.' He stared into the motion of the windscreen wipers. He hadn't made eye contact with her once, she realized.

'Please! Let me out!'

'I can't.'

'I'll get out here. Stop the car.'

He didn't look away from the whirr of the windscreen wipers. 'Everything's OK now. Don't worry.'

She felt panic rising and choked it down. She needed to stay calm. She was struggling to tell real threats from imaginary ones, and the fear was getting worse. Who was this guy? Some weird outsider on the force, exiled to work on this estate until he retired.

The situation could not be dangerous: they were in a police car, she was an officer. He must be driving her to the station, probably he wanted to take her statement about those men. He'd be one of those with no people skills; no matter how many training courses you sent him on, he'd never be able to talk to a woman properly. She watched him as he hunched over the wheel and stared ahead. It was as if he'd forgotten she was in the car. She saw traffic lights up ahead. He didn't notice when she released her seat belt. The car slowed, joining the back of a line of vehicles at the red light.

'Thanks.' She opened the door. 'I'll walk from here. This is great.'

He glanced across as she climbed out into the rain. 'But–'

'Goodbye!' She slammed the door shut and hurried across the street as the lights turned amber.

29

In the archive section, Special Constables Jones and Walker were arguing about Lenin. The rest of the station called this basement "The Socialist Republic of Filing Cabinets". The two officers were universally known by their first names, Marvin and Billy.

'Am I interrupting?' Krush said.

Billy smiled at her. 'Beth Krush! The bourgeois individualist deigns to come down to the basement. How can the proletariat be of service to you?'

'Can you help me with something? It's important. I'm not bourgeois, by the way. Not that I care.'

Billy shared a glance with Marvin, his longtime colleague and best friend. 'She doesn't deny being an individualist, you notice.'

'I don't deny it,' she said. 'Keep your collectivisation. I prefer to work alone.'

Marvin pulled a face. 'What do you need?'

'We've got an unusual killing. A woman was found dead, stabbed. Her eyes had been removed and her hands were stuck to her face.'

'Jesus.' Billy went out through the rear door, saying, 'You'll see, capitalism has reached the final stage. Violence runs amok.'

She turned to Marvin. 'Think you could point me in the direction of unsolved cases involving knives?'

'Knives? There's – I don't know – thousands of unsolved cases with knives. How far back do you want to go?'

'Not far, not yet anyway. Just in the last year.'

'That's a lot of stabbings.'

'There's also eyeballs. Knives and eyeballs. Does that narrow it down?'

'Yeah, I guess that does narrow it down. Wait a second.' He sat down at his computer and typed. 'Eyeballs… eyeballs…'

'Anything there?' She leaned over his shoulder trying to see.

'Nothing in the last month.'

'Keep looking.'

'Here's something.'

She felt a rush of excitement. 'Got one?'

'Well… This guy lost his eyes. It wasn't a knife though.'

'What then?'

Marvin twisted the screen around to show her the case file he'd pulled up. 'How about a screwdriver?'

'Can I?' She reached over and took the mouse out of his hand before he could reply, and clicked on one of the photographs attached to the file. A picture of a corpse filled the screen.

'Oh shit,' Marvin said.

'What is that?' The photograph was dark and difficult to see with the electric light shining on the screen. She leaned closer. The dead man had a screwdriver stuck in one eyeball. His other eye was a pulp. Dried blood leaked down his face like tear tracks of mascara. She stared at the image. Eyeless, it couldn't return her gaze, but it seemed to weep still at the horror of life.

'A screwdriver…' she said aloud.

'Does it fit?'

'Only the eyes… the rest is different. Our body was found with her hands up over her face; this guy's arms are by his side.'

'I could—'

'Shut up a minute.' She clicked through the attachments and pulled up a transcript of the police report. She scanned through, waiting for something to jump out.

> *Robbery at an all-night garage… Masked assailants took four thousand in cash… One security guard killed… Stolen van… Sundial Court…*

'There it is!' She almost slapped Marvin on the shoulder in triumph. 'The estate. It does fit. There's a connection.'

She kept reading. Three masked robbers had used a van that was reported as stolen by a man who lived in Sundial Court. A Mr Hunter. The stolen van was later found burned in a ditch just outside the city. Mr Hunter lived at number 5 in the estate. She flipped through her notepad to a list she'd made of all the houses on the estate. Number 5 was one of the abandoned properties.

'Ah shit.' Her excitement died.

There was a phone number for Mr Hunter, but when she tried it, nobody picked up.

'No luck?' Marvin said.

'The house listed in the report is abandoned. Nobody's answering the number. I'll keep trying.'

Marvin turned the screen back around. 'I'll have a dig and see if any other files pop up, connected to this one. I'll call you.'

'Thanks.'

As she was walking out, Billy stuck his head through the rear door and shouted, 'Keep up the good fight, comrade. They are few, we are many.'

30

Eleanor rushed across the city in a trance, afraid of every stranger she passed, keeping her head down, her face hidden below the peak of her cap. She longed for Daniel's creaky old house where nothing worked, the overgrown trees that covered the front garden and concealed everything. It was a sanctuary. If she got too attached to it, she'd never go outside again. Liverpool was wider than she'd remembered. The centre was compact, but the suburbs sprawled in wide streets where the wind gathered constellations of litter. Her mind hurried on ahead of her, already entering the front door while she crossed the boulevard. Her imagination went straight into the living room and the piled notes, looking for the newspaper cuttings.

'I'm the doctor,' that disgusting naked man had said.

Some of the cuttings were about a doctor. She tried to remember the photographs, could it be the same person? He'd said "Eleanor". He must have seen the tattoo on Daniel's wrist. If Daniel had found this guy, perhaps brought him to the estate… there must have been a reason. The answer was in the newspaper cuttings, but what did they say? Her memory used to be so clear, a mirror where guilt, the past, Liverpool, haunted, at the fringes of all the crime scenes she'd ever witnessed. The mirror was dusty now. Too much anxiety, too much running from herself. Something about a doctor, a court case, a death.

She turned onto Daniel's road and couldn't hold back. She ran across the street and through the gate, beneath the old trees… and saw the front door hanging open. Had she left it that way? She hesitated at the top of the driveway, biting down a creeping sense that all her defences were spoiled. There was nowhere else to go. Still, she hesitated... *Could it be Daniel?* Perhaps he'd come home. If it were someone else, the suspicions he'd mentioned in his email...

She snuck up to the living room window, ducked below the ledge, and peeped inside. A trickle of water leaked down from the broken gutters high above. The window was dusty, it was difficult to see in the shadow. There was nobody in the room. They might have left already. She tiptoed through the overgrown grass and came to the open front door. Hunched in the frame, she listened for a moment but there was nothing to hear above the murmur of rain. She went inside and didn't dare to close the door behind her for the sound it would make.

The hall was still and quiet. The rug was in place, covering the trapdoor. She ran past it and glanced around the kitchen, where she'd left Daniel's notes laid out on the table. They were all gone.

'No,' she cried. 'No, no, no.'

All that remained of his investigation was the map she'd kept in her bag. At the bottom of the staircase, she looked up into the gloom, braced for any sound from above. Everything was dulled by the patter of rain against the windows. She looked back towards the open door. She could run out of here; she longed to. She went back to the kitchen and found a knife.

At the foot of the staircase, she listened again, gripping the knife. She took a step upwards. The rickety banister rattled as she climbed two more steps and stopped to listen again. Nothing. She climbed another step and heard it. There was somebody up there. Caught halfway up the stairwell, she released the banister and tried to breathe. She needed to stay calm, keep her mind clear, remember her training. She'd taken part in armed raids before; she'd dealt with dangerous criminals. This was just a mouldy old house in the rain. She listened again, but whatever she thought she'd heard was silent now. With the knife in both hands, she climbed up and peered over the top step into the landing.

Everything was still. The floorboards creaked as she stepped into the shadow. Four dark doorways showed on this storey, and the staircase twisted and carried up to the attic. She held her breath and listened for any sound. The rain played on the skylight set into the roof above the attic. If there was anybody up here, they'd gone quiet. They must be hiding. She gripped the knife and stepped towards the first door, Daniel's old bedroom. If it was him, if he'd come home, he might be in there. She crept to the open doorway, cringing as the floorboards moaned under her feet.

A black cat lay on its back on the dusty duvet cover of Daniel's old childhood bed. It blinked and watched her, but it didn't move. When she took a step closer, it let out a cautious meow. The release was overwhelming, she feared to fall as the tension drained. She sat down on the bed beside the cat, and it rolled on its front. She held out one hand for it to see. When it didn't flinch, she stroked its head. The cat nuzzled against her.

'What are you doing in here?' she said. 'Do you live here now?'

Something clattered in the room next door, that used to belong to Daniel's mother. Running feet thudded across the landing before she could respond. For a moment she stayed perched on the edge of the bed with the cat stiffened against her. The intruder hurtled down the stairs. Eleanor jumped up. Before she could think, she was running out of the room in pursuit. She tripped and fell forwards. The knife skittered out of her hand and across the landing.

She crawled in the shadow, feeling for it with her fingers as the stranger's feet crossed the hall downstairs. She scooped up the knife and chased after them, running so fast down the stairs that she almost stumbled. Momentum thrown forward, her foot missed the step, she plunged down and released the knife to grab hold of the banister. The front door slammed shut. The stranger was gone. Eleanor scooped up the knife and went down to the hall, relief mixed with the adrenaline: she had lost them, but perhaps it was better that way. She opened the door and looked out, but they had vanished. The old sycamore trees creaked in the wind.

She hurried down the path and out of the front gate. The street was empty. Perhaps they'd driven away. She tried to remember if there had been a car parked out front before, but she only noticed the old, blue Datsun that had belonged to Daniel's mother. It was half mounted on the kerb and looked like it hadn't moved in years.

She returned to the house and locked the door behind her. At the top of the stairs, the cat watched. Still, she didn't feel safe. She checked through the whole building, all the way up to the attic, teeth gritted at every door, clutching the knife, while the cat followed and curled around her legs. The house was empty.

Back in the kitchen, she sat down at the table and tried to organise what she remembered of the notes and cuttings. The cat jumped up and draped itself across her knee where she ignored it.

The doctor in the news story had been in some kind of legal trouble: a court case, misconduct, a dead patient. Could it be the same man…? She felt the threads coalescing, but here she was jumping to conclusions again. A half-dead stranger in an abandoned flat who called himself a doctor. Daniel's old house, the map, the newspaper cuttings. The name "Eleanor" on that naked man's flecked lips. Connection points, but did they connect?

There wasn't time to think it all through. She had to go back to the house on Daniel's map, the last tenuous link to him. If she could get some food and drink into that man, put some clean clothes on him, he might be able to help.

Upstairs, she dug out some old, dusty clothes from the wardrobe. Would they fit? Probably not. She found the loosest items, an old hoodie, some jogging pants, a handful of underwear, and threw them in a rucksack that was hanging on the back of the door. She hid the knife at the bottom of the bag. Downstairs, in the kitchen, she filled a bottle with water and found some tins of beans in the cupboard, a tin-opener and spoon in a drawer.

The phone in the hall started to ring. The trilling sound filled the empty, echoing house. Her feet were ready to sprint away, but she mastered herself. She gripped the knife at the bottom of her bag and waited for the ringing to stop. It didn't stop. She tensed all over, her teeth grinding. It's just a phone, she told herself. It's just a phone. The ringing didn't stop. She went out into the hall and looked at it: a harmless object, absurd even, with its old-fashioned rotary. She reached a hand, picked up the receiver and held it to her ear without speaking.

'Eleanor,' said the cold, smug voice. 'Why are you standing there? You were supposed to run away, not come back home.'

She couldn't make a sound.

'You have to die now, but first, everyone you love. You'll listen to them scream over the phone. Hold on tight…'

She dropped the phone. A tiny sound of laughter played out of the receiver against the floorboards as she ran out of the door.

31

He woke screaming. He would never die, and never escape. But when he opened his eyes, something was different. There was a mug on the floor beside his head. He lay on his back on rough wooden floorboards in the hall. Twisting his neck back, he saw the door to the room where he'd been locked. He'd got out, but how? A woman… Who was she? One of them, surely, his accusers, who had trapped him in this place and would never let him be. He listened but couldn't hear any movement over the ringing in his ears.

For a few moments, he just lay and tried to fall unconscious again. He was alive. Reality seeped back into his pores. The sickness had passed, no more spasms. It was almost peaceful, lying there on the cool floor, but she would come back, that woman. She'd come and get him if he didn't escape. He had to get out, but he was naked. Could he move? Groaning with exertion, he managed to drag himself back through the wall of smell into the torture room where he'd been trapped. He pulled on his stinking, damp clothes.

He managed to walk, supporting himself against the wall. He leaned on the doorframe and rested there a moment. His body swooned, it wanted to collapse and lie down on the floor – those cool wooden boards in the shadows – but if he let himself, he'd never get up again. Keeping to the wall, he stumbled out of the room. He came to the stairwell and felt vertigo looking down. He had to sit on the top step and push himself, one stair at a time.

On the ground floor, panic set in. The front door was locked. The windows were sealed. This whole place was just an extension of the same room where he'd been trapped. He howled with frustration and banged his head against the wall. But there must be a way out; he felt a draught creep through the walls.

He followed the slight breeze along the hall into the kitchen and dragged open the back door. He crawled out into the rain and flopped on his back on the concrete, letting it patter all over him. Delight rippled over his skin, all the twisted pain that was his body. He found himself laughing. The rain pooled in his mouth, and he swallowed it down. Blinking in the drops that fell on his face, he opened his eyes and looked around. It was a barren backyard. Weeds grew between the concrete slabs. He saw a tap set in the wall and heaved himself through the puddles towards it. He twisted it open and let a burst of water stream over his head. He sucked greedily on the end of the tap and just kept drinking. He couldn't get his fill.

Voices disturbed him. There was somebody nearby. He bared his teeth. He'd never let them lock him up in that room again. He'd kill anyone who tried. The voices came closer. He twisted the tap shut. The last drops of water slipped through his disgusting beard. He pressed himself against the wall and listened. Men's voices came from the adjacent garden.

'It was a woman. Poking around. Looking for something.'

'Too many people now. It's not good. This is our place. They'll take it from us.'

'Nobody would dare.'

There was an edge to their words. One of them flicked a lighter open and the smell of cigarette smoke came winding through the rain. The doctor sucked it in. One of the men coughed. The voices moved away.

'Did you hear about her in number 14?'

'Stabbed to death, they said.'

'Was the husband, apparently.'

A strange sound, like an animal rasp, a snigger.

'Is that what they believe?'

'It's always the husband, isn't it?'

'Sure. But whose?'

They stopped talking. He thought they might be finished, but one said, 'Do you smell that?'

'What? This whole estate stinks.'

'It's like… I don't know… vomit.'

He heard the fence creak as he cowered against the side wall, out of view.

'The yard next door is full of rubbish. It's been there forever. Council won't do shit about it.'

'Fuck's sake. This place could've been beautiful.'

'Nah, it's ugly, deep down. We made it that way.'

They dropped their cigarettes. He heard them grind the butts out with their soles. A door banged shut in the neighbouring house. He let out a sigh. Perhaps there'd be a shred of tobacco left in the discarded butts, a mouthful of nicotine, but he'd have to climb the fence, and he had no lighter anyway. He crawled around the other side of the house and found a gate. Pulling himself up, he peeped over the top and saw the estate. It mouldered in the rain. There was nobody around. Where was this shithole? Why was he here?

The gate was chained shut, but he was able to climb onto a pile of soft, mushy bin bags that released rotten fumes as he pressed them. He dragged himself up and over. There was no way to get down the other side, and he wasn't strong enough to hold on. He dropped, landed with a splash in a dirty puddle and rolled on the concrete. He managed to sit up against the gate and check his legs and arms. Nothing seemed to be broken, but his ankle throbbed, it might be sprained. So what? The only thing that mattered in existence was to find a fix of heroin.

He was so light, it felt like dancing when his legs carried him down the bottom of the driveway and out into the estate. As his long-clenched muscles untightened, he straightened, and found that he could walk faster, but he was like paper – a breeze might catch him. He glanced around constantly as he hobbled, with one hand grazing the low front wall. The thought of meeting another person was terrifying, but he'd have to if he was going to get a hit from somewhere.

When did he last take it? Where did it come from? He'd been in a homeless shelter, but time fragmented, he wasn't sure if that was last week or last year. He felt as if he'd slept for a lifetime and couldn't wake up. There had been some other men, not friends exactly; they must have been homeless too. They'd been together in the shelter. They'd got the heroin from some place, God knows how, perhaps they'd stolen it. All this was too much – his head ached, his bones shivered, he was lost, he had nothing. He'd never find any drugs.

A dog's bark startled him. He tried to turn around too quickly and fell back against the wall. As he cowered backwards, he saw an old lady in a pink tracksuit with a Liverpool FC scarf, walking a bulldog. The dog sniffed and barked again.

'Shut up.' The woman kicked it. She came closer to the doctor as he flattened himself against the wall. 'Are you lost?'

The dog growled but didn't bark. It tried to sniff his foot, but the woman jerked it back on its lead.

'Jesus. What happened to you?' she said.

He tried to speak and found that he couldn't. His bottom lip jabbered.

'Are you homeless?' She took a step towards him and scrunched her nose. 'Pooh! What a stink.'

He cleared his throat. 'I… I…'

'Do you need help?'

'I…'

'Here.' She dug in the pocket of her tracksuit and pulled out a five-pound note. 'Get yourself something to eat. There's a homeless shelter. Want me to call them?'

She held out the note. It fluttered in the wind. Too light, it might blow away, the most precious thing. He leapt and grabbed it from her hand. The woman let out a cry and jumped back. The dog barked, then snapped in the air, narrowly missing his arm with its teeth.

The woman dragged the animal back. 'You're crazy,' she shouted as the doctor pulled himself up. 'You'd better leave this estate. There are kids here.'

With the five-pound note balled in his fist, he ran through the rain.

32

Krush sheltered from the rain under the fire escape outside the station. She rang Hunter again. That's what the cold-callers do, keep ringing until somebody answers. On the third attempt, the ringing stopped.

'Who is this?' a man said. He sounded afraid.

'Police Detective Beth Krush. Are you Mr Hunter?'

'Police? Nobody's died, have they?'

'What? No. It's about your van. The one that was stolen.'

'Oh, the van.' The relief in his voice was vivid. He must have been expecting a different kind of call. 'That's all been sorted now. Good riddance to it. The insurance company paid out. Jesus, you don't want to reopen the case, do you? I'm not paying that money back. Not a penny. That was my van—'

'Relax. No, it's nothing like that. I'm looking into the crime. The man who was murdered. Those thieves who stole your van, they killed a security guard in a hold-up.'

'That's nothing to do with me. They stole my van is all. I dunno nothing about the rest.'

'Mr Hunter, you were living in Sundial Court at the time of the crime—'

'Hellhole.'

'You left afterwards. Why?'

'Who would stay there? My house was broken into. The van was stolen. My wife left me. That place is sick, I'm telling you. There's something wrong with it.'

'So, you just sold up…?'

'I was renting there. The contract ended, I left. I'm never going back. I'd rather die. I—'

'Mr Hunter, do you think it was someone on the estate who stole your van?'

He hesitated. She heard his hoarse breathing down the line.

'Dunno,' he said. 'I never saw nothing. It was stolen in the middle of the night while I was asleep. Never expected to see it again. The police found it in a ditch. Burned down to just the frame.'

'You didn't suspect anyone in particular?'

'I would have told the police if I did. Is there anything else, Detective? I'd like to hang up now.'

'Wait. Did you have any enemies on the estate?'

'Enemies? No.'

'But you hated it there. Why?'

'The place was falling apart. Half the houses were burnt down. Gangs of kids running wild. I don't know. It's just wrong. There was a smell in the air. I have to go now, Detective.'

'One more question… did you know a Mrs Bennett, at number 14?'

'Never heard of her.'

'Or her husband?'

'Never heard of either of them, and I don't want to. If they live on that estate, nothing good will come of it.' He hung up.

She listened to the tone for a few moments, lost.

33

Where could he go? Where was he? Scrambling along the side of the highway – his limbs trembling and his stomach empty – he only longed for a hit. Just one hit and he could lie down here, anywhere, in the middle of the road. Let life leave him alone, let him sink. There was something in his fist. He opened it, carefully, and found a five-pound note. What could he buy with it? Not heroin, he'd need more money. If he saved this note, put it somewhere nobody would find it, he'd have the first piece, but he needed so much more, and there was nowhere to hide his money anyway. He had no home. With that realization, all of his existence returned, who he was, where he'd come from, the hopelessness of it all. He didn't have a cupboard, not even a bag. He could only keep the money in his hand, where they'd find it, and pry it from him. They took everything.

Except... the last hit he'd taken, what a ride. So pure, he almost left his body forever. Where did it come from? There must be a way, only he'd forgotten. He needed money. He used to have it; he remembered the feeling. He used to be smart, he remembered that feeling too. That's how he'd got the drug: by being smart. He got money off his sister, Alison, of course. He still had one family member in this world, one person who had to help him. That's what family's for. He'd gone to her in the past, when he was dying, and she'd helped when nobody else would.

Where did Alison live? Liverpool... this must be Liverpool. He'd come up here to find her, and she'd given him money. How much, he couldn't remember. It was all gone now. She'd give him more. She was his little sister after all. When they were small, he'd taught her everything. After their parents died, he'd helped her out. He'd always taken care of her. Yes, his sister would help. What was her name again? Alison, that's right.

He veered off the pavement into the road. A car swerved around him, almost grazing his foot. The horn blared, the driver screamed. Caught in the middle of the street, cars flew past on both sides. He stumbled across to the other side. All he had was the dim sense that he should head left. He didn't know the name of his sister's road, or the number of her house, but he'd been there before. He knew Liverpool, he'd just forgotten.

The barren periphery of the city gave way to tree-lined suburbs. There were more pedestrians in this area. They backed away from him with a look of disgust, while he plodded forwards with his head down, all his pain knotted up like a bundle that he carried in his belly; and the five-pound note clutched in his fist. The houses were bigger here, and older. He was getting closer to Alison, but he was weakening.

He came to a wide boulevard with a central walkway and recognized it. The houses were three-storeys high, but many were in a state of disrepair. He was freezing cold, his skin crawled. He hugged his arms around his chest, pushed his head down, let desire guide him forwards. Still following the sense that he'd been this way before, he followed the boulevard all the way to the end. He crossed a busy road at the traffic lights and felt that he was nearing the centre.

The Anglican cathedral was up ahead. Yes, his sister lived around the other side. He could picture it. He needed to just keep going but he was weary, his bones ached. He opened his fist, just a crack, and peeped inside. The money was still there. He followed a line of shops until he came to a newsagent. At the door, he peered in, but didn't dare enter. Several customers chatted inside around a woman with a pram. They'd despise him, they'd kill him. He was soaking wet, he stank, his beard was disgusting. They'd throw him out, they'd beat him and spit at him. It had happened before.

He waited outside in the rain, shivering, head down, until the customers left. He drew back as the woman with the pram came out, not wanting her to have to look at him. When she'd passed, he ducked inside. The man behind the counter was reading a newspaper, he didn't notice him enter. What could five pounds buy? He almost tripped and fell in his haste. He banged into the end of an aisle, causing the shelves to rattle.

'Sorry.' He froze in place, but the shopkeeper didn't respond.

A fridge on the side wall contained sandwiches. They looked awful. A leftover sense of snobbery came back to him from years back. Whoever he had been before was somebody who didn't eat prepackaged sandwiches from corner shops. The cheapest option was a plain cheese sandwich on white bread. Two pounds fifty. He'd have half of his money left. It would be painful to break the blue note in his hand, but he needed to eat. Afterwards, he'd be stronger, he'd find his way to his sister, and she'd take care of him. He took the sandwich up to the counter, head down, terrified of this man's judgement. But the man didn't look at him. He scanned the sandwich and tossed it back.

'Two fifty, mate.'

His eyes scanned the wall and saw a sign behind the shopkeeper that read "Tea and Coffee: £2.00". Tea. He'd forgotten it existed.

'Two fifty,' the man said again in a bored tone.

'Please…' He tried to find the words but couldn't.

The shopkeeper looked at him properly for the first time. Disgust showed in his face. 'Two fifty.'

'Please…' He managed to point at the sign.

'You want a cup of tea?'

He nodded.

The shopkeeper sighed. 'You homeless, mate?'

Not knowing the right answer, he said nothing.

The man got up to look closer but pulled away at the smell. 'Pooh! Don't you have a coat? It's pouring down. You're soaked.'

He tried to apologise but couldn't speak.

'Here.' The man reached below the counter and pulled out a blanket. 'At least put something over yourself.'

* * *

This world is filled with wonders. Tea, for example. Hunched on the concrete around the corner from the main road, out of view down a back alley smelly with bins, he blew steam from the polystyrene cup and sipped. It burned his lips, but he didn't care. The blanket was hugged around his neck. It was getting damp and offered meagre cover from the wind, but it was a comfort to have something around him. He drank again. The shopkeeper had given him three sachets of sugar. He ripped them open, one after the other, and poured them into the liquid. The sweetness on his tongue was spellbinding. He drank it too quickly and held the emptied cup upside down over his tongue to savour the last drops. When it was gone, he tore the sandwich open. It was dry and flavourless, difficult to swallow with his dry throat, but he forced it down. When it was gone, he leaned against the wall as his stomach churned. He hadn't eaten in so long, he feared he might throw it back up.

After five minutes with his spine pressed against the wall, he hadn't vomited. The tea sloshed in his stomach when he stood up. He felt worse than before, the fuel only lit all the agonised twists of his insides, but at least he could walk again.

He set off down the main road following the outline of the cathedral that towered over the other buildings. It was further away than it looked. A fifty-pence piece clutched in his palm, he trudged through old leaves and puddles. He turned a corner and saw the cathedral up ahead – a vast, red-brick monolith that had never felt like a church to him, more like a prison.

A long metal fence surrounded the building. He circled around, keeping a lookout for other people, but it was quiet here on the far side of the cathedral. On the horizon, he saw the tops of the city's skyline dotted over the roofs of the buildings. Epic clouds gathered over the sea that was concealed beyond the furthest towers. A place to throw himself, if all else failed.

He recognized his sister's road right away from the sensation of shame it sparked in him. These pretty Georgian houses were quiet, peaceful, not a place where he belonged. He didn't know the number, but he remembered her house was around the middle of the street, on the right-hand side. Coming closer, he recognized her car, a yellow Fiat. That was Alison, she'd always liked yellow. There was a softness in her that adulthood had not calloused. He peeked through the car window and saw a pile of books on the passenger seat. It was her, it had to be her. Walking up the driveway to her front door, it felt like only yesterday that he'd last made this journey. Yes, he remembered, he'd knocked, she'd opened. He could picture the look on her face like it was just a moment ago: despair. That's what it was.

At the yellow front door, he stopped. The memory of knocking was so intense, he was almost certain it had just happened this morning, but that was impossible. He'd raised his hand and knocked, lightly at first, then banging. He'd kept banging in terror that she might not open. Then he'd heard the bolt on the other side. The door had pulled inwards, just a crack, and she'd looked out.

'What are you doing here?' she'd said.

'Alison, I need help.'

'I gave you help last time, remember?' There had been no gladness in her voice to see her elder brother. No, no gladness at all.

He'd looked for a way to make her open. 'I'm sorry, Alison, I'm sorry about everything.'

'No, you're not sorry. You just want money.'

'If I could come in for a moment. I've nowhere to go.'

'Come in and do what? You can't stay here. We tried that before. We've tried it many times.'

'No… we'll just have a cup of tea, and a chat. We'll talk about Mum and Dad, and childhood, like old times, like a brother and sister.'

'Don't try to con me with that brother-and-sister shit.'

'What–'

'You and your mind games. You want to guilt-trip me. God, it's worked enough times. I'm a fool. I let people walk all over me.'

'This isn't like you, Alison. Where did you…?'

'I've got a new friend, OK?'

'A friend; who?'

'He pointed out a few things to me, like how I let people take advantage. How I let you use me.'

'What?'

'How much money have I given you over the years?'

'I…'

'And you spent it all on drugs, didn't you? You were here begging just last month. You conned me, like you always do. A story about sorting yourself out, getting back on your feet. You convinced me. I'm a born idiot. But, this friend of mine, he said, it's for your own benefit. I have to cut you off.'

'He said that? Who is this guy? Can I talk to him? Is he there?'

'He said I'm an "enabler". I'm actually contributing to your problems by giving you money. I'm the only one left who does. You've got no friends anymore. All your old colleagues abandoned you.'

'No, they didn't.'

'Liar. Con artist. I spoke to them. I contacted them to ask for help, to ask what I should about you. They all said the same thing: you treated them like you treated me. Used them. Stole from them. Tricked and cheated. Go away. Alright? I'm not going to help you anymore.'

'But…'

'If you come back here, I'll call the police.'

And she'd slammed the door shut. He'd stared into its yellow paint just like he was doing now. 'Go away!' she'd screamed from the other side. 'Go away now! I'm calling the police. I'm calling them right now…'

He'd staggered away. The details came back too fast in memory, with a hot burst of sorrow. He'd lost the last person. Even his sister despised him. There was nothing left to do but end himself. He couldn't even apologise. When was that? It felt like just now, but it must have been a few weeks ago. He wasn't wearing this blanket around his shoulders at the time. He remembered trudging away from the locked door with such despair in his chest, he couldn't believe the fibres of his body still strung together.

Suddenly he was afraid that Alison would see him outside her house in this state of physical ruin. If he ever wanted to win back her trust, he needed to show her that he could change, and yet here he was, worse than ever. He ran back down the driveway into the street. He veered away from the yellow car and set off in the direction he'd come from. Halfway down the road, he stopped. It was all confused, the memories didn't fit together. If Alison refused him last time… then where did the drugs come from? He remembered the drugs. He remembered holding the bag in both hands, and the glow of pleasure that came up through his loins in anticipation was more sexual than anything he'd ever known.

Where had the drugs come from? He had no money, no friends. He turned back towards Alison's car. Another memory was forcing its way through: he had gone back to his sister's house afterwards. She wasn't home. He knew how to get in. He knew where her things were hidden. He'd taken some jewellery, her laptop, some other odds and ends, and pawned them. He'd managed to scrape together just enough money.

The shame only lasted a moment before the lust came back stronger. Broken and emptied as he was, a wave of desire swelled out of his belly and spread through his chest, irresistible. He'd do anything to have that little plastic bag in his hands again. Even if he didn't use it, just to have it in his hands and know it was there. He was running back to Alison's house before he could stop himself, to remember her face when she'd screamed at him to go away. The last person in life who'd felt anything for him.

When he reached the house, he crept around the side and looked through the window. The lights were off. She might be at work, although the car was there. What time was it? He had no idea. She was usually at the university, where her work kept her busy till all hours. She might have left the car at home and gone on foot. It wasn't far from here, and it was a pleasant walk. He followed the path around the side of the house, feeling the glow of need billow in his veins; the memory, like a recurring nightmare that he must walk through again and again and again. He'd follow it until he woke.

In the backyard, he came to the window that he'd broken last time. It was covered over with cardboard. That wouldn't stop him. He looked through the pane on the left; it wasn't broken, offering a partial view of Alison's kitchen. There was nobody there. Some dirty dishes were piled in the sink, and two wine glasses rimmed with red stains had been left out on the counter. Tut-tut, Alison wasn't so neat and tidy after all. Her "friend" must have been around, whoever he was, this know-it-all who advised sisters to cut off their brothers. Alison always had poor judgement when it came to people. He knew that better than anybody.

As he edged around the window trying to see deeper into the interior of the house, he noticed the back door was open. The pleasurable anticipation was dispelled instantly; his sister must be at home. If she caught him snooping around in the back garden, that would be the end of their sibling relationship, permanently, this time.

He took a step back but couldn't bring himself to leave. There was nowhere else to go, and the door, just slightly ajar, invited him. A sickly smell eked out of there. He put his eye to the gap and looked inside. What he saw made him jump back. The fifty-pence piece dropped out of his fist.

He let out a cry and slapped his hands over his mouth. The world was still. The sound he'd made was too loud, but nothing responded. Nothing moved behind the door. He didn't dare to look again, he couldn't. Eyes averted, he pushed the door open all the way, braced for a movement, but all was still. Somehow, this was worse.

'Alison,' he said. 'Alison?' His voice, long out of use, was croaky and frightening.

He forced himself to look. A trail of dark blood seeped through the tiles. Alison – *was it Alison?* – was huddled in the far corner of the kitchen with her hands over her eyes, as if hiding. The blood came issuing from somewhere inside her.

'Alison? Are you alright?'

She didn't move. Her shoulders and chest were motionless. The smell of the blood was heady. He held the edge of a worktop to support himself as he stepped carefully around the unfurling blood.

'Alison?'

Perhaps she was only asleep or unconscious. He didn't know what to do. Just grab anything you can find of value and run out of here, straight to the pawnshop, obliterate this image, he thought. But he was mesmerized by her – the way she hid herself in the corner, not a gap between her fingers. Perhaps she was ashamed, but she shouldn't be, she'd always been kind, she was a good person. He came as close as he dared, until he could almost reach out and touch her. Something vile wormed in his heart.

It must have been him... this was the part of the memory he'd repressed. Last time, when he'd come for money, and she'd turned him away, he'd broken through the back window; he thought she was at work, but she'd run in and found him there. They'd fought... He must have hurt her. He couldn't remember doing it, but of course, that was what the drug did to him, it pushed away anything that might not lead to its own satisfaction. He'd killed his sister. The only person who ever tried to help him.

'Alison... I'm sorry,' he mumbled.

He couldn't bear it any longer, those hands covering her face; he was the one who should be ashamed, not her.

'Alison... can you?' He reached and grabbed her wrists and pulled the hands back.

He thought she might resist, her body seemed so tense, but the hands were loose. He wanted to see her face, he needed to, he needed to know that it was really her and not somebody else's lost sibling. He pulled the hands all the way down. With a slick, wet noise, her eyeballs, stuck to the palms of her hands, came free from the sockets, dangling ugly, red cords behind them. He screamed. The hands dropped from his grip as he slipped and fell hard on the tiles. Something snapped in his brain, reality split in half.

He crawled back against the cold tiles and pressed into the opposite corner. All he wanted to do was to put his hands over his face and hide there.

34

There was one key left on Daniel's keyring that she hadn't used. A car key. Eleanor climbed in the old Datsun that was parked in front of his house and tried the key in the ignition. It fit, of course. Despite his disappearance, Daniel was beckoning her forwards. She drove back to the estate and parked outside number 35. It was quiet outside, but she felt herself watched from every window. The rain had picked up and she was glad; it would keep the inhabitants of this place sheltering indoors. Still, she felt uneasy. She had the kitchen knife in her bag in case she ran into those lads again, or anybody else.

She climbed over the fence of 35 and snuck around the side of the house. The kitchen door hung open. She was sure she'd closed it behind her. Perhaps the wind had blown it loose. In the kitchen she stopped to listen, but there was no sound from the house. She tiptoed up the stairs, back into the cloud of stink, but the sick man was gone. She checked every room and almost screamed with frustration. She went back to the staircase and inspected the wooden steps. There was a trail of slime where he'd come down.

Outside, she noticed the garden tap dripping. The "doctor" must have stopped to drink. He had climbed over the fence, and he was gone. Good riddance, she thought; he wasn't her problem, never had been. *Go home, Eleanor, stop all this, before you go crazy.* She climbed back over the fence and was relieved to leave the looted house behind. Time to leave this estate entirely. She would never set foot in here again, thank God. As she was walking back to the car, a woman shouted.

'Hey, you!' An elderly lady in a pink tracksuit came towards her.

Eleanor opened the car door.

'Hey! Hey, you!' The woman came closer. Her face was coated in make-up, with thick mascara and bright red lipstick. Her white hair was done up in curlers. 'I'm the one who called you.'

'You… you called me?'

'Yeah. What are you looking at me like that for?'

'On the phone?' She noticed a bulldog at the woman's heels.

'Get back, little bastard.' The woman kicked at the dog, and it retreated. 'You're from the homeless shelter, aren't you? I rang about the old tramp. He was here creeping around. A right mess. He's a bad one, I can tell. Heroin addict. I've seen them before. They get that smell. The skin turns green.'

'Oh, him. I know who you mean.'

'Well, you're too late. He's gone. Ran off, didn't come back. I gave him a fiver.'

'You gave him a fiver?'

'What do you expect? We're not a bad lot on the estate, you know. It's not our fault everything's fucked.'

'You're right. Do you…'

The woman turned around and started walking back in the direction she'd come from. The dog barked and waddled after her. Eleanor climbed in the car, closed the door, locked it, and tried to feel safe inside its flimsy metal shell.

35

Voices woke him. Where was this? He lay on a mattress. His head ached. He tried to open his eyes, but the pain was too much. He lay still and tried to remember what place this was, how he'd got there. Voices muttered, just out of earshot. A musty smell in the air. There was something in his memory that flared, something awful had happened. All the world's vileness was there in that hole in his head. If he looked, he'd see it. Alison... what happened? He screamed and jerked in the bed. Footsteps came running over. Somebody shouted.

'He's awake,' a woman said.

Hands pressed him down on the bed. A cold palm pressed his forehead.

'Are you alright?' the woman said. He recognized her voice. 'Can you hear me?'

'Where am I?' he said.

'You're back in the shelter. We thought you'd left us for good this time.'

'What?' He forced his eyes to open.

Through a red patch of blurred pain, he looked into the light and saw the kind nurse who'd treated him in the past. He was in the homeless shelter, where he'd spent countless nights over the years, and always swore he'd never return. Thirty bunk beds filled a wide room like a school gym, grey with grimy light through the windows. A smell of sour sweat soaked through the mattresses. In the bunk above his head, somebody groaned. The frame of the bed rattled. He sniffed himself; they'd taken his foul clothes off him and put him in clean things.

'Does it hurt?' the nurse said.

'What?'

'You banged your head. Must have had quite a fall. They found you lying unconscious on the pavement. Somebody rang us. We came and picked you up.'

'I can't stay here.' He tried to sit up, but his bones ached.

She tutted. 'You need to rest a while. Just lie down there. The others will be glad to see you. "Where's the doctor?" they ask me. You're popular here, you know.'

'Oh great.'

'You've been back on the drug, haven't you? You're in withdrawal. You're shaking.'

'I don't know. I guess I must be.'

'We agreed you weren't going to do that anymore, remember? You can't come here to the shelter if you're using. Where did you get it from? If it was from someone in here, you have to let us know.'

'I have no idea.'

'Try to.'

As soon as she was gone, he grabbed hold of the bunk bed frame and dragged himself into a sitting position. Something awful had happened. Alison was dead. Was he the one who killed her? Who else could it have been? He was responsible for all the bad things that had happened. The police would be searching for him.

'Psst, Doctor.' From the neighbouring bed, a man poked his head out. 'It's me, Lanky. You came back.'

Lanky had black teeth and wispy tufts of white hair.

'I banged my head,' the doctor said.

This was the hell of the shelter – there was no solitude, he was surrounded constantly. To discourage conversation, he lay back down on the bunk and closed his eyes.

'I wanted to talk to you.' Lanky crawled out of his bed and squatted beside him.

'I can't talk. My head's spinning. I fell over in the street.'

'I'll give you something.' He took the doctor's hand and placed something in his palm. 'As payment. I need you to decipher this dream I keep having.'

The doctor looked and found a small penknife in his hand. 'Where did you get this?' He opened the blade and held it to the weak light of the windows.

'Found it in the street, didn't I? It's sharp. I tried it out. It'll be good for you, Doctor, keep you safe while you're living rough.'

'Don't you need it yourself?'

Lanky grinned. 'I've already got one.'

'Alright. Tell me your dream.' He folded the knife and put it in his pocket.

'It's a nightmare. I've been having it every night recently. I wake up screaming, and then everyone goes mad. They say they'll kick me out of the shelter if I don't stop it.'

'What's it about?'

'I'm driving a car. When I turn around and look in the back, my parents are sitting there, but they're small, like little children. Then I get scared. My dad's supposed to be the one who's driving, not me. Suddenly I can't control the car. The pedals don't work. The steering wheel is going crazy. Up ahead, there's a giant truck coming towards us. My parents start crying. I'm struggling with the wheel, my feet are like mad on the pedals. I scream and wake up.'

The doctor fingered the penknife in his pocket. 'That's the end?'

'That's it.'

'You have this dream every night?'

'Most nights, yeah. Sometimes I manage to drink enough that I don't dream at all.'

'And this worries you?'

'Of course, it worries me. I feel like I'm losing it.'

'Are your parents dead in reality?'

'They died years ago, but even before that, I stopped seeing them. They gave up on me.'

'You know, nightmares can feel terrible, but they're often positive.'

'What do you mean?'

'It shows the mind dealing with some problem and making progress. It's a kind of breakthrough.'

'A breakthrough?'

'It's about accepting your parents are gone forever. You're on your own now, but you're in control. You're free, but you're afraid to be free. You have to accept it.'

'But how do I do that, Doctor?'

'Steer the car into the truck. The only reason you can't control the car in the dream is because you're trying to avoid crashing. But you need to crash.'

'How can I do that? I don't understand. It's a dream, I can't control it.'

'You can. Before you go to sleep each night, repeat to yourself ten times, "Drive into the truck. Drive into the truck." Try to visualize it as vividly as you can. Then, in the dream, your mind will know what to do. You'll press on the accelerator, grasp the wheel, go straight through the truck, and drive out the other side. When you look back behind you, the car seats will be empty. Your parents are gone forever.'

Lanky said nothing. After a few moments, the doctor opened his eyes and looked to see that the man was silently weeping next to his bed.

'Hey, it's alright,' he told him. 'Here, take the penknife back. It's yours.'

'No, Doctor, you keep it.' Lanky got up and walked out of the dormitory, his shoulders shaking.

36

Eleanor couldn't go back to Daniel's house. The phone receiver would still be lying on the floor, laughter leaking out. She couldn't go anywhere, couldn't stay in Liverpool where the voice had found her, and couldn't leave it, not without Daniel.

She needed to think, but in the city streets she was too exposed, she longed for a place of shelter. She found a hotel just outside the city centre, overlooking the river mouth, and booked a room. She didn't kid herself that it was safe. The voice would find her there as well; it was clear they could track her. If the police were involved, they'd have technology to hunt her down. Still, she took money out of a machine and paid for the hotel room with cash in case her credit card was being monitored. The precaution was only for show, she no longer believed she could escape, she only wanted to keep moving for as long as possible.

The room was empty. She sat on the edge of the bed and watched the vast grey sky that filled the window. Looming clouds unfurled in slow motion, driven by the sea's breath. She'd left her laptop behind in the old house. She was helpless without it, but she couldn't go back – she just couldn't. Daniel was gone. She'd followed his trail, found the locks for the three keys he'd left her, but she'd reached the end and was empty-handed.

'Where are you?' she said aloud. 'What do you want me to do?'

Nobody answered. Or perhaps they did. She knew the answer. She was a detective, she only had to do her job. She had lost Daniel's investigation room, but she could make a new one. She took his map of the estate out of her bag and laid it out on the table. The answer was there, she was certain of it; the solution was somewhere in the estate. She took out her notepad and jotted down every detail she could think of. The doctor, his sickness, the locked room. She tore the page out and placed it at the top of the map. The stool that she'd found, and the red eyes painted on the wall. She added these notes beneath the first.

What else had she seen? The gang of lads, she'd learned one of their names... Lee. She jotted it down and set the page next to the others. What else? A police officer who had seemed strange – he'd just driven away, and didn't listen to her. Scott, or something like that. She added him to the growing set of notes. There'd been a woman as well, with a bulldog. She'd seen the missing doctor and given him five pounds. What else did she say?

37

At dinnertime they lined up to receive bowls of soup that they ate on benches. As the doctor was receiving his, one of the women who volunteered at the shelter pulled him aside.

'Can I have a quick word with you, Doctor?'

He inhaled a mouthful of steam from his bowl. His stomach gurgled. 'Sure.'

They sat down on the corner of a bench on the far side of the room, and he ate while she talked.

'It's about my boyfriend. We've been together about a year now. Last month, he hit me. Not too badly, I didn't bleed or anything, he just sort of punched me in the side of the face. He was sorry about it. He swore it wouldn't happen again.'

The soup was tasteless, potatoes and water, but it was hot. Too hungry to wait for it to cool, he swallowed the stuff down and let it burn his throat.

The nurse stopped talking. 'I'm sorry, I should let you eat.'

The doctor shook his head. 'Leave him,' he said with his mouth full.

'I… I don't know. That's what my friends said.'

'So why didn't you?' He ate another spoonful.

'He begged me. He said he's suffering from depression. He said he needs help, and he's going to get help. He said I can help him, but that if I leave him, it could make things worse because he's in a really bad mental space at the moment.'

'Leave him.'

'But… I googled depression. They say anger can be a symptom. If he really does have depression, then… I feel like I should help him. I don't know what to do. I heard you were back at the shelter, I thought maybe I could ask. I know we're not supposed to. It's not your job here to give advice. But I just wanted to ask, is it true that depression causes anger?'

'Yes, it's true.'

'So, it's true then. He really does need help.'

'Anger and violence aren't the same. Lots of people feel anger, but they don't hurt others.'

'He says I could help him.'

'Manipulation. You have no obligation to help. It's his responsibility to control his emotions, not yours. If you stay with him after he's hit you, he won't get better, he'll get worse. He's got away with it once, he doesn't need to change. Why would he?'

'You don't think he can change? Maybe if you met him… he's not like it sounds. He's not a bad person, really.'

'Everyone can change, but they have to do it on their own, they can't ask someone else to help them.'

'But… I…'

'Leave him,' the doctor said.

* * *

Maybe he'd eaten too much soup. His stomach wasn't ready for it. Trembling all over, sweating yet freezing cold, he stumbled back to his bunk and lay down. The spinning of the world slowed but didn't stop. He gulped the sour air of this place and tried to think. What was happening? How did he get in that torture room, and how did he escape? Where did the drugs come from? And Alison... he couldn't bear it. Everything was the torture room. He was locked inside, and he'd never get free.

'Psst, Doctor...' A raspy voice snaked out from one of the other bunks.

He rolled on his side, away from him. He couldn't bear to listen to any more of these people's problems. He couldn't help them, he couldn't even sit up straight. He kept his eyes shut and let his limbs go slack. Let them believe he was asleep. He wouldn't wake for anyone.

'Doctor...' The voice was closer. There was something sinister in its cadence, a repressed hilarity.

He heard somebody sidle up to the bed and crouch next to him. He smelled a mist of stale vodka and rotten teeth. He didn't move, and he wouldn't. Something pressed against his neck.

'Feel that?' the voice said. 'That's a syringe. There's blood inside. Dirty blood.'

He flinched and gave himself away. He opened his eyes to see a man leaning over him, wearing what appeared to be a bedraggled clown costume: multicoloured waistcoat, polka-dot bow tie, dried smudges of face paint around his eyes. It was as if one of his patients' nightmares had come to life.

'Who are you?' he said. 'What do you want? I'm sick. I can't help you. I'm sorry.'

'Oh, don't be sorry.'

'What do you want? Tell me.'

'I just want you to listen.'

'What?' He watched as the man slipped a pair of old headphones with twisted wires from around his neck and placed them in the doctor's ears.

'What is this? Some kind of joke?'

'Clown music. Shush. Listen.' He pressed play on a tape cassette Walkman.

An electronic jingle played in the doctor's ears. It sounded tinny through the old headphones but it was a cheerful, satiric tune like a fanfare. It stopped. A voice sounded.

This is how you die.

The voice was ancient, deep, throaty with malice.

Under my stare... You're naked, stretched out, helpless... I look at every part of you... Nothing is hidden... I tell you how ugly you are. You're disgusting. You make me sick. You're vile... And you cry, because you know it's true.

'Turn this shit off.' He moved one hand to grab at the wires, but the clown pressed the knife deeper into his throat.

'Don't you move, you cunt.' He closed his other hand over the doctor's mouth. The palm of his hand tasted salty. 'You lie still like that, and don't make a sound.'

The voice in the headphones kept probing into his ear, slow, patient, inevitable.

First, I cut your eyeballs out... I start with the left eye. Your lids are held open, you have to watch, you have no choice. I slip the edge of a spoon underneath and pry the ball loose. I pull it out, gently. I don't want to break it yet. I want you to see. The ball in my palm watches as I set it down on a petri dish. It can't blink anymore. I swivel it around so it witnesses as I remove the other eye.

The doctor's hand found the penknife that was in his pocket. He eased it out and opened it.

> *…Watching is everything. Everything must be seen… Everything must see itself seen. This is how you die. You witness every part of you removed, inch by inch, until there is no part of your vileness left…*

'Turn it off,' he said.

'Don't you want to listen to the end? Don't you want to know what happens?'

'No.' He grabbed the clown with his free hand and slashed the penknife at his face.

The clown let out a cry and dropped the syringe. The cassette player fell to the floor and broke open. A battery rolled away under the bed.

'What's happening?' someone shouted from the top of one of the bunkbeds. 'Stop that!'

A spurt of blood came from the clown's arm. The doctor barrelled past him. He ran out into the hall and didn't look back. All he desired was to get out. He'd jump out of the window if need be.

'Hey.' One of the volunteers grabbed his arm. 'Why are you running?'

He shoved her away and kept running. In the reception area, he saw the front exit, just ten yards away. A few staff members and a handful of homeless people stood about, blocking the way. He roared as he ran through them, blindly swatting at their faces until they skipped back.

'What are you doing?' someone said.

'Hey, stop.' One of the volunteers tried to catch him.

Their voices were calm; this kind of occurrence was normal in the shelter. He was almost at the door when a man grabbed hold of him with two arms, a strong grip.

'Hey, Doctor. Where are you running off to like that?' It was the shelter supervisor, a large man, whom he knew to be unflappable.

'Let go of me!' He writhed in his strong arms and looked back towards the hall, but there was no sign of the clown. 'Let go!'

'Alright, just relax.' The supervisor released him. 'Are you calm now? Just be calm.'

'I have to get out.'

'OK. You know you're free to leave. But first, there's someone who wants to speak to you.'

'No!' He felt his neck, but there was no puncture. It seemed the syringe hadn't pierced his skin. Still, the thought of it made him dizzy.

'You don't know who it is yet.' The supervisor turned to a woman who was standing at the front desk. 'Sorry, love, he's not normally like this. The doctor is one of our best-behaved guests.'

He looked at the woman. Medium height, brown eyes and hair. She was wearing a tracksuit. 'Who is she? I don't know her.'

'Yes.' She studied his face. 'Yes, it's him. He's the one I'm looking for.'

'Who are you?' he said.

'Police Detective Eleanor Rose. I'd like to talk to you for a moment.'

The name Eleanor resonated. He tried to pin down the memory of that word, but it slipped away. 'Police?' he said. 'You don't look like police.' He stepped away, but there was something there… he had seen her before, but where?

She showed her badge. 'Don't worry, you're not in any trouble. Will you talk with me?'

He glanced around wildly, but there was no sign of the clown. The volunteers watched him with a hint of amusement, and turned away. They'd seen everything before in the shelter.

'I hope there isn't any problem,' the supervisor said. 'The doctor's never caused trouble here. The others like him, the staff as well. He's helped some of us.'

Eleanor's expression was sceptical. 'No, there's no problem. I just want to have a chat, that's all.'

'Alright, we can chat,' the doctor said. 'But not here.'

38

Elliot met her outside the front gate of the house.

'Come round the back,' he said. 'The killer came this way.'

Krush followed him around the house to a little garden. The back door hung open. Forensics officers were taking photographs and dusting the surfaces.

'It's like your murder scene on the estate. I thought you'd want to see it before we box it up.'

'Who's the victim?'

'Alison Stray. Lecturer in biology at the University of Liverpool. This is her house.'

Krush looked through the door. 'Can I go inside?'

'Go ahead.'

She put on her crime scene gloves.

'You'll need these too.' He handed a pair of foot coverings. 'Need to keep the floor scene intact.'

Inside, the smell of blood was intense. In the corner of the kitchen, a woman's body leaned against the wall. Blood ran through the tiles.

'What the hell?' Krush took out her torch and shined it over the woman. 'What happened to her eyes?'

'Seems they were stuck to her palms. When the palms came down, the eyeballs came out.'

'It's similar to the one on the estate, but not exactly the same. The hands were up over the face last time. Has somebody moved the body?'

'Not police. It was like this when they arrived. The hands could have been pulled down by someone else.'

'By the person who found the body?'

'Could be. It was a man who phoned the police. He used the landline in the hall.' Elliot pointed. 'Didn't give a name. He wasn't here when the police arrived. We've dusted the phone, found some prints, but they could be the victim's. This is her house.'

* * *

The woman next door, a Mrs Williams, couldn't stop crying. 'I just can't believe it…' She dabbed the corners of her eyes with a tissue.

Krush was getting impatient. The neighbour was short, maybe fifty years old, she wore dungarees and had grey dreadlocks, perhaps an artist, a bohemian type.

'Did you know Miss Stray well?'

'Oh, you know. We were neighbours, we used to say "hello"; we'd stop and chat, that kind of thing.'

'How long have you lived next door?'

'I moved here around five years ago, but Alison was already living here. She…' Mrs Williams broke off into a new fit of tears.

Krush waited for what she hoped was a compassionate amount of time, before continuing, 'Is there anything you can tell us? Did you see anything? Hear anything?'

Mrs Williams sobbed and shook her head.

'Please,' Krush said. 'Try to concentrate. Was Alison threatened by anyone? Did she have a jealous ex? Did she ever…?'

'Oh well, there was that brother of hers.' Mrs Williams pulled the tissue away from the red corner of her eye. 'You don't think he could have…?'

'Tell me about the brother.'

'He's a heroin addict. Homeless, according to Alison. He drifts around. For months – a year sometimes – she wouldn't hear from him. Then he'd turn up, asking for money.'

Krush flipped a new page in her notepad. 'Do you know his name?'

'Sorry, no.'

'What does he look like?'

'I don't know. I never saw him.' Her upper lip twitched; she looked like she might start crying again.

'And this brother,' Krush said, 'was he dangerous? Did Alison ever say she was afraid of him?'

'She didn't say so, not to me, but whenever he turned up, she'd be different. All on edge. She was such a kind lady…' A new tear came trickling down from Mrs Williams' eye. She raised her tissue, but it was saturated.

'Had the brother been around recently?' Krush said.

'Yes, last week. This time it was different. Alison told him she couldn't help anymore. She wouldn't give him any money. He went away. But yesterday, when I saw her, she was very upset. She said… she said…' The woman's voice dissolved into tears.

'Mrs Williams.' Krush almost shouted but managed to soften her voice. 'This is important. It's a murder investigation.'

The woman's shoulders shook. 'I'm sorry.'

'You saw Alison yesterday?'

'Yes. She said she'd had to get the glass fixed in her kitchen window. That brother of hers had broken in and robbed her. Taken her laptop, some jewellery, I don't know, some other stuff. To pawn for drug money, Alison said. Can you believe her own brother would do that…?'

'Oh, siblings are capable of all kinds. They're not like other family members. I've got a sister myself.'

39

'My name is Raymond Stray,' the doctor said. 'I'm a psychiatrist, or I was. It's been a long time since life fell apart.'

They sat in the front seats of Daniel's Datsun while the rain pattered on the windscreen. Eleanor glanced around, checking each side of the car, but there was nobody outside; nobody had followed them.

'What are you afraid of?' Stray said.

'Nothing.' She looked in the rear-view mirror and adjusted it slightly.

He figured she must be investigating Alison's death. There was no other explanation for the detective's sudden appearance at the shelter. But then why did she keep glancing around? Was she afraid of him? He decided to play for time.

'Your car's a collector's item,' he said.

'It's not mine.' She took out a pack of cigarettes. 'Smoke?'

'I'd kill for one.'

His hands fluttered with anticipation as he accepted the cigarette that she lit for him. She said nothing as he inhaled, but he sensed her watching. He couldn't hide the pleasure from his ravaged face. A moment of perfection. He coughed, gagging on the smoke.

'Whoa, slow down,' Eleanor said.

He couldn't speak, he only wanted to smoke the whole thing down alone. The detective seemed to understand this; she kept quiet and looked away. He wanted to make it last, but he couldn't stop smoking, and the cigarette burned down fast. Soon it would be gone. He coughed painfully, his lungs felt raw, but he didn't care. He sucked it all the way down to the last mouthful and stared into the twining strands of smoke.

'I guess you needed that,' Eleanor said.

He sighed and threw the butt out of the window.

'Here, take the rest. I'm supposed to have quit.' She tossed the packet over and he failed to catch it with his quivering hands.

He snapped it up greedily and looked inside. Half the packet was gone. It was a treasure. He stuffed it in his pocket and let his head rest on the car seat.

'You're an empathetic type,' he said.

'What?'

'That's not ideal for police work. You don't want to be too sensitive. Police is more suited for practical types, the ones who don't take things to heart.'

'You're wrong,' she said. 'I'm cold.'

'I don't believe you.'

'OK, I didn't get you out of that shelter for therapy. I don't need it.'

'Everyone needs therapy,' he said.

'I'm going to take those cigarettes back.'

'You define yourself as a cold person, but your element is earth. That's why people need therapy: to discover who they really are.'

'I don't believe in "elements".' Her feet hovered over the pedals as if she was readying to drive away at any moment.

Sensing her fear, he grew more confident in himself. People who were fearful could be manipulated.

'The elements are just symbols,' he said. 'Are you afraid of symbols?'

'And what's your element?'

'Fire,' he said.

'You didn't talk like this last time we met.'

'What?'

'You really don't know me?'

'I recognize something. Are you… a former patient of mine? No. I'm sure I'd remember.'

'You were locked in a room in an estate. I let you out. I brought you water. I went home to pick up a change of clothes and some food for you, but when I came back, you were gone. A woman from the estate said she'd called the homeless shelter. Honestly, I really didn't expect to find you there.'

'I remember you now. The room. I wondered how I got out of there. I woke up on the floor in the landing.' He released his grip on the door handle. 'Do you… do you know why I was locked in that room?'

'I wanted to ask you the same question.'

She didn't trust him, he could tell, but she wanted to. Why? Perhaps she had nobody else. She was afraid of something, that much was clear as she glanced in the mirror again. He began to believe this really wasn't about Alison. The body might not have been discovered yet.

'Beats me,' he said. 'I woke up and I was trapped. I couldn't remember anything.'

'I don't believe you. Why would someone lock you in a room in an abandoned house? There has to be a reason.'

'You're the one who found me. You must have been looking. How did you know I was there?'

She took a breath. He sensed her internally questioning, wondering if she could trust him or not. She glanced around again. She kept looking out of the window, but nobody had passed the car this whole time.

She let the breath out. 'Alright. I'll tell you the story. A friend of mine, a police officer, Daniel, he's gone missing. Maybe. I'm not sure. Nobody's seen him around. He left a strange message for me, said he was afraid, in trouble. I'm trying to find him. I think it might have been Daniel who took you to the estate.'

The doctor fought to keep the release from showing in his face; this police detective wasn't here about Alison. He was safe. He frowned to keep from smiling. 'Why would your friend do a thing like that?'

'I was hoping you could tell me.'

'I never heard of him before in my life, honestly. I'd tell you if I had.'

'But you knew my name. You said it at the estate.'

'What? Really?'

'Yeah. You said "Eleanor". My friend had the name tattooed on his wrist.'

He closed his eyes and saw it. 'Crossed out, with a line through the name? A red line...'

'That's it. That's his tattoo.' Something like excitement showed in her face just for a moment.

He felt a wall had been crossed. He wanted to trust this detective, he wanted to cooperate with her, but he knew he had to resist, otherwise she would have all the power, and he would have nothing with which to defend himself.

He looked for a ruse and said, 'Got your name tattooed on his wrist? Sounds like more than just a friend.'

Eleanor turned her head away. He had made a false step.

'Sorry,' he said. 'It's none of my business.'

'No. It's not like that. I haven't seen Daniel in five years. Haven't spoken to him, haven't replied to any of his messages. You see? I told you I was cold.'

'How does this connect to me?'

'He was working on a case. I found his notes. There was a map of the estate, and photographs of it. There's something hidden there he wanted to find. If he brought you there... he thought you could help... or...'

The doctor watched horrified as the thought played out nakedly across her face. She couldn't finish the sentence.

He finished it for her. '...or I was the thing he was trying to find. I promise I'm not.'

She took out a kitchen knife. 'Tell me the truth now.'

'Jesus.'

He grabbed for the door handle, but she reached over him and pushed the lock down. He was so weak, he couldn't fight.

'I'm on your side, alright?' he pleaded. 'I want to know what's going on, just like you do. You saw the state of me in that house. Someone locked me in that room. The key was on the other side. I couldn't have locked myself in.'

'There was blood on the wall downstairs in there. Was it Daniel's?'

'I don't know.'

'Why were you running out of the shelter?' she asked. 'It was like you'd seen a ghost. Tell me the truth.'

'I was attacked. I was running away when you came in. I figured I'd be safe with police, so I went with you.'

'Attacked by whom?'

'Some crazed lunatic.'

'He was homeless too?'

'I guess so. He must have been staying in the shelter.'

'Why did he attack you?'

'He was nuts. He wore some old, disgusting clown outfit, and he had this tape player that he made me listen to. It was weird, violent stuff.'

'Hold on.' Still holding the knife, she took out a mobile phone. 'I'll call the shelter and check.'

'Be my guest.'

She must have had the number saved; she pressed a button and set it to speaker mode. Electronic ringing sounded.

Somebody answered. 'Hello, Liverpool Homeless—'

Eleanor interrupted them, 'It's me again, Rose, the detective who called earlier… I just wanted to check, do you have someone staying there dressed in a sort of clown costume…' Her voice trailed off; she must have felt ridiculous asking the question.

Stray nodded to reassure her.

The voice of the shelter supervisor spoke through the speaker. 'Clown costume? That's Mac. He stays with us from time to time. He does an act in the streets. People give him a quid.'

'Is he there now?'

'He was here, but he left. I don't know where. There's blood on the floor in the dormitory and the bathroom. Must have been a fight. Do you think…?'

'Do you have an address for Mac?'

'No address. I can tell you his full name, it's Alistair Macintyre. That's what's written here, anyway.'

'Thanks.'

She rang off. She looked at Stray. 'Maybe you're telling the truth.'

'Can you put the knife away, please?'

'What am I doing?' She put it back in her bag. 'Am I losing my mind? Running around with a kitchen knife…'

'Are you asking for my professional opinion?'

'No.' She stared out of the window and seemed lost.

He feared she might kick him out of the car; he'd proven to be no help in finding her friend, she didn't need him, he'd be back on the street with nowhere to go. He didn't dare to return to the shelter after what had happened there.

When she didn't say anything, he tried. 'Maybe I can help you.'

'How?'

'Let's say it's true your friend brought me to the estate. The reason might be connected to one of my old patients.'

She turned from the misted window; he sensed her imagination flicker. 'Go on,' she said.

'It's been years since I worked. Things went wrong, I got addicted to heroin. Lost my home, everything. I won't bore you with the details. I don't have my office anymore, but my former secretary is still around. If we… if I go to her, she might still have copies of my old case files on a computer. We might find a connection in the files to your friend Daniel, or perhaps to this Alistair Macintyre, or somebody at the estate.'

'Alright. That could work. Where does this secretary live?'

'Ah, that's the problem. We'd have to track her down. It's been years.'

'I can find her. That's my job.'

40

Krush heard the siren and turned to see the flashing light of Carmichael's car as he drove up to the murder scene. She met him as he was ducking under the crime scene tape.

'The same killer?' he said.

'Looks like it.'

'Shit.' He went up the driveway.

'Two bodies, both found with their hands over their eyes. This is looking like a serial killer. We need to—'

'Serial killer, in Liverpool? I won't have that. Let them have their serial killers down south. We're not that kind of city.'

'I think we should—'

'The suspect from the first killing, the husband… think he could have done the second one as well?'

'Not likely. He's in a coma.'

'What if the second murder happened first?'

'The crime scene looks fresh. We'll have to wait on forensics to come back with a timeframe.'

'Fuck my life. If it's not that idiot in a coma, who is it?'

'The second victim had a brother. Drug addict, apparently.' She followed as he rounded the house, circling a few officers who were taking pictures.

'Drug addict? That could work. Ah shit.' He stopped in the back doorway with his hands on his hips, surveying the scene. 'What a mess.'

'Supposedly, he used to hassle his sister for money. Real piece of work. Recently she cut him off, refused to help any more.'

'Well, there you go. That's him. He's the guy. Got a ready-made motive and a connection to the victim. We'll put out a search. I'll speak to the press people.' Carmichael left the doorway and sucked up the clean, leafy air of the garden. 'This kind of thing is bad for my blood pressure. Doctor says I'm supposed to be avoiding stress.'

'The problem is,' Krush said, 'why would the homeless brother kill Mrs Bennett?'

'Don't overthink it. The motive was the same in both killings: drug money.'

'Why would he kill them in the same way? He'd want to cover his tracks, wouldn't he? Not draw attention to himself.'

'He's out of his mind on drugs, that's why. Stop complicating things.'

'I don't know, this stuff with the eyeballs, the positioning of the bodies, it's too deliberate, too staged. It's like a game somebody's playing. Listen, I looked in the unsolved cases—'

'Jesus. You'd actually look for a serial killer on purpose. You enjoy this shit, don't you? You're only happy when life is difficult.'

'I just—'

'Is it because Daniel left you? Is that why you're screwed up, taking it out on the rest of us?'

'There's an unsolved case from six months ago, but it's not exactly the same. The body was found with a screwdriver in his eye…'

'And his hands?'

'By his side.'

'It doesn't fit. It's irrelevant.' Carmichael raised his voice as she tried to speak again. 'Don't you dare, Krush. You go find this drug addict brother. He's the killer, I promise you, it's him.'

41

'What's the name of your old secretary?' Eleanor said.

'Lydia. Lydia Hargreaves.'

She caught a slight lilt in Stray's voice, as if the name brought back happy memories. But his face showed no emotion. Could she trust him? He didn't seem dangerous. He was weak, gaunt, his hands trembled when he lifted them. But he was smart, she sensed him calculating behind his words while he spoke. She'd have to be careful.

She jotted down the name. 'Where was she living, last you heard?'

'In London, Camden. But I doubt she's still there. It was a small flat, something for young people. She's not young anymore.'

'Could still be worth checking.'

'No, I tried there, back when I was desperate for drugs. I tried every person I ever knew – friends, family, colleagues. I went and knocked on her door, but she'd left. I heard she'd moved back up north to Manchester, where she's from.'

'What was the name of your company?'

'Blue Skies Psychiatric Practice.'

'Blue Skies?'

'We imagined at the time we were pushing the boundaries with our work. That was before…' He trailed off.

'What?'

'Heroin.'

His answer was too quick. She sensed an ellipsis, something he wanted to hide. He was too smart, he wouldn't give his secrets willingly; she'd have to catch him out.

'Alright, I–' Eleanor broke off as the mobile phone in her bag started to ring.

She must have been staring at it with horror; Stray sounded concerned when he said, 'What is it?'

'Nothing. Nothing.'

'Why don't you answer?'

She picked up the phone. 'It's an unknown number.'

'So?'

'Nobody knows my number. I got rid of my old phone. This one's disposable, I just bought it at a garage. I haven't given the number to anyone.'

'So, answer it and see what they want.'

She raised the phone and felt the vibration in her palm. 'I can't.'

'Why not?'

'I just can't.'

'Eleanor, you have to answer it.'

'Why? They'll stop.'

But the phone didn't stop ringing.

'In life, we have to face our fears,' he said. 'It's important. It's the only way we can grow.'

'I'm not afraid.'

'Think I can't recognize fear? I'm more afraid than anyone.'

'It'll stop ringing now.'

It didn't stop. She should reject the call, but she was paralysed. It was worse with Stray watching her. She didn't move as he reached over and took the phone out of her hand. He accepted the call.

'Hello?' He held it to his ear. 'Who is this, please?'

She cringed, watching his face as he listened.

'Insurance?' he said. 'No, I don't need phone insurance. Hold on a moment.' He passed the phone to her. 'You should speak to them.'

She stared but didn't take it from his hand. It was close enough that she could hear the quiet voice say, 'Sir, are you sure you don't want to take advantage of this fantastic offer? Today is the only day...'

She pressed cancel. 'Just a cold-caller,' she said.

'Who did you expect?'

'Oh God, I'm going crazy, aren't I? I'm losing my mind.'

'No,' he said. 'You're anxious. It happens to all of us.'

'Let's just... let's get back to work.'

'Alright. How do we track down Lydia?'

'There's a guy at the station in London. Trevor. He finds people online,' she said. 'He can come up with any address or phone number in the blink of an eye.'

'So, call him.'

She stared at her mobile. 'I don't want to call the station. Truth is, nobody there knows I'm in Liverpool. I sort of ran away. I told my boss I was stressed. Why am I telling you this? You're analysing me now, aren't you?'

'It's fair enough. People get stressed. You're allowed to take time off for that.'

'Yeah, but there's more. I... I can't talk about it.'

'You're afraid of someone down there? You don't want them to know where you are?'

'Will you stop this, please?'

'Sorry.' He raised his hands and seemed sincere. 'Alright, here's an idea. That phone's disposable, right? So, call Trevor, and then throw the phone in the bin. Buy another.'

'That could work.'

She called the station in London, and was put through to Trevor.

'Eleanor?' His cheerful, cockney voice in her ear made the anxiety seem ridiculous, and Liverpool non-existent. 'Where are you? Everyone's worried.'

'I'm fine. Listen, sorry to call you out of the blue like this...'

'The boss said you're stressed or something.'

'I'm… err… I'm working on a case. I'm not in London.'

'You're not in London? Does the boss know? You should call him. Look, I understand, everyone's stressed. It's the targets, the pressure…'

In the passenger seat, Stray stared out of the window, pretending not to listen.

'Hey, Trev, I need your help.'

'I'm confused,' he said. 'Are you off work, or are you working?'

'I'm sort of working from home.'

'But you're not at home.'

'I just need you to trace a name for me.'

He chuckled. 'Of course. That's all anyone wants. It'd be nice just occasionally if someone rang to ask how I was. Just once, you know?'

'I'm sorry, Trev, you're right. How are you? Tell me.'

'It's too late now. Forget it. What's the name?'

'Lydia Hargreaves. She worked as a receptionist at a psychiatric practice called Blue Skies. They were based in London. The company closed down ten years ago.'

'Too easy. I'll send you a message. Is this your new phone number?'

'Err, yeah, I guess so.'

'What's the deal with this Lydia? Is it urgent?'

'I… I don't know. Just… please don't mention it to anyone.'

'It's that kind of job, is it? Alright, Eleanor, I've got to go.'

The phone went lifeless in her hand. She stared at it. What had she done? They'd know she was in Liverpool now. She'd never escape.

42

'Is Raymond in trouble?' the shelter supervisor said. 'We're quite fond of the doctor here. He's helped a few people out.'

'I don't know.' Krush showed him a photograph. 'Is this the man who was at your shelter?'

The supervisor put on glasses and squinted at the picture. 'That's an old one.' He laughed. 'Wow, he looks so different, it's the black beard. This must be from when he was still working, before he was homeless.'

'But it is Raymond Stray?' she said. 'You're sure?'

'Oh yeah, that's him. You can tell right away; it's the eyes, like they're staring into your soul.'

'Good.' She put the picture away. 'Has he spent a lot of time in the shelter?'

'He comes and goes. Sometimes we don't see him for six months or a year. Then he'll be back for a while. Every time he leaves, I hope he won't have to come back. He's talented, you know. They say he was a brilliant therapist before everything went wrong.'

Krush jotted the details down in her notepad. 'And he was here today?'

'Yeah. I'm surprised you didn't know already. He left with a police officer.'

She looked up from the pad. 'An officer? Which officer?'

'Erm, I think it was Eleanor.'

'Eleanor? Eleanor Rose?'

He snapped his fingers. 'That's it. Rose. I remember it was a pretty surname.'

'Wait. You're telling me Eleanor Rose came by here today and picked up a homeless guy.'

'Err… yeah, I guess. Is something wrong?'

'Did Detective Rose give an explanation?'

'She said it was connected to an investigation.'

'How did she know Raymond Stray?'

'She didn't. They'd never met before. I had to introduce them to each other.'

'So… why?'

'Like I say, she came here looking for him.'

'And he just went with her, willingly?'

'Well, funny thing about that. It seems there'd been an altercation. The doctor, that's what we call him around here, for fun, he came running out of the dorm like he'd seen a ghost.'

'Why? What happened?'

'There'd been a scuffle with another individual who was staying in the shelter.'

'What caused this "scuffle"?'

'That's the funny thing, the other guy disappeared. I couldn't ask him. He hasn't been seen since, but he left a trail of blood. It seems he climbed out of a window and went down the fire escape and out the back.'

'What was his name?'

'Fellow named Mac. This may sound ridiculous, but he's dressed sort of like a clown, only his outfit is all ragged. He's been around. Some of our staff have seen him before. He performs his clown routine in the city centre for the tourists sometimes, makes a bit of money.'

'I know who he is. He's from Sundial Court. Did you check there?'

'No, Detective. I wouldn't send my staff over there, it's too dangerous. We get phone calls sometimes, asking us to come and pick up drug addicts from that estate, but it's off limits.'

Krush rubbed her forehead. 'Our missing doctor had a fight with a homeless clown, then ran away with a police officer.'

'That's it,' the supervisor said. 'I wish I could be more helpful.'

'If any of those three turn up again, you call me right away. I'll leave my card.'

The supervisor took the card and looked at it doubtfully. 'I hope the doctor isn't in trouble. Honestly, he's got a good heart. He may not seem that way, but he's helped me personally.'

'That's nice for you.' She walked out.

* * *

On her way to the estate, she called Carmichael. He wasn't at the office. She tried his mobile.

'Krush? I'm busy.' To judge from his mumbling, he was eating a Pot Noodle again.

'I got a lead on our missing doctor. He had an altercation with a guy from Sundial Court.'

Carmichael swallowed loudly. 'Shit. Again, this fucking estate. Why do they always give pretty names to the worst places? Is there even a sundial there?'

'Not anymore. I'm on my way over now to see if I can find our suspect.'

He took a bite out of something and chewed with a grunt of pleasure. 'Don't go there on your own. Take Scott.'

'We've been through this; I can't work with him. He's weird.'

'Take Scott. End of conversation. I'm busy. I have to hang up now.'

'Wait!' she shouted down the phone. 'There's more.'

'Jesus. More?'

'Eleanor...' She almost choked on the name. 'Eleanor was seen with our missing man.'

'Eleanor Rose. Of course. I'd say crazy runs in the family except you two aren't really related.'

'What's she up to?' Krush said. 'You spoke to her. Why's she involved with this?'

'I told you, she was looking for Daniel. That's all. I wish I knew what was so special about this guy. He's got every woman in the city chasing after him. Is it the red hair?'

Krush hung up.

43

It was dark when they left Liverpool in the old Datsun. Rain battered the car as they coasted along the motorway towards Manchester. The text message had come through from Trevor fifteen minutes earlier with Lydia's address.

'We should wait until tomorrow,' Stray said. 'The weather's terrible. It's getting late.'

'It's only an hour's drive. We'll be fine.'

They continued in silence until the mobile phone started to ring in her bag on the back seat.

'No. Not again.'

'It's alright,' Stray said. 'I'll answer it.'

'Don't.'

He reached through the gap between the seats and pulled the phone out.

'Leave it!' With one hand on the wheel, she swatted at his arm, but he didn't stop. 'I said, leave it.'

'It could be important.' He accepted the call and set it to speaker.

The voice of her boss in London came through into the car. 'Eleanor? Is that you?'

She froze. Stray gave her a thumbs-up that was presumably supposed to be encouraging.

'Oh hey, yeah, it's me,' she said.

'I got this number off Trevor.'

She shook her head silently.

'What are you up to?' the boss said. 'Where are you?'

'I'm… I'm in Liverpool at the moment.'

'Liverpool?'

'I came home to take a break. I seem to be suffering from stress.'

'Did you talk to a doctor?'

'Err…'

Stray cleared his throat and said, 'Hello, sir, I'm actually Eleanor's doctor. She's in my office now.'

'What?' the boss said. 'Who is this?'

Eleanor clawed at him with one hand, horrified, but Stray pulled the phone out of her reach and spoke into it.

'My name is Dr Raymond Stray. Eleanor came to see me. We discussed her symptoms. I've prescribed two weeks off work and a course of Valium. I'll have a form sent through to you. Is that alright?'

'I… you say you're a doctor?'

'Yes, I–'

Eleanor grabbed the phone. 'I'm fine,' she said. 'I'll be back in work in a few days. I have to go now. Goodbye.'

'Are you–' the boss said.

She grabbed the phone from Stray's hand, turned it off, and shoved it in her pocket.

'Sorry,' he said. 'I only wanted to help.'

'You're not my doctor. You're not a doctor at all. Let's just get this over with. I feel like I'm losing my mind.'

* * *

When they arrived in the outskirts of Manchester, Eleanor pulled an old A-Z map out of the glove compartment.

'Can you navigate?' She tossed it in Stray's lap.

'This thing's from the sixties. The streets have probably been knocked down and renamed.'

'Yeah well, try anyway. I don't want to get stuck out here all night.'

They found the house in a row of Victorian semi-detached properties on the far side of the city. It was nothing like Sundial Court. In the dark, in the rising panic, she didn't feel as if she was anywhere at all; she had crossed a line somewhere and entered unreality.

Peering through the rainy windscreen, Stray pointed. 'That's it. Number 71.'

'There's a light on inside, that's good. Come on.'

She parked up outside the house and climbed out of the car. When she looked back, Stray hadn't moved from the passenger seat, he hadn't even unbuckled his seat belt.

She stuck her head in the door. 'What are you doing? Come on.'

'I'm scared,' he said.

'Why?'

'It's been so long since I saw Lydia... I don't want her to see me this way. She'll remember me as someone successful. I don't want her to see me now as a homeless junkie.'

'Come on, you'll be fine.'

He stared through the windscreen. Suddenly he looked so weak – skeletal, demented.

'I smell like shit,' he said. 'Do you have deodorant?'

'No.'

'Is there anything...?' He rooted in the glove compartment. 'What about this?' He took down an old air freshener shaped like a pine tree that was attached to the mirror.

'What are you doing?' She watched as he lifted his shirt and rubbed the air freshener into his armpits, across his chest, and neck.

'I just need a minute.' He took out the packet of cigarettes she had given him and lit one. 'A lot happened since I last saw Lydia.' He stared through the window as he inhaled.

'Well, in that case, give me one too.' She followed the direction of his gaze to the dark doorway of Lydia's house in the shadow behind a row of privet hedges.

44

Krush drove in a slow circuit around the estate, looking for Mac. Night was falling. Without streetlights, the surrounding houses faded into the rain's background murmur.

'This is hopeless,' she said.

'Maybe if we left the car and looked on foot,' Scott said from the passenger seat.

'What's the point? He's not going to be sat outside begging in the dark and the rain.'

'I would, if I were him,' Scott said.

'Why?'

'He would look sad. People might feel sorry and give him more money.'

She considered the idea. 'Is that how people think?'

'Dunno.'

'Me neither,' she said. 'I never give money to homeless people. It traps them in a cycle of dependency.'

'Oh.'

She stopped the car. 'Does Mac have a place around here where he goes? Maybe someone who lets him come inside to shelter from the rain? Does he have a friend on the estate?'

'Dunno.'

'Your local expertise is pretty thin. Have you never seen him inside someone's house? Like, through the window, or in the doorway?'

When Scott stared blankly, it was hard to tell if he was thinking or just existing. 'No,' he said.

'Alright, you know what, maybe he shelters in one of the abandoned houses. Let's try them. One at a time.'

She parked outside number 3 and climbed out. 'Come on, the rain's picking up.'

The front door of number 3 was boarded up, as were the windows. She shone her torch through the boards but couldn't see anything inside. Behind her, Scott stood motionless in the freezing wind.

'You know what?' she said. 'I'm starting to like working with you. You're quiet. You keep out of the way. You do what you're told without arguing.'

'That's nice,' he said.

'Wait there, I'll check round the back.'

The gate leading to the backyard was broken, it hung off one hinge. She pushed through into a stink of ash. The remains of an enormous bonfire had left a black stain on the concrete. The back doors and windows were locked. She heard voices in the street and came back around to the front of the house. Scott was talking to a woman with a bulldog.

'Here again?' the woman said.

'We're looking for Mac,' he said. 'You seen him around today?'

'No. You could try number 28. It's hollow. Drifters stay in there sometimes to shelter.'

They got back in the car and drove to the other end of the estate. In the car headlights, the pavements were empty, the houses floated away.

'Hey.' Krush glanced at Scott in the mirror. 'Do you ever go to those parties?'

'Which?'

'At number 21, the karaoke parties.'

He thought for a moment. 'I don't think they're parties.'

'What do you mean?'

'It's not multiple, I think it's just one party that doesn't end. It carries on every day. They're not different parties.'

'I guess that's one way of looking at it.'

'I don't like to sing,' Scott said.

She glanced at him in the mirror but she already knew by now, there was no point trying to read Scott's expression. Either he was brilliant at deception, or he had no inner thoughts at all.

'Alright, we're here.' She parked outside number 28.

This building was the most ruined on the estate; there were no doors or windows, it was just a hollow frame through which the wind blew freely. From the front yard, Krush could see all the way into the back garden.

'What happened to this one?' she said.

'I dunno. I heard the owner killed himself. But, sometimes, when people say that, they mean he left Liverpool and moved to London.'

'That's not death. People come back from London. They don't even warn you; they just arrive like magic.'

Walking up the driveway she smelled alcohol, urine, and rancid waste on the wind.

'Someone was here.' She stopped at the hole where the front door should have been, and called inside, 'Anyone home?'

Rain leaked through the two storeys, drumming on the bare concrete foundations. She went inside. 'Hello?' Her voice echoed off hard surfaces. She took out her torch and flashed it over dripping gaps in the skeleton of what had been a building.

'Don't go in there!' A voice from the street took her by surprise.

She jumped around to see a man in a tracksuit and trainers with a sweat band, watching from the end of the driveway.

'The kids use it as a toilet,' he shouted through the rain. 'It's full of piss and shit.'

'Who are you?' Krush shone her torch over him. 'Do you live on the estate?'

The man shielded his eyes from the light and set off running again.

'Hey!' she called after him.

'That's just Mr Church,' Scott said. 'He lives on the corner. He jogs. Even in the rain. Even in the dark.'

'In this estate, there's nobody here when I knock, but as soon as I turn my back, the place is full of people.'

Scott shrugged. 'They don't like police.'

She entered the hallway of the derelict house into an intoxicating reek of urine.

'He wasn't lying.' She kept one hand over her nose while with the other she flashed her torch over corners filled with waste. The walls were marked with graffiti. An enormous pair of red eyes, covering a whole side of the living room, stared at her with malice.

'That sign again,' she said.

Scott appeared behind her. He looked at the eyes and blinked.

'What does it mean?' Krush said.

He didn't reply. It was like he couldn't drag his gaze away from the red eyes.

'Come on,' she said, 'we're wasting time.'

She checked through every room on the ground floor and found nothing. The toilet was disgusting. A hole in the ground overflowing with shit.

'There's nothing down here,' she said.

Scott didn't reply.

'Where are you?' She went into the kitchen and found him staring out of the hollow space where a window should have been into the backyard. The wind blew rain into his face, but he made no move to wipe it off.

'What are you looking at?' Krush said.

He pointed. A body lay twisted on the paving slabs among thickly overgrown weeds. Blood seeped out into the cracks.

'Shit!' She ran outside. 'It's him. It's Mac.'

The clown clothes were soaking wet and stained with blood. He lay on his front, his face turned to one side as if averted, one glassy eye open to the rain, unable to blink.

His limbs were splayed all wrong. His clothes stank of vodka. A pair of headphones were still attached to his ears.

'Is he dead?' Scott said.

'Stand back. Don't touch anything.' She knelt over the body and tried his pulse. 'This goddamn estate.'

Scott stood in the doorway. 'How did he…?'

She looked up to the first-floor window, a wide, jagged hole in the wall. 'He must have jumped, or he was pushed. The blood looks fresh. Shit, we were just too late. We might have found him alive.'

She put on crime gloves and found the tape cassette Walkman in his jacket pocket.

'What are you doing?' Scott said.

'I want to listen.'

One of the headphones was soaked in blood, the other one was clean. She put it to her ear and pressed play on the Walkman. A fanfare sounded through the crackling earpiece; trumpet and trombones played a brash, grotesque funeral march.

Scott crouched next to her, trying to hear. 'What is it?'

'Clown music.' She pressed stop.

45

Lydia Hargreaves answered the door wearing yoga pants and holding a glass of red wine.

'Hello?' Her mouth dropped open as she stared at Stray.

'Lydia,' he mumbled.

Eleanor felt she should say something. 'Mrs Hargreaves? Sorry to disturb you. I'm Detective Rose…'

Lydia didn't notice. She couldn't take her eyes off Stray. 'It's you,' she said.

He looked bashful. 'It's been a long time.'

'I didn't think I'd ever see you again, after… after everything.'

'I'm sorry,' he said.

'If you're here to beg for money, forget it. I've heard how you treated your friends. Stealing, using people.'

'I'm not here for money.'

Eleanor stepped between them. 'Mrs Hargreaves, I'm a police detective. I can assure you, this man isn't going to cause you any problems.'

'Police?' The dreamy expression on Lydia's face contracted. 'What's this about?'

'Can we talk inside?' Eleanor said.

Lydia looked over her shoulder into the unseen hall. 'I suppose so…'

They followed her into a neat home smelling of incense. It was dark.

'Sorry, the light bulb's gone in the hall,' Lydia explained as she led them through into a kitchen at the back of the house.

She kept up the strained conversation with Stray while she made a pot of tea. 'People said you'd changed, but I recognized you straight away.'

'I have changed,' Stray said. 'But you haven't.'

'Oh, shut up.'

'I can't believe all that was ten years ago.'

'Well. The past is gone.' She set the teapot on the table and pulled out a chair. 'Good riddance to it.'

Through the window behind her head, the back garden was shrouded in darkness. The branches of a few tall trees swayed in silhouette.

'The things that happened,' Stray said, 'I'm sorry for what you went through. I never suspected… if I'd known… I would have done it differently. We could have avoided…' He trailed off.

They both gazed through the window.

'I'll get to the point,' Eleanor said. 'It's late. We don't want to waste your time. We were wondering if you still have any of the old files from the psychiatry practice? Maybe on a pen drive or something?'

'Files…' Lydia said. She glanced at Stray, who didn't respond.

'You know,' Eleanor continued, 'names of clients, that kind of thing.'

An odd expression crossed Lydia's face, confusion mixed with distaste, and something else. 'What would you want with those?'

'It's for a case I'm working on,' she said.

Lydia rubbed her forehead. 'I'm sorry, who are you again?'

She took out her ID and showed it. 'Eleanor Rose, police detective.'

'It's alright,' Stray said. 'You can trust Eleanor, she's helping me.'

Lydia picked up one of the empty teacups and put it down again. 'What's this all about? What do you want? Why are you here? I don't understand.'

There was a note in her voice; bewilderment, verging on panic.

'Please,' Eleanor said, 'don't worry. Mrs Hargreaves, I realize this must be a lot, us barging in here at this time. And you haven't seen Raymond in so long. Let's just sit for a moment and drink this tea. There's no pressure at all.'

Lydia's hand shook as she gripped a teacup. 'It's the past you're interested in?'

'Yes,' Eleanor said. 'But really, don't worry. It's not a big deal. Raymond thought you might still have a copy of the files from back then. It's not important if you don't.'

'The files are upstairs. I'll show you.' Her voice changed abruptly, it was now firm and cold. Her hand stopped shaking.

'We don't have to rush.' Eleanor took one of the teacups and was about to pour some tea, but Lydia had already got up.

She walked across the kitchen. From the door, she said, 'Let's do this now, before it's too late.'

She disappeared into the darkness of the hall. Stray got up and started after her, but Eleanor stopped him.

'Is something wrong here?' she whispered.

'I don't know.'

'She seems upset. What happened between you? Was there...?'

'Nothing. Nothing ever happened. We–'

'Are you coming?' Lydia called from the foot of the stairs.

'Yes. Sorry.' Stray hurried after her.

Eleanor poured some tea and took a sip. It was bitter and tepid.

'Sorry,' Lydia shouted down through the stairwell. 'The light bulbs are broken up here. I never bother to change them. What's the point? Nobody comes here anyway.'

They climbed through the shadow to an attic, where, thankfully, the lamp worked. The room served as an office, with an out-of-date computer set on a desk that was dusty with disuse. Lydia opened a drawer to one side and pulled out a box of old floppy disks.

'I couldn't bring myself to throw these away,' she said. 'Gosh, it's hot in here.'

In fact, Eleanor was shivering from the cold. The heating was not turned on in the house, despite the weather. Lydia opened the window. A chill gust blew into the house.

'That's better.' She sat down as the computer blinked to life and began to slowly load. 'This thing's an antique, I'm afraid. You'll have to be patient.'

Eleanor went to the window and looked out into a spray of rain. Tall trees in the garden sighed in the wind. A concrete square of patio, three stories below, was lit by the light from the kitchen.

'I forgot the tea,' Lydia said.

'It's alright,' Stray said. 'Really.'

'No. You sit there and check the disks. I'll bring the tea.' She pushed him into the wooden chair in front of the screen. 'The disks aren't labelled, unfortunately. Truth be told, I never thought I'd look at them again. But you can have a go, see what you can find.'

She went out of the room, and they heard her feet go quickly down the stairs.

'Was she always like this?' Eleanor said.

'Like what?' he asked.

'I don't know. Weird, I guess. Her house is freezing cold and pitch black. Her tea is awful.'

Stray shrugged. 'Maybe she can't afford the bills.' He put the first disk into the drive and clicked.

'What do you see?' She leaned over his shoulder into his musk of sweat, and caught a whiff of pine air freshener.

'It's empty,' Stray said.

'What?'

'This disk, nothing on it. Maybe it's been wiped, I don't know. Let's try another.' He popped the disk out and skimmed through the box. 'None of them are labelled. How about this red one...' He picked it up and inserted it into the drive.

The staircase creaked as Lydia's feet climbed up from the ground floor. 'Coming now,' she called.

'This one's blank as well,' Stray said. 'I'll try another.'

'Find anything?' Lydia shouted from the landing below.

'Not yet.' He pulled out another disk. 'Blank. Are they all blank?'

Lydia came up the final staircase and entered the room. It looked at first as if her fist were empty, but the lamplight flashed on a blade; the kitchen knife was held point downwards.

'This one's blank as well,' Stray said.

Eleanor back-pedalled. 'Are you alright?'

Lydia moved slowly forwards. Her eyes were fixed on the back of Stray's head.

'This is pointless,' he said. 'I'll try one more.'

She raised the knife.

'Stop!' Eleanor jumped on the woman as she leapt forwards. 'What are you doing?'

Lydia let out a scream like a cat. Stray jerked around and pulled his head back as the knife scraped down his shoulder.

'Let go!' Eleanor pulled at the knife.

Lydia's face was a mask of childish hatred. She leered and laughed and gasped, like she couldn't believe the emotion passing through her. The knife dropped from her hand.

'Lydia!' Stray shouted.

Eleanor scooped up the knife. 'Why…?'

Lydia pushed past her, wavering on her feet. She looked so drowsy she might topple into bed and fall asleep. She staggered to the open window, grabbed the ledge, and threw herself out. Her cat's scream pierced through the wind, and stopped dead.

46

Next door to number 28, now marked off with crime-scene tape, the owner was a bald, middle-aged man. He wore a stained dressing gown with just a pair of pyjamas underneath. The flashing lights of the squad cars in the street danced in his brown eyes.

'Been empty from the start, 28,' he said. 'Nobody ever moved in.'

'Have you seen anyone in there?' Krush said.

'Recently?' He fished a packet of cigarettes out of the pocket of his dressing gown. 'Can't say I have.' Smoke drifted out as he inhaled lazily. 'It was picked clean. Fucking vultures. They took everything. Carpets, light bulbs, pipes. Anything of value, even a penny's worth, was ripped out ages ago.'

'It's true,' Scott said. 'All the empty houses have been looted.'

The neighbour shrugged and exhaled. Krush flashed a look at Scott to keep his mouth shut, but he didn't seem to notice. He watched the ribbon of cigarette smoke.

'Ripped out by whom?' she said. 'Who are these vultures?'

'Oh, you know.' The man switched the cigarette to his left hand and scratched his groin beneath the dressing gown with his right.

She thought she heard laughter somewhere inside the house.

'Is someone back there?' she said.

'No.' He wafted the smoke away. 'Vultures. Bad'uns. Where do they come from? Where do they disappear to? God knows. Some hole in the ground somewhere. They're like rats. Turn your back for a moment, they'll steal it off you.'

Krush waved the cigarette smoke away. All of this was a waste of time. 'Alright. So, you haven't seen or heard anything from that house in months. Is that it?'

'That's it, Officer. Cross my heart and hope to die.'

Somebody in the hall behind him let out a titter. He turned inside and shouted, 'Shut up, go away.'

'Who's that?' Krush said.

'Nobody. A friend of mine.'

The laugh sounded again in the hall, but the view was blocked by the neighbour who stood in the doorway. 'Get lost. Go on,' he shouted again. Turning back to Krush, he said, 'Sorry. You know what friends are like.'

'I don't have any friends.'

'Oh.' The grin disappeared from his face. 'Is this about the murder at number 14?'

'No,' Scott said.

She gave him another look that fell unseen. 'Why do you say that?' she asked the neighbour.

'I don't know,' he said. 'Why else would you be stood out there in the rain?'

'I asked you about number 28. What connection is there between 28 and 14?'

He stared. The cigarette burned down between his fingers, forgotten. '14 is a factor of 28.'

'We're not talking about maths,' she said. 'Do you know anything about what happened at number 14?'

'No.'

'Did you know Mrs Bennett?'

'Was that her name, the dead woman?'

'Can you tell me anything at all that might be helpful?'

'I can tell you, you shouldn't leave your car parked out in the estate like that. Kids will have the wheels.'

'What's your name?'

'John.'

'Your full name.'

He coughed. 'Sorry, John Jones.'

'John Jones?' She jotted it down.

'My mum had a thing for the letter J. My sister's called Janice, my brother's Jason.'

'Alright, Mr Jones.' Krush took out a card and handed it over. 'If you think of anything, you call me.'

'Right you are, Officer.'

He ducked inside and shut the door. The sound of laughter leaked out through the frosted glass.

47

'Oh, Jesus.' Eleanor leaned over the window ledge and looked down. Lydia's body lay on the lit concrete, three stories below, her bent limbs slack.

'Lydia!' Stray cried. He ran out of the room and went tumbling down the stairs.

Eleanor chased after him. 'Slow down, you'll fall.'

'Lydia!' He raced ahead. 'Why? Why?' Blood seeped down his arm onto the banister and the steps as he ran.

Just a few steps behind, Eleanor kept pace. 'You're bleeding. Stop. You're hurt.'

He didn't hear and didn't slow down as he reached the foot of the stairs and barrelled along the hall, sliding off the walls. Eleanor took her phone out as she ran and started to dial 999, but she was running too fast, it slipped out of her grip and the battery flew out as it clattered on the floorboards. She collected the pieces and was reassembling them while she heard Stray go out of the back door onto the patio.

'Lydia!' he shouted as if trying to wake her. 'Lydia!'

Eleanor ran out to find him hunched over the broken body of his former colleague.

She kneeled and checked the pulse. 'She's gone. I'm sorry. She will have died instantly.'

Stray clawed at his face. 'What is happening?'

'Your shoulder.' Eleanor pointed. 'You're bleeding badly.'

'What do we do? Do we call an ambulance for her...?'

'There's no point.' Eleanor turned her phone back on.

Stray wailed. 'Oh, Christ, this is my fault. It's my fault.'

'What do you mean? Why is it your fault?'

The phone in her hand vibrated and started to ring. Startled, she almost dropped it. They both stared at the ringing phone.

'What do I do?' she said.

'Answer it.'

'I... I can't...'

Before she could react, Stray grabbed the phone from her hand and accepted the call. He set it to speaker.

The voice came creeping out into the wind. 'Eleanor... I told you to run. Remember?'

Speechless, she watched the phone in Stray's shaking hand, as the voice said, 'You really messed up now.'

Stray looked at her with a question that she couldn't answer.

The cold voice chuckled. 'You just stand there. Don't you know we're watching you?'

She looked wildly around the garden, but it was dark, the trees were tall and overhanging in the rain.

Stray mouthed at her, 'Who?'

'Why don't you speak?' the voice said. Suddenly, it screamed, 'Run! Run while you can!'

She grabbed the phone from Stray's hand, cancelled the call, and set off sprinting through the house, barely conscious of where she was going.

'Wait!' He chased after her. 'Who was that?'

She pulled the front door open and ran out into the street, splashing through a puddle on the pavement. She jumped in the car and slammed the key in the ignition. It was moving as Stray opened the passenger door.

'Wait!' he shouted as she shifted gear. He dragged himself into the seat. 'Jesus Christ.'

With the passenger door still hanging open, she leaned on the accelerator, only wanting to get as far away from that house as possible. They sped too fast down to the main road, and she turned left at random, with no idea which direction she was supposed to take.

'Who was that voice?' Stray kept talking beside her, asking questions, but his voice was weak. Blood poured out of his shoulder while he struggled to wrap the sleeve of his sweater around the cut.

'Use this.' She took off her jacket.

They came to a dual carriageway, and she followed a sign to Liverpool. As she steered along the right-hand lane, with one hand she took the mobile phone apart and threw the pieces out of the window. Only after the last part was gone, she exhaled. 'Oh shit.'

Rain battered against the windscreen as the wipers toiled. She kept glancing in the rear-view mirror, but she could only make out the blank eyes of car headlights speeding by.

She looked across at Stray, who was breathing heavily. The jacket was wrapped tightly around his shoulder.

'Are you alright?' she said. 'You're pale.'

'It's just a scratch.'

'I have to take you to hospital.'

'No. It's better now. I just have to keep pressure on it.'

'Are you sure?'

'It's too exposed at the hospital. It's not safe.'

She looked for an argument but couldn't find a good one. She was supposed to work for the law, she should ring the police right now, she should go to the hospital, but she felt herself sliding further across the invisible line to the other side of wrong and right. Everything was different here, and none of it made sense.

'Who was that voice?' Stray whispered.

She shook her head. 'I can't explain.'

'Try anyway. I'm a patient listener.'

'There's some kind of conspiracy. That's why I ran away from London. I was working on a big operation; we were tracking this drugs outfit for months. I started getting weird messages. Warnings. Then I got a phone call. I found a message in my desk at the station. Someone there is part of it. Whatever's going on, someone from the police is involved.'

'But that voice, it didn't sound like a drug dealer… it didn't sound like police…'

'It must be police. Nobody else knew my number. The only people I spoke to on the phone were Trevor and my boss back at the station.'

'You think it's one of those two?'

'I have no idea. It could be anyone. That's the worst thing about it. Trevor and the boss are in London, this person is following us, from Liverpool all the way to Manchester.'

'How do you know that?'

'They were watching, in the garden, weren't they? How else could they know? They rang as soon as I came out to find the body…'

'Do you have an enemy you know of?'

'Nobody. Well. There's something else, but I can't tell you. I can't tell anybody. Least of all, you. Christ, I don't even know you. I can see why you were a shrink, you're good at making people talk; even when they don't want to.'

'That's not actually how we describe our work.'

'There you go again.'

'You may as well tell me. I'll probably die of blood loss anyway. If not, someone will murder me. That's twice today they tried to kill me.'

She felt a frightening urge to share with this stranger. She had never opened up to anyone. She'd carried these secrets and this pain around for so long. She glanced across at him, but he wasn't looking. His eyes were closed. His head rested against the window. He said nothing. His breathing softened.

After a few moments of silence, she was astonished to hear herself say, 'Something happened in Liverpool.'

She looked to see what his reaction would be, but he didn't open his eyes. He only said, 'Alright.'

'Five years ago, before I left, I found out about corruption in the police. I did some digging, on my own. What I found out changed my life. Around that time, there was a drugs bust; we seized a huge amount of material on the docks. Drugs, weapons, cash, cars, all kinds of things. Fifty grand went missing from the haul. Nobody could account for it. But I found it. My fiancé, Daniel, he'd split it with my half-sister, Beth.'

She thought Stray had passed out, but he spoke without opening his eyes. 'And they were punished?'

'Nobody ever knew. I took the cash and dropped it off anonymously at the station. I never told anyone what happened. I couldn't bring myself to turn them in, but I couldn't speak to them either. I transferred to London and never saw either of them again.'

'That must have been difficult for you.'

'I think I never got over it.'

'So, your fiancé and your half-sister, were they having an affair?'

'I don't know.' She felt a tear forming in the corner of her eye and gritted her teeth to restrain it. 'I never suspected anything at the time, now I found out that they did get together, after I left. Maybe they were together all along.'

'Was that worse for you, the betrayal? Worse, I mean, than the fact they were corrupt?'

She fought to keep the tear back, but it burst free and rolled down her cheek while her teeth ground together. Stray wasn't watching anyway; his eyes were closed.

'I don't know anything,' she said.

'But you came back home.'

'But I came back home.'

48

Krush spoke to some of the other neighbours, but it was the usual story on the estate: nobody knew anything, nobody had seen anything, nobody had heard anything.

The last squad cars pulled out and drove away while she sheltered beneath her umbrella in the doorway of number 28. There was nothing left to do here, but she didn't want to leave. She felt a secret just out of reach behind these blank windows. Rain danced in the puddles all around while her mind worked backwards through each house that she'd seen here, each person who lived inside them. One of them must be a killer.

A few feet away, Scott also stood in the rain, smoking, but without an umbrella. The water streamed down his face and soaked his jacket. She guessed he didn't want to leave either. The growing sense of kinship with him disturbed her; Scott was weird.

She felt her phone vibrate and took it out. Carmichael.

'You found another one?' he said.

She threw the butt of the cigarette down and stamped it out. 'It's been packed away. You missed it.'

'They ought to bulldoze that estate and pour concrete over the whole thing.' His voice was distant; he might have been driving.

'I'll send my report as soon as it's ready,' Krush said.

'Don't bother. Elliot already filled me in. It's a suicide. Wouldn't you, if you were a homeless clown? Jump out of a window, I mean.'

'I couldn't say. I've never been one.'

'He still had his eyeballs, didn't he?'

She pictured the glassy eye looking up into the rain. A mirror where infinity danced. 'Yeah. He still had them.'

'Well, there you go. Listen, Krush, I can't talk, I have to be somewhere. I was just checking to make sure you weren't about to connect this death to the others and declare a serial killer.'

'We should go to the press now, before anyone else dies.'

'I already reached out to my journalist guy. It's in hand,' he said. 'But this clown suicide is nothing to do with it. Leave it alone. Leave the poor bastard in peace.'

'I don't know, it's on the estate…'

'It's late, Krush, we're all tired. God, I feel like I could sleep for a week. Go home and get some sleep. We'll find the drug addict brother tomorrow. We'll pump the story out of him, put all this to bed.'

Krush raised her voice before he could hang up. 'The thing is, boss, I'm worried. I'm worried about Daniel. Nobody's seen him in weeks. I'm worried about Eleanor. She turns up now after all these years. She's seen hanging around with our missing suspect. What the hell is she up to?'

'She's looking for Daniel,' Carmichael said. 'I don't know why.'

'Have you seen her again? Have you spoken to her?'

'No. I told you. She sat in my office and asked about Daniel. That's all. Stop stressing out. Go home. You've done enough today. Go home and relax, if you know how. Otherwise, just go home.' He hung up.

Krush put the phone away. Eleanor was in danger, she could feel it; she tasted it on the wind. She set off towards her car.

'Hey!' a voice called after her.

She looked back to see Scott waving in the dark.

'What do you want?' she shouted.

'Should I...? I don't know what to do. Should I stay here? Do I go with you?' He wiped rain from his soaked face.

'Go home,' she said. 'Go to sleep.'

'Sleep. Alright.'

She started to walk away but stopped. 'Hey, Scott, don't you have an umbrella? You're saturated.'

'I lost it.'

'Here.' She closed hers and tossed it to him. 'I've got another.'

49

By the time Eleanor had parked the car outside the hotel, Stray was asleep in the passenger seat. She shook him by the shoulder.

'Come on, wake up, we're back in Liverpool.'

He mumbled, head lolling, as she dragged him out of the car. Blood seeped out beneath the jacket wrapped around his shoulder.

'Can you walk?' She grabbed him under the armpit and guided him forwards. He was surprisingly light, like a child. Holding his side, she felt how skinny he was; his ribs stuck out through his skin.

'Never felt better,' he said, but his head rested on her shoulder, his feet moving drunkenly as they walked together into the hotel.

The receptionist at the front desk looked up from her register with a quizzical expression. Eleanor tried to smile at her, but she found she'd forgotten how. The receptionist yawned and looked back down at the desk.

Eleanor manhandled Stray into the lift and let him flop on the floor as they floated up to the sixth storey. Back in the room, with the door locked, the first thing she did was pull the phone cord out of the wall. She checked all around but there was no trace of any intruder.

She found a plastic sachet of shower gel in the bathroom and carried it over to Stray, who was stretched out on the couch.

'Let me see the cut,' she said. 'It's alright, it doesn't look too bad, doesn't need stitches. I'll just clean it.'

She dabbed it with gel and wrapped a makeshift bandage of torn bedsheet around his shoulder until it was completely covered. Stray appeared to be asleep, and she was relieved to be alone with her thoughts.

She laid the map and her notes out on the table. She began to feel a sense of order as she arranged the pages neatly, but before she could sit down, Stray said, 'What happened to Lydia?'

'Shit, you scared me. Thought you were asleep.'

He raised his head over the edge of the couch. 'Why would she try to kill me? Why would she jump?'

'You were her colleague, you tell me.'

'I swear, I never harmed Lydia. I don't know any reason she would have done that. We always got on well at work, and she wasn't one of those people whom I stole off afterwards. At least, I don't remember stealing off her. Shit, did I? Is that what happened? There are whole years in my brain that are just blank. I don't remember anything.'

His voice was weak, sleepy. His head dropped back on the pillow. 'I feel dizzy,' he said.

'What about the files?' Eleanor said. 'All those disks were blank. Somebody might have got there before us and wiped them.'

'But why?' Stray's voice was fading.

'Go to sleep now,' she said. 'We'll figure it out in the morning.'

'I don't want to. I just need to…'

A moment later, he was snoring.

50

Krush was sitting at home, staring out of the window into the wild sky, when her phone rang. It was Marvin, from the Socialist Republic of Filing Cabinets.

'Sorry to call you at home, Krush, I just thought you'd want to know.'

'What?'

'That case you were interested in, the stolen van. I ran a few searches. Found something, it's not much, probably nothing.'

She jumped up. 'What is it?'

'Thing is, it's kind of confidential. I'm not supposed to share this. I'm not supposed to know about it myself.'

'Are you messing? Don't call me at night and then tell me you're not allowed to talk.'

'Calm down, comrade, I'll tell you. Just promise you'll keep this to yourself.'

'I can't promise until I know what it is.'

'Like I say, it's probably nothing.'

'Alright, I promise. Just tell me.' She was gripping the phone so hard, she felt the muscles tighten along her forearm.

'Let's say, for argument's sake, I looked at a file I wasn't supposed to see…'

'That's why I like you, Marvin.'

'I can't share it with you, but if you can guess what I read, then, technically, I never told you; you came up with it by yourself.'

'How could I do that?'

'The man whose van was stolen, Mr, erm, Hunter, he's on this other list, the one that's secret.'

'He's an informant,' Krush said. 'His identity is only available for officers cleared on whatever case that is.'

'You said it; I didn't tell you anything. The business with the van is separate, that was a real police report. His van got stolen, the insurance paid out.'

'What's the other case, the secret one?'

'Can't tell you.'

'Which officer did he report to as informant?'

'Can't tell you that either.'

A single gull outside drifted on the howling gale, alone in the storm.

'Was it Daniel?' she said.

'You said it; I didn't tell you anything. That's all I've got. I have to go now before I get fired.'

'Thanks, Marvin. What's your saying? We are few, they are many…'

'No, that's the wrong way around.'

She hung up.

* * *

As Krush drove through the night-time city, her thoughts drifted back to Oslo. The bright winter trees and the snow. She walked with Daniel, pressed together for warmth, their breath merged into one cloud of steam, lit by the streetlamps. This was a forbidden memory. Everything started to go wrong from that moment. At the Viking Ship Museum, he'd let slip a comment about Eleanor – a joke she'd made in the same spot, six years earlier – and Krush realized, all of this trip was just Daniel's way of trying to go back in time, back to her sister who had abandoned both of them. Suddenly, it was so obvious. He still loved the dark-haired sister, the elder; the younger, the blonde, was just a substitute. She'd argued with him then. The trip was ruined. When they got back to Liverpool, nothing was the same. She would always associate winter with Oslo, loss, and rage.

She tried calling Hunter, but his phone number no longer existed. Too late. To her amazement, she was glad to return to Sundial Court. As soon as she steered along the curved drive leading inside along the tattered wooden fence, she felt the streetlights of the highway disappear, and let the darkness swallow her. Here was the place where she belonged, the well of loneliness.

She parked outside number 5, where this Hunter had lived, but she saw right away it was abandoned. The windows were broken, the whole front of the building was covered in graffiti. She parked outside the house and climbed out of the car.

She pulled her coat tightly around her shoulders as she went up the driveway of the neighbour's house, number 7. An argument was taking place inside. She heard voices screaming in the hall, so shrill that she couldn't make out the words. She knocked on the door, and the voices stopped. An elderly lady answered. She wore thick glasses and a red shawl.

'Police.' Krush showed her ID. 'Is everything alright in there?'

'What?'

'I heard shouts. Sounded like an argument.'

'Oh no, that's just my husband. We were joking around. We like to joke.'

Krush leaned closer. 'Are you sure?' she whispered.

The woman looked at her strangely. 'What do you mean, am I sure? Of course I'm sure. It's my house, isn't it?'

'Alright, fine. What's your name?'

'Olivia.' She managed to make the name sound like a threat.

Krush made a note. 'Olivia what?'

'Mickelson. Why do you care? Is it about the murder at number 14?'

'Not exactly.' She glanced over Olivia's shoulder for a sight of the husband, but the hall was empty. 'But if you know anything about number 14—'

'I don't. Is that all? It's cold. I want to go inside.'

'Just a minute. Did you know the victim?'

'I couldn't even tell you her name.'

'OK. I actually wanted to ask you about next door, number 5.'

'Nobody lives in number 5.'

'It used to be owned by a Mr Hunter. He had a white van. It was stolen by thieves and used in a robbery. Does any of this ring a bell?'

'Hunter, Hunter. Sure, I remember a Hunter. Miserable bastard. Wore a high-vis jacket, even indoors. Didn't stay long. Six months maybe.'

'Can you tell me anything else about him?'

'No.'

'Do you know where he moved to after he left the estate?'

'No.'

'What about your husband? Could I speak to him?'

Olivia hesitated. 'Erm, not really.'

'What do you mean? Why not?'

'He, he doesn't speak English.'

'Where's he from?'

'China.'

'Can I see him?'

'For God's sake.'

The woman shouted something back along the hall and an old man came out to the door.

'Hello,' Krush said.

He nodded.

She turned to Olivia. 'Can you translate?'

'No.'

'I just want to ask if he knows anything about Hunter.'

'He doesn't know anything. He never spoke to Hunter. Can we go to bed now, please? It's getting late.'

'Sure.'

Olivia slammed the door shut. Krush started to walk away but she doubled back to listen. Along the hall, they were arguing again, furious voices, words she couldn't quite catch. But this was fruitless, they didn't want to speak to her, and she couldn't force them. If they wanted to yell all night in their own home, that was their choice.

She returned to the car weighed down with the load of wasted time and dead ends, foreknowledge of insomnia waiting in the early hours of the morning. Seagull's wings. Memories of Oslo, the snow, Daniel's red hair. She opened the car door but couldn't climb in, the dark interior was like a pit. Looking across the estate, she saw the lights turned on at number 21, where the party never ended. She locked the car and walked away from it.

The music hit her from the bottom of the driveway. Somebody was screaming out another Beatles song, *Ticket to Ride*. She straightened her coat and her hair and rang the doorbell. She had to ring it several times before somebody came to the door. Davey opened and looked out. He blinked and squinted, seeming to recognize her, without being sure where from.

'Can I come in?' she said.

'I… I'm not sure. Are you police?'

'Not right now. I'm not here for work, I just wanted to sing a song.'

'A song… is it by the Beatles?'

'Why not?' She saw his hesitation as he looked back inside. 'Don't worry, Davey, I don't care what you're all getting up to. If you want to take drugs, or whatever. Honestly, I'm lonely and bored and I've got nowhere to go. You told me last time, everyone's welcome.'

'Alright, alright, come in.'

She shook the rain off her coat and went inside. The living room was full of people, most of whom she recognized from her previous visit. Some elderly, some young, all of them wearing paper party hats, their red faces glistened with sweat in the airless, overheated room. A mist of cigarette smoke stung her eyes.

'We've got a new singer,' Davey announced.

Nobody seemed to care, they were busy singing or swaying from side to side.

'Are you hungry?' Davey gestured to a pile of pizza boxes on the table.

'Actually, yes.'

While she was eating a slice of cold, greasy pizza, a young man with glasses came over to her. 'Here.' He put a crown of silver paper on her head.

She tried not to flinch.

'What are you going to sing, love?' He showed her a list of names.

'Erm…' Her mind went blank. She'd always hated The Beatles. 'Is there a catalogue or something?'

He handed over a laminated sheet covered in song titles. She scanned through, lost, until her eyes snagged on a single word.

'*Yesterday.*' She pointed. 'I'll sing that one.'

He smiled. 'That's my favourite. I'll put your name down here. Your name is…?'

'…Eleanor. Hey, is there a toilet I could use?'

'Just along the hall. Hold your nose. Some of the old-timers have rotten bowels.'

It was cooler in the hall, but no quieter. The floorboards vibrated from the music and dancing. She ducked her head into the next room, the back living room that was painted entirely red. A young girl was sitting in the corner.

'Hey, you should be in bed. It's school tomorrow. Do you live in this house?'

The girl shook her head.

Krush kneeled and saw her dirty face close up. 'What are you doing here?'

The girl shrugged.

'Where do you live? I'll take you home.'

The girl shook her greasy hair and turned her face to the wall, hugging her knees against her chest.

'You're not a talker, hey.' Krush got up and went back into the corridor. She went past the toilet, holding her nose, and into the kitchen. A skinny man with long hair was seated on a stool by the window at the opposite end of the room.

'Aren't you singing?' she said.

'I sing by myself,' he stuttered, 'back here.'

'Oh.'

The kitchen was messier than the last time she'd seen it. Dirty plates and glasses covered the worktops among bottles and ashtrays. She saw the residue of cocaine on the table. A big glass bowl of some kind of punch, pink-coloured, filled with melting ice, was set on a chair.

'You can help yourself,' the man said. 'There are plastic cups over there.'

'Thanks.' Just for show, she took a cup and scooped up some of the punch. It smelled of chemical fruit flavouring and alcohol. 'What's your name?'

'Carl.'

'Why do you stay back here on your own? Are you shy?' She stepped towards him, but he backed against the wall in fright.

'I can't be near to people,' he said.

Krush stopped, seeing the agitation in his face. 'Alright, don't worry, I'll stay over here.'

His brown hair was so long it reached down his back. It was smooth and straight, as if it had been combed obsessively.

'Do you often come to this party?' she asked.

'Sometimes. Can you go away, please? I want to be alone.'

She felt a surprising stab of hurt at this rejection. 'Why did you come to the party then?'

'I want to hear people. I just don't want to see them.'

'I'll leave you in peace.'

She went back into the hall and put her head in the red room. The girl was gone.

'Shit.'

She came to the foot of the staircase and looked up to the first floor. It was dark. Over the rumble of sound from the living room, she couldn't hear anything from the rest of the house. She checked back over her shoulder that nobody was watching before she ran up the stairs. As soon as she reached the top, she heard a cry and a thump across the landing. Something rattled. A dull, violent blow struck flesh. She followed the sound to a closed door. Music from downstairs rattled the surfaces up here. She put her ear to the wood and heard a muffled grunting. She gripped the door handle and opened it gently.

It took a moment for her eyes to adjust to the darkness inside, but she knew from the smell that leaked out through the open door. Four people were having sex on either side of a double bed. Hypnotic, their bodies moved in constant, aggressive rhythm, their faces, beneath party hats, transfixed with hatred or joy. One of the women let out a gasp of pleasure.

A man saw her in the doorway. He might have been sixty years old, with flabby skin and thick white hair all over his chest and shoulders. He beckoned to Krush and smiled. She closed the door and ran back down the stairs.

She was still holding the plastic cup of punch. She slugged it back in one gulp. *Fuck this place.* She was headed towards the front door when Davey came out into the hall.

'There you are,' he said. 'It's your song next.'

She hesitated. The taste of the punch, sickly-sweet and yet with a bitter aftertaste of cheap alcohol, clung to her throat, and all she wanted was to drink another one.

'Wait a second.' She went back into the kitchen, where Carl was still pressed against the far wall, and poured herself a large measure of punch.

'Careful,' Carl said. 'It's strong.'

'I've been careful my whole life.' She drank half the cup and returned to the living room.

'Give me that.' She grabbed the microphone. The others applauded.

The music started. What the hell was she doing? The man with the list pointed towards a screen on the wall where the lyrics came up. She had no idea of the melody, but at the first word, the entire room took up the verse. The word "yesterday" was like a wound in the sweaty, smoky air. As the crowd sang the sad song, it was as if they knew her pain – Oslo and Daniel, and her sister who'd left her without a word of explanation, without a goodbye. She couldn't sing, she simply spoke the words aloud as they lit up on the screen. In the open door, she saw somebody new looking inside. He had a thick beard, and he wore a suit, he looked different to the others. He gazed at her.

The next verse began; that word again, "yesterday", a knife thrust. Somebody took the empty cup out of her hand and replaced it with a new one, filled with punch. She took a gulp between lyrics, there was something about this drink that was oddly refreshing. The song didn't end. Another verse started up. She felt drowsy. She looked at the door but the man with the beard was gone. Somebody wrapped a tinsel boa around her neck. She drank and sang.

51

Eleanor woke early. Stray was snoring on the sofa as she crept out of the hotel room and went downstairs to buy a newspaper. Perhaps the death of Lydia Hargreaves had been reported. A sense of guilt lingered at the back of her mind; she was police, she should have called the murder in. She could still do it, but the thought of speaking on the phone terrified her. Any phone, even a public one; they were all connected along the same network. There was nothing in the national news. She picked up a copy of the *Liverpool Echo*, flicked through, and was stunned to see an image of Stray looking back at her. It was Stray, but younger. She almost didn't recognize him. He had a black beard, wide glasses, and neat dark hair with a side parting. But it was him, the same inquisitive eyes that saw through people's words.

The headline said, "FORMER PSYCHIATRIST SOUGHT BY POLICE".

Fear caught in her throat. She read:

> *Merseyside Police are requesting that Raymond Stray, a former clinical psychiatrist, come forward for questioning related to the death of his sister, Alison Stray, who was found murdered yesterday. Dr Stray is reported to have been homeless in recent years. Members of the public are encouraged to share any information about his whereabouts.*

She kept reading in the lift as it carried her back up to the sixth floor of the hotel. What was she supposed to do? She could call the police and let them know where he was sleeping; she could go back in the room and ask him about his sister; she could leave now, drop everything and run; but she was pulled back to the news article with a desire to know everything, even the worst.

> *Dr Stray, formerly a successful therapist, once attracted high-paying customers, boasting several celebrities among his clients. In 2013 the company was shut down after a court case that shocked the psychology community. Stray's partner, Dr Vincent Dreyer, was convicted of abusing patients. The abuses came to light after the death of a young woman in Dr Dreyer's care. He was jailed for twenty years. In the trial, Dr Stray testified against his associate and received immunity. No charges were pressed against him. Families of the victims protested his special treatment but were ignored by the prosecutors and judge.*
>
> *After the collapse of his practice, Dr Stray's life unravelled, according to former colleagues of his. Lydia Hargreaves, who worked as a secretary at the firm, spoke to one of our reporters over the phone. She said, 'Raymond was changed by what happened. Unfortunately, he became addicted to heroin. Although many of us tried to help him, he cut off his old friends.'*

Like speaking to the dead, this woman had been alive just a moment ago. Eleanor could see her, the yoga pants, the glass of red wine. She had failed her. Lydia's voice spoke from the page, accusing her:

> '*Sadly, he was living homeless, the last I heard. He was always kind to me, and always had a smile. I believe he really did care about his patients.*'

She closed the newspaper, revolted. The poison spread, everything was connected. They were all corrupt. Stray was part of it; the court case sounded like a clown show, he'd cut a deal and walked free despite the abuse of his patients. There was no end to the corruption. She crept back to the suite and put her ear to the door: silence. She opened it just an inch. The room was so quiet, it might have been empty, but she could smell Stray. She stepped inside.

'You're up,' Stray said from the couch. 'I was going to put coffee on, but I didn't want to wake you.'

'Stay there. Don't move!'

'What?' He sat up on the couch. 'What's the problem?'

'Who are you? Tell me truth.'

'I don't understand.' He looked at her and she recognized those piercing eyes from the photograph in the newspaper.

'I just read the news,' she said. 'The police are looking for you. Your sister's been murdered.'

His face turned vacant, but his eyes widened. 'What? Alison? Could I... could I see that news story?'

He started to get up from the couch, but she shouted, 'No! Stay down there. Don't get up.'

'It wasn't me, OK? People are trying to kill me. You saw what happened yesterday... Whoever killed Lydia must have... must have... Oh, God, Alison... it's my fault, somehow, all of this.'

'If it wasn't you, who did it then?'

'I have no idea.'

Her hand shook as she pointed at him. 'You're a liar. You manipulate people. You use your psychological tricks–'

'I promise, I don't have any tricks. I just try to help, that's all. It's just therapy.'

'Bullshit. The newspaper said your practice collapsed because the patients were abused. A young woman died–'

'But that wasn't me!' He tried to stand up again.

'No! Stay on the couch. Don't get up.' She inched along the wall, keeping her back against it, not taking her eyes off him.

'I swear,' he said. 'That wasn't me. It was my colleague, Vincent. I had no idea what he was up to. I was as shocked as everyone else. He's in prison now. I never faced any charges.'

'No. You cut a deal. You got immunity in return for giving evidence against your friend. Think I don't know how these things work? I'm police, I've seen all kinds of trials. I know what deals get made. I've seen murderers, guilty as sin, walk free because their lawyer played the game. It's all corrupt, all of it.'

'Eleanor, I swear, I never did anything wrong. The police investigated thoroughly. You can read about the case. Look it up online or call one of your colleagues. You can ask the officers who worked on it. They went through my work and didn't find a single irregularity. My patients defended me. Not one of them wanted to bring charges.'

'I don't believe you. You're rotten. There's something about you. You reek, man.'

'I'm an addict, OK? And homeless. I stink, it's true. Think I can't smell myself? I've got no clothes of my own. I've done bad things. I stole money to pay for the drug. I took advantage of friends, used people. You can hate me if you want. I deserve it. But I never killed anyone. I swear.'

'Don't move!'

He gestured at the newspaper that she clutched against her chest like a shield. 'Can I read that?'

She didn't leave the security of the wall against her back, but she lowered the newspaper. It felt true, everything he said, she couldn't help believing him and yet, he was tricky, she'd seen how quick he was at reading emotions.

'It's not for me to judge,' she said. 'You have to speak to the police about what's happened. Let them decide.'

'You are police, aren't you? I thought that was the whole point of this. I thought I was helping you search for a missing officer.'

Is that what was happening? Everything was so muddled, tangled up with corruption. She studied his face for a hint of manipulation, but his bland expression was non-threatening, his body language was loose, arms down by his sides, palms held open.

'Please,' he said. 'Can I read the news story? Can I read about Alison? She's my sister…'

'Alright, but don't move. You stay there, don't get up.'

She went across to the built-in kitchen and looked for a makeshift weapon. There was only a butter knife. Brandishing this, she edged against the wall, not taking her eyes off Stray on the sofa. She came to the phone cord that she had disconnected during the night, and plugged it back into the wall.

'What are you doing?' Stray said.

'What I should have done yesterday. I'm handing you over to the Merseyside Police. They can deal with you.'

'Please don't. I'm not the killer, I swear.'

'Maybe I believe you; it doesn't matter now. The police will question you; they'll find out the truth. I can't.'

'Listen… if you'd just let me read the newspaper, I could get my mind straight. The killer must be one of my old patients. Whoever it is, they went to Lydia and wiped the records because they didn't want to be traced.'

'I don't care anymore. I want this to be over.'

'I'll give you a name, OK?' he said. 'You can check it. There was one patient, his name was Carl – Carl Rank. He came to me because he was suffering from violent impulses. He was in and out of mental institutions. He always signed himself in. He was afraid of hurting people. He was terrified of what he might do. He cut off his family and friends so that he couldn't hurt them… what if it's Carl? Could it be Carl?'

'I…' Eleanor reached out to the phone, but before she could pick up the receiver, it started to ring. The butterknife fell from her hand.

52

Krush woke in her car with a sickly headache, the taste of punch and vomit on her tongue. Her mobile phone was ringing. She had a silver paper crown on her head, and a tinsel boa around her shoulders. Rain tapped on the roof of the car. Looking through the window she saw the dirty houses of Sundial Court.

'What the fuck…?'

She found her phone on the floor under the seat, it was Carmichael calling.

'Shit.' She glanced at the time – just after 8 a.m. She accepted the call.

Carmichael's voice burst into her headache. 'Where are you?'

'I'm just… I just got up… was I supposed to…?'

'Our suspect's been spotted.'

'What suspect?'

'The psychiatrist. The brother of the dead woman.'

'He's been spotted?' She sat up straight in the car seat and looked for the keys.

'He's staying at a hotel by the docks. A receptionist recognized him from the newspaper photo. She just phoned in. It's the Waterfront Hotel.'

'I'll go now.'

'Wait. Don't go alone. I'm getting a team together. Meet me…'

'Bye.' She hung up.

53

Eleanor stared at the ringing phone. 'Who is that?'

'Nobody,' Stray said. 'Probably the desk downstairs.' Seeing her panic, he got up from the couch and took a step towards the phone. 'I'll answer it.'

'No!' she screamed. 'Stay back there! Don't move!'

'Alright, sorry. You answer it.'

She put a hand to the phone but couldn't touch it. 'I unplugged the phone last night. It's been unplugged the whole time. Now as soon as I plug it in…'

'It's a coincidence,' Stray said.

'Did somebody follow us last night…?'

'No.'

The phone kept ringing. Stray was sure the other person would hang up, and he felt a creeping urgency to answer. It had been years since he owned a phone. Nobody ever called him.

'Answer it,' he said. 'Face your fear.'

Eleanor shook as her hand closed around the receiver. She didn't pick it up. Stray was certain now, she was paranoid. He'd worked with patients like her before.

'You have to answer it,' he said. 'Don't be afraid. It'll just be the reception desk to ask when you're checking out. I promise…'

'The reception desk,' she muttered to herself. 'It's just the reception desk.' She picked the phone up and put it to her ear without speaking.

Stray strained to hear the person on the other end, but he didn't want to move closer; she was already in a state of panic. She stood with the phone pressed against her ear and the cord caught around her arm, transfixed, as if listening to beautiful music.

He mouthed, 'Who is it?'

She didn't move, but the receiver fell from her hand and clunked on the floor. Stray jumped. Eleanor slid down the wall with horror in her face, as he scooped up the phone and put it to his ear.

A cold, smug voice was speaking. 'You go in circles, Eleanor. Down and up. Away and back again. When will you learn? There's no path backwards.'

'Who is this?' Stray said.

The phone went dead in his hand. He looked at the plastic contraption that was suddenly silent. He put the receiver back in its place.

'It's alright,' he said. 'They've gone.'

Eleanor didn't respond or look at him. She was breathing too fast. Her hands moved up around her throat as if she were choking.

'You're having an anxiety attack.' He kneeled next to her, but she screamed and crawled along the wall into the corner of the room.

'Stay away!' she shouted.

'Eleanor, I've seen anxiety attacks before. You need to calm down. You need to breathe. Can you do that?'

'Who are you?' she screamed.

'I'm a psychiatrist. You know who I am. Imagine I'm your doctor, you're a patient. You're suffering from anxiety. I'm here to help you. All you have to do is listen to my voice.'

'I don't know you. I don't anything about you.' Her words were throttled, her face was turning deep red, she was shaking all over.

'The voice is a powerful medicine,' he said. 'If you let it in, if you let it speak to you deeply, it can cure all kinds of things.'

She didn't respond, but at least she had stopped screaming at him. Perhaps he could get through to her, he used to be able to connect with the most troubled patients, he'd become famous for it, they called him "the whisperer", but that was long ago. He couldn't do it anymore. He was a wreck himself; he was in no shape to help anybody.

'I'm sorry,' he said. 'I'm sorry you got caught up in all this.'

Eleanor gulped. 'Keep talking. I feel like I'm having a stroke. Keep talking to me, help me, please.' Her voice was breathless. She hunched in the corner with her hands over her face.

'Just breathe,' Stray said. 'Breathe. Let my words guide you. Put everything else out of your mind and just listen. Breathe in now – yes, that's good. Now breathe out. Good, good. Another big breath now. Breathe in, deep, slowly – that's good.'

He sensed her calming, and he moved closer, gently, not wanting to scare her. He needed to be closer so that he could lower his voice. It used to be a subtle instrument, full of tones he'd mastered, but now it was a croak. The years had turned him into an old, battered raven.

'Now, Eleanor, I want you to think of somewhere you were happy. Don't try to force it. Don't push. Just release control, let your mind flow backwards, let it take you to a happy memory. The first place that comes to you. What is the place?'

'...Oslo.'

'Oslo? Good. Oslo. I've never been there. Tell me about it. Don't force it. Let your memory go back, let it find the way. Tell me about Oslo.'

'I was… I was… with Daniel, it was our first holiday together. It was cold, freezing… it snowed… it was wonderful. I was in love…' She sobbed.

Stray crouched next to her. 'Are you OK?'

'Yes.' Her shoulders shook. 'I'm OK. I thought I was dying for a moment, but now… I just feel sad. I…'

She froze at the sound of a knock on the door. Somebody outside banged with their fist.

'Who…?' She grabbed his sleeve.

'It's alright. It'll be room service.'

Eleanor shook her head. 'It's not room service.'

'I'll check.' He jumped up and went tiptoeing towards the door as another bang sounded.

'Stop,' she said, but she didn't follow him.

He came to the door and looked through the peephole. On the other side, a woman was holding up a police ID.

She knocked again, and shouted through the door, 'Open up. Police.'

Stray looked back to see Eleanor had crept out of the main room. She held back against the wall a few feet behind him.

'It's police,' he mouthed, as the door banged again.

'Police?' Eleanor said.

'I'm going to open.'

'No, wait…'

He opened the door. 'Hello, Officer.'

'Beth Krush, police detective. I'm looking for a Raymond Stray. Is that you?'

'Yes. I don't have any ID, I'm afraid, but I can…' He broke off seeing her stare past him towards Eleanor.

'You.' Disbelief showed in Krush's face, that was drawn, with dark bags under the eyes.

Eleanor just shook her head.

'What are you doing here?' the detective said.

Eleanor's shoulders shook. 'I'm… I don't know. I guess I came home.'

'You came home, but not to see me.'

'I'm sorry, Beth. I just… after everything that happened…'

'*What* happened? Nothing happened. You walked out of our lives for no reason, that's all.'

'It did happen,' Eleanor said. 'It's been five years. How could you not have worked it out? I found out your secret, that's what happened.'

'What secret? I don't have a secret. I never had one.'

They stared at each other.

When neither spoke, Stray said, 'This feels like a family reunion. Should I leave you in peace?'

'No.' Krush grabbed his arm. 'I need you to come with me. Your sister has been murdered. You're a primary suspect. You're coming with me to the station now.'

'It wasn't him,' Eleanor said. 'I trust him. Whatever's going on, he's not guilty, he's a victim. I found him locked up in a housing estate.'

'Which housing estate?'

'It's called Sundial Court.'

Krush's bloodshot eyes dilated. 'What the fuck, Eleanor, are you investigating my case?'

'I was just looking for Daniel.'

'And did you find him?'

'No, but I will. I need more time.'

Krush shook her head. 'Sorry, Eleanor, I'm going to need you to come to the station as well.'

'What?'

'You were found in the same room as the prime suspect in a murder case. You're a potential accessory to the crime.'

'But… I'm police. I told you, I was investigating. He's not a suspect, he's a witness.'

'This isn't your beat. You're supposed to be in London.'

'Are you crazy? I'm your half-sister. You know me.'

'Do I? Come on, let's go. A team of officers are on their way. You'd prefer to come with me, honestly. Those guys can be rough.'

Stray read the look on Eleanor's face before Krush did. He'd seen it already the night before, it was the look of somebody about to run for their lives, blindly, with no direction, just forwards, just running.

'Wait,' he cried, a moment too late.

Eleanor shoved past Krush in the doorway and went sprinting down the corridor.

'Hey!' Krush started to chase after her, but she glanced back at Stray as he came out of the door and took a step in the opposite direction. 'You!' she called after him. 'Stop! Ah shit.'

She came back and grabbed hold of him. At the end of the corridor, the fire door slammed shut behind Eleanor. She was gone.

54

In the back seat of the car, Stray watched as Krush drove through the morning traffic. He was surprised to notice a silver party hat and a tinsel boa on the passenger seat.

'Your sister is suffering from paranoia,' he said. 'I've seen similar cases before.'

'*Half*-sister,' Krush said. She glanced at him in the rear-view mirror. 'What are you, Eleanor's doctor?'

'Unofficially.'

'Well, officially you're the prime suspect in a murder case, so I'd ask you to keep quiet. Anything you say can be used as evidence, *et cetera*.'

She put on the radio. A song by The Beatles was playing. She turned it off.

'You're upset because she abandoned you,' Stray said.

'Are you analysing me now? Please don't.'

'I'm not analysing you; I just think you should understand what happened five years ago. Why she left you.'

'She's crazy, that's why.'

The car came to a stop in a line of traffic at the lights. Krush drummed impatiently on the wheel.

'I think you need to know,' Stray said. 'Your sister believes the police are corrupt, she thinks there's a big conspiracy with the criminal world. She thinks you're a part of it.'

'She has no reason to.'

'In fact, she does. She found stolen money from a crime scene hidden at your place.'

'What?' Krush turned to look at him over the back of her seat.

'It was part of some haul taken during a drugs bust at the docks. Fifty grand was missing. Eleanor found the money and returned it anonymously. She never told anybody. She transferred to London as soon as she could after that.'

'That's a lie,' Krush said.

The lights had turned to green and the cars in front were pulling out. Staring into the past, Krush didn't notice the green light until the driver behind them beeped his horn.

'Ah, shit.' The car stalled as she released the clutch too fast. 'What am I doing?'

'I know you didn't take that money,' Stray said. 'But Eleanor believes it's true. That's what counts.'

'You're saying she imagined the whole thing?' The car started and Krush pulled out as the lights turned amber.

'No. I'm saying she really did find the money and returned it, but I think you were set up. That case really happened, didn't it, five years ago? The drugs bust, the missing cash?'

'Maybe… I remember something like that, but it turned out to be an accounting error. Someone put the wrong number in the wrong box.'

Stray sat forward, warming to the game. 'I think it really happened. Somebody framed you. Eleanor found the cash and gave it back. Then the accountants covered it up.'

'Somebody framed *me*? Why?'

'It's not about you. It's about Eleanor. Someone's manipulating her. They've been doing it for a long time.'

'Shut up a minute, I have to get this straight in my head…'

'There's more you need to hear. Eleanor's been receiving phone calls. An anonymous weirdo calls her up in the middle of the night and threatens her.'

'Who?'

'Eleanor thinks it's connected to this criminal gang she was tracking in London. She thinks corrupt police are involved. She found some stuff in her office back in London.'

'Maybe she's right. Could that be–?'

'No. Someone wants her to believe there's a giant conspiracy.'

'Why?'

'To alienate her from everybody. A way of controlling her. Some people get off on that – manipulation.'

'I think you're bullshitting. You're trying to buy time, or to get in my head, because you murdered your sister, and you think you can get away with it.' She steered into the police station car park. 'We're home. This is the end of the road for you.'

'But, Eleanor–'

'Don't talk about my sister. She can find me if she wants to. If she doesn't want to… I lost her once before. I grieved her already.'

Krush parked at the far end of the car park. In the entrance to the station, some officers were watching. She released her seat belt.

'But, please, listen to me,' Stray said.

'I'll listen to you in the interview room upstairs. You can tell me all about your sister. What was her name? Alison.'

'There's a way you can find out,' he said. 'If I'm telling the truth, you can verify for yourself.'

A fierce wind blew through the car when Krush opened the door, catching her blonde hair. She wasn't as attractive as her half-sister, but she must have been more academic. He wondered about the tensions between them.

'Come on.' Krush climbed out and went around to the back door where Stray was locked in.

He allowed himself to be pulled out into the cold. 'The man who calls Eleanor, you can find out who he is.'

'How?'

'She bought a new phone yesterday, a burner, she just got it. She only had two calls. One was a guy called Trevor who works at the station in London. The other was her boss, he got the number from Trevor and phoned her not long after. That was all. Later that night, the secret person called. How did he get the number? Either he's Trevor, or her boss, or he got the number from one of them. Ring them, find out who they gave it to.'

'Bullshit. If it was that simple, Eleanor would've done it herself.'

A tall, broad officer came striding across the car park towards them. 'Krush!' he shouted. 'What did you do? You were supposed to wait for backup.'

'No,' Stray whispered. 'Paranoiacs don't want their delusions to be broken. It's how they order the world. It gives them a sense of meaning. Without the delusion, it's worse, they have no meaning at all. Their mind falls apart. They'll fight for their delusions. I've seen it.'

Krush took a breath of the freezing wind and wiped the blown hair out of her eyes. 'Stop talking now. I don't believe a word you say.'

55

Eleanor was halfway across the city before she stopped running and dropped to her knees, exhausted. The sound of the phone still played in her mind – an insistent, relentless ringing. It was too much, and Beth... loneliness emanated from her half-sister, Eleanor couldn't bear to see her. She'd aged in the five years since they last met. The abandonment had corroded her. She couldn't let herself stop to think of the past, the mistakes and missed chances; she'd fall apart entirely. The only way forwards was to keep running, stay one step ahead of whatever was behind her, the voice, the net of killers and corrupt police, and wasted love.

Stray had given her a name: Carl Rank. It wasn't much to go on, just a name. "Violent compulsions," he'd said. "In and out of mental institutions." It could be a fit. He had a connection to Stray, and an issue with violence. If she could check online... but she'd lost her laptop, and she'd thrown the phone away last night. She'd left Daniel's car at the hotel. If she kept this up, she'd end up homeless like Stray. All she had was her bag, some money, and her ID. It was enough, just.

She bought another mobile phone, a sandwich, and a coffee. She looked up psychiatric institutions in the North West and found an NHS mental health centre in Liverpool. She dropped the sandwich, ran out of the café, and crossed the city. Running was taking over. She found it hard to slow down now. Her feet wanted to break into a sprint every time she got out of a chair.

At the NHS centre, she showed her police ID and asked about patient records. The woman in charge of the files seemed half asleep, but she sparked to life when Eleanor mentioned the name Carl Rank.

'Oh, Carl, yeah he's been through a bunch of times.'

'Is he here now?'

'No. Haven't seen him in a while actually. Let me check...' She typed something into her computer and scanned a few pages. 'Last time was almost a year ago. He's doing better it seems.'

'OK, could I...'

'The thing about Carl is it's all in his head. He's not really violent, he's just afraid he might do something. He brings himself here because he's sure he's going to hurt someone. But he really doesn't want to. He cut off all his family and friends because he was afraid he'd do something terrible to them. But he never did. He's a gentle soul, skinny, he wouldn't hurt a fly.'

'He never hurt anybody up to now?'

'No. Well, not that I know of. He's not in trouble, is he, Detective? Honestly, he's like a lamb when you know him.'

'Do you have an address for Carl?'

'Let me see... the last address he left was... Sundial Court, number 23.'

'Sundial Court?' Eleanor leaned over the desk. 'Can I see?'

The woman pursed her lips as she swivelled the screen around. 'There you go. Sundial Court.'

Sundial, the word was soothing cruelty, a node where all her frenzied anxieties met. It all connected – everything. Daniel, the murders, Stray, the corruption, the voices, the estate. It was all real, exhilarating, horrifying. She only had to put her finger on the spot.

'Is there a problem?' the woman said.

'That's one of the most dangerous estates in the country. Do you think someone like Carl should be living there?'

'Detective, if you're suggesting we're at fault, I can only say our powers are limited. We can't just wave a magic wand…'

'Thank you, you've been helpful.' She ran out into the rain.

56

On the other side of a two-way mirror, Stray was slouched alone at the table of the interview room. He stared at the wall.

'The bastard's guilty as hell,' Carmichael said. 'I just a got phone call from the Greater Manchester police. They found a woman dead this morning. Lydia Hargreaves. Turns out she used to work for this piece of shit.'

Krush looked through the glass. 'Does it fit the pattern? Her eyes…?'

'We're waiting for them to send through the files but, no, I don't think so. She fell out of a window. Could be a suicide.'

'Like the clown. It does fit. Somehow, there's a connection.'

'Don't overthink things,' Carmichael said. 'The important thing is he's the killer. You get the confession out of him, or I will.'

'It's just…'

How could she explain? Eleanor trusted this doctor, for some reason. Based on what Stray had said in the car, he knew her sister well. Maybe they were friends. Krush hadn't told anyone that Eleanor was at the hotel. Why not?

She must have hesitated too long; Carmichael said, 'Do you want someone else to do the interview?'

'No. I'll go in now.'

She filled a plastic cup with water before she entered the interview room. Stray didn't look up when she sat down in front of him.

'Here.' She pushed the cup across the table.

'Thank you.' He stared at the cup but didn't touch it.

'I want you to listen to something.' She took out a recorder and set it between them.

Stray was calm. A bad sign. She pressed play on the device.

A woman's voice came out of the speaker: "Emergency services. How can I help you?"

A man replied, "She's dead. Oh, God. She's dead. What do I do? What do I do?"

Krush pressed stop. She studied Stray's face for a reaction, but he was looking at the water with fascination.

'Was it you who made that call?' she asked.

'It sounded like me.'

'You don't know?'

'I don't remember making the call. But it was my voice. I believe it must have been me.'

'Dr Stray, do you know what that phone call was about?'

'Evidently, I'd just discovered the body of my sister. I was in a state of shock, as you can imagine.'

'What did you do after you put the phone down?'

'I haven't a clue.'

Krush glanced at the mirror. Stray's answers were too glib. Carmichael would be tightening his fists now; she knew the way he watched, he'd be ready to hang this guy.

Stray blinked at the reflection of light on the surface of the water. 'All I remember,' he said, 'is waking up in the homeless shelter. Apparently, I'd been lying in the middle of the street. There was a bump on my head. I must have passed out and fallen down.'

'Why did you pass out?'

'Shock. Exhaustion. Hunger. I'm homeless. I'd hardly eaten in days. Finding Alison like that… it was too much.'

'You don't seem shocked. You seem calm, given the circumstances.'

'This?' For the first time, he looked up and held her eye. 'This is a shell. When you've lived rough, you grow a shell. My shell is so thick, I can't come out from inside it.'

Krush held the eye contact. It was difficult to read this man. She could see the truth in most suspects' faces, she only had to read it aloud to them. Their eyes shone when they heard it, they couldn't keep the relief from showing. *Thank God*, they thought; she read it in their lips, *Thank God, I don't have to pretend anymore. She knows, she knows everything.* But nothing showed in Stray's face except an aura of suffering. She wanted to trust him. The feeling was dangerous. Eleanor had trusted him; Eleanor was crazy.

'Tell me about Alison,' she said.

Stray picked up the water and drank it in a single gulp like he was dying of thirst. Yes, she thought, she had found the way inside: Alison. His shell would break.

'Alison.' He wiped his lips. 'She was… she was… good. She was a good person.'

Krush said nothing. She had to resist the urge to sit forward as she sensed herself close to the edge of something.

'You already know,' Stray said, 'I'm not good. I'm an addict. I admit it. I'd do anything for the drug, and I have done. I've stolen and lied and cheated and used people I loved. I never wanted to hurt Alison, she was the last relative I had alive. I only ever visited her when I was desperate. I'd come to her house and try to look presentable, and I'd beg for money. She was so warmhearted, she always helped. But recently, she made a new friend at the university, I don't know who. This new friend told her she should stop helping me. The friend was right, of course, whoever he is.

'Last time I went to Alison for help, she refused. She was different; she was firm. I waited until she was in work, then I broke into her house. I knew where her stuff was

202

kept. I pawned her laptop, some jewellery, I can't remember what else. I got what I wanted. But there was something wrong with that fix. Maybe the dealer cut it with something; maybe it was too strong. It messed me up worse than ever. For days, I couldn't move. I just lay and vomited and wanted to die.'

'That was the last time you saw her?'

'No. The last time I saw her, she was sitting in the corner of her kitchen. Dead. Her hands covered her eyes like she was ashamed of something. I couldn't understand. I pulled the hands away… and…' Tears glistened through the weathered pathways of his face. He didn't dry them.

'It's alright. I know what happened next.'

'So, you believe me?'

'I didn't say that.'

'Listen, Detective.' He sat forwards. 'I think maybe the person behind this was a patient of mine. As you'll know, my practice ended after a court case. We were shut down. Rightly so. My partner's in prison now, but I never faced charges. I was given immunity in return–'

'I'm familiar with your back story,' Krush said.

'I think one of those patients, one of those who were abused, maybe they're out for revenge. Maybe that's why Alison was killed. I can't think of any other reason. She was innocent. She was kind. She had no enemies; she never could have.'

Stray's green irises, surrounded by bloody filaments, were bright with intent and calculation. Krush pulled back on the other side of the table, resisting his implied cooperation.

'It's our job to solve the case,' she said. 'Not yours.'

'Of course. I only meant, I could write up a list of those patients' names, if I can remember.'

Krush glanced at the mirror. Carmichael would say this was just a ploy to buy time.

'Who's behind there?' Stray said.

She took out a pen and paper and slid them across the table. 'Write your list. You have ten minutes.'

She got up and left the interview room.

57

Eleanor went back for the Datsun that was parked outside the hotel, but she didn't dare go upstairs. They might have left somebody to watch for her. Of course they had. They were watching now; how else had Beth found her? She shook the fear off and drove out of the city centre. The new mobile phone was beside her on the passenger seat. She hadn't given the number to anybody. There was no way it should ring, but she couldn't help glancing across to make sure it was silent.

Everything led back to Sundial Court. She steered around the bend of the entrance driveway, back into the grey circle where the rain filled the potholes and saturated the ashy debris of bonfires. She parked outside number 23, Carl Rank's last known address, and lowered the window to check the front of the house through the rain. It was still intact, unlike the house on the left. The front yard was a mess, filled with bin bags and junk. She looked around. There was nobody to be seen in the street, but she felt them watching.

She got out of the car and walked slowly up the drive, looking around for any movement. The curtains were closed downstairs. There were no lights on inside. Dread tightened her stomach into a knot so that she could hardly stand. Daniel had brought her here, he'd been in this estate, and he'd brought Stray here. It all led to this door, painted white, with an inlay of frosted glass, really the most banal of doors.

She rang the doorbell and was amazed at how trivial it sounded, a pleasant chime that echoed through the house. Somebody moved inside. She braced, ready to set off sprinting, but she knew she wouldn't this time; she had to find the end, or she'd lose her mind. If she kept running, she'd end up like Stray, homeless on a street corner, alone, without any belongings; every shred of identity discarded so that the voice, when it called, would find nobody.

The door opened to reveal a grill blocking the way inside. The man who looked out was not at all like she'd expected. He was skinny and had long brown hair that reached down his back over a dressing gown. He peered out through the bars of the grill and adjusted his glasses.

'Do I know you?' he said.

'Detective Eleanor Rose.' She showed her ID. 'I'm looking for a Carl Rank.'

'That's me.'

She stared at him. The threads that she'd felt closing together, joining to a final point, now released with a sigh. It didn't feel right, his face didn't fit.

'Can I talk to you for a second?' she said.

'What about?'

A smell came leaking out through the grill. Beneath a layer of stale cigarette smoke and damp, there was something else, just a touch of something rancid, and a sickly-sweet chemical odour.

'It's a case I'm working on,' she said.

'What?' He seemed not only short-sighted but also hard of hearing as he frowned, turning one ear towards her.

'It's for a case,' she said.

'Oh, a case.'

'Can we talk without this grill between us?'

'This?' He fingered the bars of the grill. 'It's for your safety, Detective. I have a disorder. Violent impulses. I'm afraid to hurt people. I shut myself in here to keep the world safe.'

'Are you feeling a violent impulse now?'

He adjusted his glasses and blushed. 'You're safe out there.'

Eleanor looked over the top of his neatly combed hair trying to see inside. It was dark. A door on the left was closed. She sniffed and caught a trace of rotten meat, hidden beneath the sweet chemical smell that she identified as artificial lavender. She felt Daniel nearby. She had to get inside.

'I'd like to come in and talk to you,' she said. 'If that's alright?'

'Are you sure?'

'Yes, I'm sure.'

'Alright.' He took out a key and unlocked the grill. 'Please, come in.' He moved back along the hall giving her plenty of space.

'Thanks.' Eleanor stepped into a dim interior. The carpet smelled of lavender cleaning product. The rancid trace was buried beneath it, almost undetectable.

'Shall we sit in the living room?' he said. 'It's safe in there. I make sure there's nothing that could be a weapon – no knives, nothing.'

'It sounds cosy, sure.'

The living room was practically empty. A couch and a chair under plastic dust covers faced the closed curtains. He opened them now, letting grey, rainy light into the room. There was a grill over the window, just like the door. The scent of lavender was strong.

'You sit there.' Carl pointed to the couch. 'I'll sit over here.'

When she sat down, he moved his chair to the opposite corner of the room and perched on the edge of it.

'Have you been cleaning?' Eleanor said.

'What? Oh, yeah, I like to keep things nice.'

'You're sort of far away. We won't be able to hear each other.'

'It's safer like this.'

'Really, I think…'

He raised his voice. 'It's OK, I'll shout.'

'Alright.' She looked around the grey, empty space. This was hopeless. She was no closer to the meaning at all. There was a horrible absence on the other side of this smell... if the pieces didn't fit together; the voice, Daniel's disappearance, Lydia Hargreaves' suicide, all the mistakes of her own making... it had to fit together, it had to, or the world might cease.

'What's this about?' Carl shouted.

'First of all, a police officer called Daniel Reynolds. Have you ever met him?'

Carl turned his ear towards her. 'Can you speak louder?'

'Daniel Reynolds,' she shouted. 'A police officer. He was on this estate. Did you meet him?'

'Never heard of him, sorry.'

She shook off a feeling of futility. 'Alright. Second question: a psychiatrist called Raymond Stray. You were his patient.'

Something changed in Carl's face. He sat up straight and stroked his smooth hair.

'You do know him,' Eleanor said.

'The doctor.' Carl stood up.

Frightened, Eleanor jumped up as well. They stared at each other across the room.

'Dr Stray,' Carl said. 'He helped me a lot when I was younger.'

'That's good. Can you tell me–'

'I have something of the doctor's. I'll show you.'

He moved forwards and Eleanor instinctively edged away.

'That's alright,' she said. 'I just want to talk.'

'It'll only take a minute.' He ran out of the room.

She heard him go up the stairs. In the room above, his feet moved and stopped. Something heavy shifted, perhaps a wardrobe. Eleanor tiptoed out of the room. With no idea what she was looking for, she opened the first door she came to along the hall. It was an empty space with no furniture, just a window behind closed curtains, and that smell of lavender cleaning fluid. She went back into the hall and listened at the foot of the stairs. There was no sound from up there. *What is he doing?*

She kept going along the hall. The next door disclosed a bathroom that was so clean, it might have never been used. Carl was evidently a neat freak... but there was something else, something concealed beneath the obsessive cleaning, a residue of decay. She followed the barest whiff of rotting meat to a small kitchen at the end of the house.

She stopped to listen for Carl, but the house was silent. It was as if he'd forgotten she was downstairs. Her throat was tightening. She feared another anxiety attack, and could only think of Stray's words. *Listen to my voice. Breathe...* She tiptoed across the kitchen to a set of cupboards and opened them slowly, one by one, trying not to make a sound. They were all empty. She checked in the drawers and shelves, but there was nothing. It seemed nobody lived here. She came to the fridge and felt an overwhelming desire to turn away.

Breathe. Stray's voice echoed at the back of her mind. *Breathe.* She opened the door of the fridge. Somebody stared back at her. Not somebody, just a stare. A pair of eyeballs were set on a dish on the top shelf. Blue. Daniel's eyes. With that tiny dot in the corner of his left iris. She could never fail to recognize his gaze, even after these five years. Streetlamps reflected on snow.

'What are you doing?' Carl said behind her.

She tried to turn but something closed around her neck. She looked down to find a rope looped beneath her chin. She grabbed at it as it tightened, cutting off the air. She screamed but couldn't make a sound.

58

Carmichael was waiting for Krush outside the door of the interview room.

'What the hell was that?' he said.

'The suspect offered to write a list of his former patients. It might come in useful. Give him ten minutes.'

'He's playing you, for Christ's sake. It's obvious. He's a psychologist. That's his job. He knows how to twist people's minds.'

'Sure,' Krush said. 'Which would make him a useful asset in solving the case, if he's not guilty.'

'He's guilty. Who the hell else would kill her? She wasn't harming anyone. You know the rule. It's always the husband. If there is no husband, it's the dad. If there is no dad…'

'How far does this rule stretch?'

'I'm one inch away from pulling you off this job, Krush.'

'Why?'

'Something's got to you. It's because Eleanor came back, isn't it? You're not focused. It makes sense, I get it. After all these years…' Carmichael smiled.

The prick.

'I don't care about Eleanor,' she said. 'I moved on. I'm an only child.'

'Her boss called me, you know, yesterday. He's worried about her. He heard she was back in Liverpool. He rang me to ask if I'd seen her.'

Half-turned to walk away, Krush froze. 'Her boss rang you? And did he… I don't know, did he have a phone number for her?'

Carmichael frowned. 'Why do you ask? You want to ring her? I don't think that's a good idea.'

'No… I guess you're right.' She stepped away, keeping her face neutral. 'I need to get something from my office. I'll be back in ten minutes when the suspect is finished.' She went out into the corridor before he could stop her.

'Watch yourself, Krush,' he called after her. 'One more slip-up, and I'll have someone else take over this case.'

She turned the corner and ran down the stairs to the basement. In the Socialist Republic of Filing Cabinets, Marvin was eating a sandwich with his feet up on the desk.

'I'm hard at work,' he said with his mouth full. 'Honestly.'

'Marvin, you remember a case, around five years ago, big drugs bust on the docks, bunch of cash was seized, some of it went missing…'

He nodded and swallowed what he was eating. 'Sure. But it turned up again. They said someone made a mistake in accounts.'

'That's the one. Do you know who signed off on that case?'

'Want me to check? I'll drop it by your office later.'

She looked outside the room, but the corridor was empty. She closed the door over. 'Can you do it now? I'm in a rush.'

He eyed the closed door, her obvious panic. 'Is something wrong?'

'No. I just need to check. It's probably nothing.'

'Alright.' He sat down at a computer and clicked through some files. 'Here it is.'

'You got it?' She hunched over his deck, magnetized.

'Carmichael signed it off.'

'Carmichael.' She rubbed her eyes. 'I need to think.'

'You know the money was all there in the end? Strange business. Fifty grand was missing, but then it wasn't. I was actually one of the officers who did the final count. It was all there, honestly. There was no theft, in the end.'

'There was no theft, you're right. You're right.' She opened the door and peeped out into the corridor. It was empty, just like before.

'Are you sure everything's alright?' he said.

'I'm not sure about anything. Do me a favour. Don't tell anyone we had this conversation.'

'Solidarity.' He raised a fist.

She ran out of the room and back up the stairs.

59

When Krush came back upstairs, she found Scott with Carmichael, looking through the two-way mirror. On the other side of the glass, the suspect was leaned forwards at the desk, writing. She wanted to scream in Carmichael's face what he'd done, how he'd pushed Eleanor away, how he'd broken their family… but she couldn't. She needed to find out why, she needed more time, it would have to wait.

Biting down her rage, she pointed at Scott. 'What's he doing here?'

Carmichael grinned, but the smile was forced. 'There's a connection to the goddamned estate, isn't there? Your suspect was attacked by a homeless guy who ended up dead in one of those shitty houses. I thought we should get the local expert in.'

'Hi,' Scott said.

'No,' Krush said. 'You're trying to control me. It's what you do. You want to control everyone.'

'You're treading on thin ice, Krush,' Carmichael said.

'I'm going in to talk to the suspect now. On my own. You can watch if you want.' She turned away before he could argue, and entered the room.

Stray looked up. 'I've got a list here. There are twelve names. I put down everything I could remember: what they look like, where they're from, what age they should be now, roughly.'

Krush snatched the list and scanned the lines of wavering handwriting. 'OK. This is a start. Why did you draw a circle around this name, Carl Rank?'

'I told Eleanor about him. She might have gone to look for him. If so, well, he could be dangerous…'

She saw Eleanor in the hotel room, pushing past her, running away down the corridor. The fire door slamming shut. It was too late. She should have gone after her, she should have stayed with her, but she'd let her escape.

'You sent Eleanor after a suspect?' she shouted.

'I didn't send her anywhere. Your half-sister does as she pleases. She is a police officer, by the way.'

'And this man, this Carl Rank?'

'He suffers from violent thoughts. He fantasizes about hurting people.'

'Jesus Christ, and you sent Eleanor to him…?'

'Detective, please, calm down. Carl has never actually hurt anybody, to my knowledge. They're just fantasies. He controls them–'

'Don't go anywhere. I have to check this out.' She stormed out of the room.

Outside, Carmichael was waiting with his hands on his hips. 'He's playing you, Krush, he's manipulating you. Don't you see?'

'Shut up a minute.'

'He's using Eleanor against you. He knows she's your sister. It's a way to get under your skin.'

'Maybe. Maybe not. I have to check these names. Don't do anything until I get back.' She ran to the door, where she stopped and look back to point at Scott. 'And send him back to his estate. He's just getting in the way here.'

She sprinted down the hall and up the stairs to her office. Along the way, another officer stuck his head out of a doorway and said something that she didn't hear. In her office, she closed the door and sat down at her computer.

'Carl Rank... Carl Rank...' She typed the name into a browser. It wasn't a common name; something might come up on social media. She found a LinkedIn account for a computer programmer in Liverpool called Carl Rank and clicked with a rush of adrenaline. There was a thumbnail profile picture that she clicked on to resize. As soon as she saw him, with his long brown hair that reached down his back, she knew him: he'd been at the karaoke party on the estate.

'Oh, Christ.' She ran out of the office. For a moment she considered telling Carmichael, but he'd only insist she took Scott with her. *It would slow everything down, and anyway, fuck Carmichael, given what he's done...* She hadn't decided yet how to deal with him, but she would do something. She'd have his job, one way or another, when this case was over; when she'd found Eleanor and explained it all.

A blast of wind and rain hit her when she burst into the car park, but she didn't care. She climbed into her car and looked back upwards once at the empty windows of the police station. Carmichael might be watching; he'd be wondering where she was headed. *Let him wonder, the bastard.*

60

Stray tried to compose his face as the door opened and two men entered the interview room. The first was Carmichael, the chief, whom he'd met before. The second was a stranger, and yet he felt a spark of recognition, or perhaps he was just exhausted, sleep-deprived, and hungry. He had been trapped in this room for over an hour now.

Carmichael pulled out a chair. 'We're going to do things differently.'

Stray ignored him. He turned to the other man who sat down next to the chief. 'Have we met?'

The man looked at him vacantly but didn't respond.

'This is Scott,' Carmichael said. 'He's assisting me.'

'Scott…' He turned the name over in his memory. 'I feel like I know you from somewhere.'

'I don't think so,' Scott said.

'Look at this.' Carmichael took out a newspaper and placed it on the table in front of him. 'Today's news. I want you to read it.'

Stray picked up the newspaper, the *Liverpool Echo*. The front page was dominated by a picture of his sister. She looked young, and happy. The journalists had found a good image, and he was glad. The headline said, "UNIVERSITY LECTURER SLAIN". Below, in a smaller heading, he read, "FORMER PSYCHIATRIST SOUGHT BY POLICE". There was a picture of him underneath. *Bloody hell, where did they get that one?* Ten years younger, he had a full head of hair and a black beard.

He skimmed the brief paragraph on the front page and turned to page two where it continued. 'Should I read the whole thing? It's quite long?'

'Is that your only reaction?' Carmichael said. 'That's your goddamn sister.'

Stray was about to put the newspaper down when something caught his eye. The name Vincent Dreyer would always jump out at him. It still frightened him; he still dreamed about Vincent. One of the last paragraphs on page two said, "Stray's former associate, the disgraced therapist Vincent Dreyer, was released from prison two years ago…"

'What?' He jumped out of his seat.

'Hey, sit down!' Carmichael grabbed his shoulders and pushed him back forcefully. He snatched the newspaper out of his hands. 'Alright, enough of this.'

'Wait… I need to read that. It's about Vincent.'

'We're here to talk about Alison. Remember Alison? She was your sister…'

'You don't understand…' he stuttered. 'Vincent was supposed to be in prison. He was given a twenty-year sentence. They let him out already. Why…?'

'Stop trying to change the subject. Your mind games won't work with me. I'm not a woman like Krush.'

Stray covered his face with his hands. 'Oh, God. It's Vincent, it's been Vincent all along. I thought it had to be one of our old patients, but of course not. How could I be so stupid?'

'Shut up!' Carmichael swept the table clear of paper and pens and empty plastic cups. 'You need to start cooperating now, pal, or things are going to get a lot worse for you.'

Stray sat up straight, he took a breath to calm himself, and stared into the narrow eyes of the police chief. 'I'll say this carefully, so you won't misunderstand. Your colleague, Beth Krush, and her half-sister Eleanor, whom I believe you also know, are in terrible danger. You need to call Krush now and tell her. Is she in the station somewhere?'

'She left. She drove away. She can't help you now. You have to deal with me, so stop stalling.'

'She left? Oh, Jesus. Call her. Call her now.'

'What are you talking about?'

'Chief Inspector, you have to call your officer right now and tell her to come back.'

'What?' Carmichael's bluster faded. 'You're trying to mess with me…' He turned to look at Scott who stayed silent. 'I won't–'

'I'm trying to help you,' Stray said. 'Call her. Call her now and I promise I'll cooperate fully. I know who the killer is, I can explain everything, but there's no time. Krush is in danger.'

Carmichael took out his phone and stared at it. 'This is insane. I can't believe I'm doing this.' He dialled the number and put the phone to his ear.

'Oh, thank God, thank you, I promise you won't regret it.'

In the strained silence, he heard the quiet ringing from Carmichael's phone. It rang and rang, but Krush didn't answer. Stray looked again at Scott, trying to pin down where he remembered him from, but Scott's face was like a pencil drawing – he hardly resembled anybody at all. The chief inspector hung up and lowered the phone. He wiped sweat from his brow.

'She's not answering. I'll try again in a minute. But first, you tell me the story. If you're bullshitting me, I swear…'

'Vincent and I were partners. We were successful for a while; even had some celebrities among our clients, whom I can't name for confidentiality reasons. Vincent was an expert at hypnosis. He could do anything with it. He'd cure smoking, alcoholism, arachnophobia, you name it. He was obsessed, he kept pushing the limits, experimenting, trying to do more. In the end, he was like a magician, he could get people to do whatever he wanted, and they'd never even know.'

'Go on…' Carmichael said.

'That's when I started to worry. I spoke to him about it more than once, but he assured me he'd never use it unethically. For a while, I had no idea what he was up to. He was good at it; he never left a trace. But he was abusing our patients in all kinds of ways. Under hypnosis, he'd get them to transfer money to his account, and forget they'd done it. He'd get women to sleep with him and then erase the memory. Just for fun, he'd have his patients steal things and bring them to him. He started to think he was a kind of god…

'As soon as I found out, I called the police. I had no choice. I testified against him. That was the end of our friendship. Even before the verdict, he let me know that he despised me, and he'd ruin me. I guess I hoped that prison would give him time to reflect. Maybe, by the time he got out, he would have understood why I did what I had to do. But he's out already. More than ten years before the sentence should have ended.'

'Let me see this.' Carmichael picked up the newspaper from the floor. He turned to Scott. 'What do you think? Do you think he's bullshitting us?'

Scott blinked. 'Me? I don't know anything.'

'Do you have any proof this Vincent of yours is the killer?' Carmichael said.

'Yes. That homeless man who attacked me in the homeless shelter... He was acting under hypnosis. After the attack, he went back to the estate and threw himself out of a window.'

'So what?'

'That's how Vincent was caught out the first time. There was one woman he was abusing... he'd hypnotized her so many times, he kept wiping her memory of what he'd done to her. Finally something broke in her mind. She jumped out of a window.'

'That doesn't prove anything.' Sweat was pouring from Carmichael's brow. He wiped it again, but his sleeve was already damp.

'It's hypnosis, I'm telling you. Vincent probably sent that homeless guy to kill my sister. Then he sent him after me. The poor bastard would have no memory of what he'd done or why. But the guilt was still there. He must have known he'd done something awful, something unspeakable, only he couldn't think what it was. This is the kind of thing that makes a man jump out of a window. Vincent's dangerous. He can hypnotize people without them ever suspecting.'

'How do I know you're not the hypnotist?' Carmichael said. 'I feel like you're trying to hypnotize me right now.'

'Because I'm trying to help two police officers whose lives are in danger. Vincent only helps himself. He wants revenge. He's ruthless...'

'Shit!' Carmichael threw the newspaper down. 'Shit. Shit. Shit. I'll try Krush again.' He took out his phone and put it to his ear.

Stray fixated on the phone, willing her to answer at the other end. Scott stared into space.

'No answer.' Carmichael lowered the phone. 'Alright, I'm not saying I believe you, but just in case, just to be safe, this is what I'll do. I'll talk to somebody upstairs and get them to track down Krush. And I'll have them look into this Vincent character. But after that, no more excuses or diversions. We're going to talk about you. You're still the prime suspect in a murder case.'

'Very well.'

'Don't move.' Carmichael wiped sweat from his brow and went out of the room.

As soon as he was gone, Stray felt his shoulders release. 'Thank Christ. I really didn't think he'd listen to me.'

Scott stood up.

'What are you doing?' Stray said. He stared as the policeman came slowly around the side of the table. 'Wait… please…'

'You shouldn't have said his name.' Scott grabbed his hand as he tried to pull back.

'I do know you,' Stray said. 'You were a patient of mine, weren't you. Where did Vincent find you?'

He tried to wriggle away but the chair fell backwards. He clattered onto the floor with Scott on top of him. The man's blank face was electrified by frenzy; neither a smile nor a snarl, his mouth was caught in a rigid mask. They wrestled on the ground, but Scott was stronger.

'Please…' Stray spluttered. 'I remember you now. It was after your mother died; you were suffering from grief… you couldn't carry on living… You…'

'I'm nobody.' Scott closed his hands around Stray's throat. 'And neither are you.'

61

Krush drove through a mist of confusion and loss, and the rain. Sundial Court emerged out of the grey traffic like an apparition. She steered around the curved driveway with an acrid taste like punch on her tongue. She knew this would be the last time. She parked outside the house of the everlasting karaoke party. Looking out from the passenger seat she saw the front window was lit, silhouetted figures moved inside. What song would they be singing? *Yesterday.*

She climbed out of the car and felt exhausted. Her body was burning fuel too fast, it held nothing back; her blood sensed the end of the race, she would cross the finish line and collapse. She followed the path again – the way a familiar dream plays over in a loop – through the concrete front garden between the bin bags, up to the door with its frosted glass, where she knocked.

Davey opened the door. 'Oh. You came back. I didn't expect…'

'I'm looking for Carl. Is he in there? I need to talk to him.' She looked over his shoulder and noticed several faces peeping around the edge of the living room door, further along the hall. They ducked out of sight when they saw her looking.

'Carl?' Davey said.

'Carl Rank. He was here last night, in the kitchen. I spoke to him.'

'Oh well, if you spoke to him. But, Detective, I don't think Carl's here. He doesn't come every day.'

'Can I come inside anyway? I'll look for him myself.'

Davey peered back along the hall. 'Can we keep singing? Everyone's having fun.'

'Sure.'

Davey let her in and set off ahead of her down the hall. 'It's OK,' he shouted to the others. 'We don't have to turn it off.'

At that moment, a woman was singing a strange song that Krush didn't recognize. It didn't sound like The Beatles, but it must be. She entered the living room and couldn't believe what she was looking at: Eleanor held the microphone in a loose grip, it almost fell out of her hand. She sang quietly, with concentrated emotion. She wore a gold party hat and a tinsel boa.

'Eleanor?' she said.

'I read the news today, oh boy,' Eleanor sang. She turned around and saw her. The microphone dropped from her hand. The song stopped midway through a verse.

Everything went silent. Some of the others booed. Davey knelt and picked up the microphone.

'Beth,' her sister said. 'What are you doing here?'

'I was… I was looking for someone. Why are you…?'

Melinda stared angrily at her. They were all angry. She heard Davey's eighty-year-old father whisper, 'What does that tramp want?'

The young girl from the red room ran out of the door and up the stairs.

Out of a daze, Eleanor grabbed her hand. 'Thank God you're here. Let's talk in the kitchen.'

It was quieter at the back of the house, with the door shut. The music from the living room vibrated in the floorboards. Several women in there were chanting *I'm Only Sleeping*.

'This is crazy…' Krush said. 'I never thought… Do you know these people?' She reached for Eleanor, without knowing why, from instinct, need, or memory, or just from loneliness.

Eleanor skipped back out of reach.

'They're my friends,' Eleanor said. 'You're not going to stop the party, are you? They'll all worried you'll turn the music off.'

'No. I just… what the fuck? Eleanor, what are you doing here?'

'You should leave.' Eleanor backed away. Her tinsel boa came loose, showing a dark welt around her neck.

'What's that?' Krush said.

'What?' She looked down and noticed the welt. 'Oh. I don't know.' She stroked the sore place on her neck. 'Where did that come from?'

'I need to understand,' Krush said. 'How does this fit together? I know it must make sense somehow, but it just keeps getting weirder.'

'You should leave,' Eleanor said.

'Are you alright? You seem… different. Earlier today, when you went running out of that hotel room… I thought I'd never see you again.'

'I'm fine. I just want to sing my song. Everyone sings. Everyone gets a turn.'

'I know what happened five years ago,' Krush said. 'When you left. You thought I'd stolen that cash from the crime scene. Daniel as well. But…'

'Daniel.' The name was like a chime. Eleanor's distracted face came to life. She turned her back and looked for something on the kitchen worktop.

'I know what you think happened,' Krush said. 'But it wasn't like that. We were framed. We…'

Eleanor turned back to face her. She was holding a small, sharp knife.

'What are you doing?' Krush said.

'You shouldn't be here.' Eleanor stuck the knife into her sister's side. It sank between two ribs. 'You don't belong here.'

'I…' She sank to the tiled floor as all the air was sucked out of her body. Agony shivered through her. She lifted one hand and saw it soaked in blood.

She tried to speak. 'Carmichael... it was Carmichael...'
But no sound came out.

Everything went black. In the darkness, knowledge flooded with the whooshing pain: Eleanor had always hated her. Even when they were children, she must have always wanted to stab a knife into her. She must have been jealous of the newcomer to the family who had her own living father. All these years in between, so much wasted time, so much loneliness – they could have done this back at the beginning. Two young girls, hatred, and a knife.

Far away, somebody sang, 'Please don't wake me... I'm only sleeping...'

62

It took three officers to drag Scott off him. Over the sound of shouts and scuffling feet, Stray curled into a ball on the floor and tried to protect himself as they moved around him.

'Get him out!' somebody cried.

Stray opened one eye and saw Scott being wrestled out of the interview room, screaming like a child, all the while his stare fixated on Stray's face. The door closed over him.

'Jesus Christ.' Carmichael set the fallen chair upright. 'Everything's falling apart.'

Even with Scott out of the room, Stray couldn't bring himself to move from the corner. The instinct to protect himself was overpowering. Carmichael knelt and pulled his hands away from covering his face.

'Come on,' the chief investigator said. 'Get up.'

'I can't. I feel sick.'

'Are you hurt? Nothing looks broken. You're OK. I'll get someone to check you over.'

'No. Don't leave me,' Stray said. 'Call Krush, please. Did you manage to find her?'

'She still won't answer the phone, but they traced the GPS of her car. She's at that fucking estate. Where else?'

'At the estate?' Stray said. 'It's too late then.'

'I keep trying to ring but she doesn't pick up. I've left two messages.'

'Call her again.'

'There's no point.'

'Call her again.'

'Shit.' Carmichael sighed. 'Get up and sit in that chair. Stop cowering like a baby. I'm sorry you got attacked in here, alright? That shouldn't have happened. There'll be an internal investigation. I had no idea Scott was like that.'

'You might have noticed, Krush didn't trust him.' Stray shook all over as he climbed to his feet. With one hand over the welts in his neck where Scott's fingers had pressed, he took hold of the chair and let himself fall into it.

'I'll drive over to the estate now,' Carmichael said. 'If she's there, I'll find her.'

'Take me with you,' Stray said.

'No chance.'

'You must realize now, I'm innocent. It was Vincent who sent that man to kill me.'

'I don't realize anything.'

'If he's got Krush, or Eleanor, I'm the only one who can help. I know how to stop Vincent, that's why he wants me dead. I'm the only one who can undo the hypnosis. If you run into him, he'll click his fingers and have you under his spell.'

'Bullshit.' Carmichael headed towards the door, but he hesitated, looking back at the mess, the blood on the wall.

Stray sensed doubt in him. 'Please, call her one more time, before you do anything.'

'Ah shit.' Carmichael rang the number and put the phone to his ear.

Stray stopped breathing, focused on the ringing. It stopped. Carmichael's fat face showed astonishment.

'Hello…?' he said. 'What?'

Stray leaned forward across the table trying to hear, but the voice at the other end was too quiet, just a hint of electronic noise.

'Is Beth there?' Carmichael asked whomever it was. 'Beth Krush? This is her number. I'd like to speak to Beth Krush.'

Those words were too naked. Stray felt horror seep through him, and he could only let it soak into his bones.

'What?' Carmichael said into the phone. 'What did you say?'

Stray no longer even wanted to hear.

'Hold on a second,' Carmichael said. He turned to Stray. 'They want to speak to you.'

'To me?'

It was too late to refuse. Carmichael set the phone on the table between them and switched it to speaker. Stray stared at the device.

'Say something,' Carmichael hissed.

He cleared his throat, and said, 'This is Raymond Stray.'

A little girl giggled. The sound came through the phone so clearly, it was as if she was in the room with them.

'Who is this?' Stray said.

The unseen girl giggled again.

'Is Beth there?' he said. 'Can I speak to her, please?'

The girl kept giggling, as if he had told a joke. 'Why do you lie?' she said.

'What?'

'You're such a big, fat liar.'

'Listen, I need you to…' He stopped as the phone line went dead.

Carmichael snatched it up. 'What was that?'

'Oh, God.' Stray covered his face with his hands. 'Beth Krush is dead.'

'Come on, get up.' Carmichael grabbed him by the shoulders and heaved him to his feet. 'I'll take you to the estate. But you're going in handcuffs. I still don't trust you.'

'What if you're the hypnotist,' Carmichael said as he was attaching the handcuffs, 'and now I'm taking you to the estate, exactly where you want to be?'

'If I was going to hypnotize you, we'd already be in the car on the way, instead of wasting time while a police officer's life is in danger.'

Carmichael fastened the cuffs tightly. 'I swear to God, if you're fucking with me, I'll go outside the law. I'll shoot you in the head, bury you somewhere, cover the whole thing up. Nobody will miss you. You've got no friends left to come looking for you.'

63

They drove to the estate in a squad car through sleet and a tunnel of wind, Stray in the back seat with his hands cuffed behind his back.

Halfway there, a phone call came through to say that Scott had committed suicide in the temporary holding cell where they'd left him. As soon as he'd hung up, Carmichael let out a scream of rage.

'Please, calm down,' Stray said. 'I need you to be calm. We're both in great danger.'

'Go fuck yourself. How many more are going to die today? This is all your fault. It all started when you turned up.'

'Please, Chief Inspector, you're a man who needs to control things. You enjoy controlling people, don't you? You're powerful, successful. You're used to everyone doing whatever you want. But you fear chaos. When you lose the sense of control, your identity starts to fall apart. There's a darkness beneath the control.'

'You'd better shut up now or I swear to God I'll crash this car and kill both of us. I don't care anymore.'

'You stalked Eleanor, didn't you?'

'What…? Where did you get that from? You're insane.' Carmichael's voice had become a squeak.

'You couldn't help yourself,' Stray said. 'You knew it was wrong. You knew you'd get caught one day. You framed Beth and Daniel to separate Eleanor from her loved ones. You needed her to be isolated, defenceless.'

'Not another word. This is your last warning. Not another word.' He was breathing heavily, his face was dark red.

'Those creepy phone calls; you got off on frightening her, manipulating her emotions. Creating a fiction in her mind and possessing it.'

'I love her!' Carmichael roared. 'Alright? I love her. She'd never touch me, I'm old and fat and disgusting. It was only Daniel she had eyes for. A weakling. A softie, with his long hair; more like a woman than a man.'

'And now he's dead,' Stray said.

'How do you know that?'

'Daniel must have been onto Vincent. It's to do with the estate. Somehow, he learned about the hypnosis. He thought I might be able to help, so he tracked me down in the homeless shelter and brought me to the estate. He realized Scott was hypnotized. He started to think others could be. He didn't trust anybody. That's why he contacted Eleanor…'

'You're the hypnotist,' Carmichael said. 'You're infecting my mind with your words. I don't know what's true or false anymore. I don't know what's happening.'

'You do know. We're–'

'Stop talking. Please, just stop talking, let me think for myself. This is the estate. We're here now. I don't care anymore.'

He drove too fast around the curved entranceway. Stray sat up in his seat, twisting his handcuffed arms, sending waves of pain up the shoulder. He saw the grey houses, the burned cars, the piled bin bags, and felt that he was returning home.

'There's Krush's car,' Carmichael said. He slammed the brakes.

'Don't park next to it,' Stray said. 'They'll see us coming. Park further along and we'll walk.'

'I thought I told you to shut up.' He parked the car alongside Krush's and pulled Stray out of the back, sending another jolt of pain through his arms.

Loud music was playing through the windows of the house up ahead. 'Sounds like a party,' Carmichael said. 'What the hell?'

'Can you take these cuffs off me, please?'

'No.' Carmichael set off up the path. 'Let's get this over with.'

'Wait, wait, wait.' Stray hurried after him. 'We have to be careful.' He crept to the living room window. 'There's a gap in the curtains. Look inside.' He put his eye to the gap, blinking at the bright light inside.

'What do you see?' Carmichael said.

'Nine or ten people… wearing party hats… they're singing karaoke.'

'Do you see Krush?'

'No. But… wait… I recognize some of these people… there's Carl. Shit.'

'Alright,' Carmichael said. 'Enough. I'm going inside.'

'Wait, wait. I recognize some of the others as well. Shit, are they all patients of mine? Patients of Vincent's… he must have brought them here to live.'

'Why would he do that?'

'Slaves for him. He could make them do whatever he wanted. Give him their money, cook food for him, buy him clothes… they could steal for him, kill for him… and he'd have his revenge. Some of these are the patients who testified against him at the trial.'

'It's just a karaoke party,' Carmichael said. He walked up to the front door and rang the bell.

'What are you doing? Stop!'

The music turned off inside. Stray cowered back against the wall, but Carmichael straightened himself. He took out his police ID and held it up. Footsteps came along the hall. The door opened.

'What the fuck?' Carmichael said.

Stray, crouched beneath the window ledge, looked up to see Eleanor in the doorway.

'You came!' she said. 'We weren't sure if you got the invitation.'

Carmichael took a step backwards. 'Eleanor… what are you doing here?'

'Waiting for you, of course.' She took out a gun and raised it to his head. 'You're a bad man, Carmichael.'

'No!' Stray's scream was torn from his throat by the deafening blast of the gun.

Carmichael's head released a plume of blood. His body tumbled and collapsed. Stray didn't see it land, he was already running in the opposite direction.

'Catch him!' Eleanor shouted.

He heard several people sprint out of the house, but he didn't dare to look. With his hands cuffed behind his back, he had no balance, he slipped in the puddles as he sprinted. They were close behind him; he heard their laughter. He slipped and started to fly forwards, but hands grabbed hold of him from behind and held him upright. More hands reached around his neck, his shoulders, his legs. They dragged him backwards.

'Come on,' Eleanor said. 'The doctor's waiting for you.'

64

He found himself in a room that was painted entirely red: red ceiling, red floors, red walls. He was manhandled into a chair with his cuffed hands pulled tightly behind his back. Two women, former patients of his whose names he couldn't recall, secured his legs to the chair with duct tape.

'Why are you doing this?' he said.

They hummed a bland melody but didn't answer.

'Where's Vincent? He's here, isn't he? I want to speak to him.'

'Of course I'm here.'

And there he was. Prison had changed him, but the same painful intensity showed in his dark eyes. Vincent's hair was silver now; it was long, he had tied it back. His beard had turned white. It was long and thick. He wore an expensive suit; he had always had a taste for fine clothes. The other patients scurried out of the room, leaving just the two old friends, along with Eleanor, who held the gun aimed at Stray's head. From the other room, the music started up again. A pop song that he didn't recognize.

'Hello again, Raymond.' His former partner closed the door over. Painted red, it completed the unity of the room.

'You're insane,' Stray said.

'Sane and insane are just two strands out of many in the mind, you know that. All I do is comb the strands, weave them, and unweave them.'

'You've enslaved those people.'

'I've given them a better life than they ever dreamed of. Their fears are cured. They know pleasure now. They're free.'

'Eleanor!' he called to her, but she didn't hear. Her face was empty.

'Leave her in peace,' Vincent said. 'She's complete now. I've relieved her of her anxieties. You would never have been able to. You're weak, Raymond.'

He came closer and kneeled until they were face to face.

'You must have known,' Vincent said. 'You must have known this would happen. You betrayed me. Betrayal always ends with suffering.'

'I betrayed our patients when I let you treat them. If I'd known… but I did know; on some level, I always knew. I just didn't want to because we were friends. After all we'd been through, it felt meaningful, friendship. But I was a fool. You used me the same way you used everybody else.'

'Yes, you were useful to me once. It's important to be useful, Raymond. If we're not useful to anybody, who will love us?'

'I've got along fine without love.'

'No, you're not fine at all. You're a mess. Think I don't know how you've been living? You're sick, Raymond. You're a sick animal that needs putting down.'

He opened his jacket, revealing an expensive silk lining, salmon-pink, and took a cloth bag out of the inner pocket.

'What's that?' Stray said.

'You'll see. Oh, you'll see everything. That's what this room is for. It's a hall of mirrors.' He took out a scalpel, a set of callipers, and a kind of metal spoon from the bag.

Stray bellowed and writhed in the chair, but his legs were fastened tightly, he couldn't budge the duct tape. 'Eleanor!' he shouted. 'It's me! You know me, don't you?'

Vincent chuckled. 'She knows you. I explained everything to her before you got here. She knows exactly who you are, and what she has to do.' He put on a pair of surgeon's gloves. 'Eleanor, hold his face.'

'What are you doing?'

Eleanor pocketed the gun. She walked around slowly until she was standing behind the chair, then grabbed his face below the jaw with both hands.

'Eleanor, please… it's me… you remember…'

Vincent put a hand over his mouth. 'Shush, Raymond, shush now. Hold still, this might hurt a bit. It'll be worse if you struggle.'

While Eleanor held his head in place, he watched, horrified, as Vincent raised the callipers. One gloved hand took firm grip of the lids of his left eye, prising them apart, while the other attached the callipers, locking the eye open. Stray gritted his teeth, but the lids on that eye couldn't close, he could only watch as Vincent took the spoon. Slowly, gently, it slipped under the rim of his defenceless eyeball, into the socket.

'Careful does it,' Vincent said.

The metal spoon was cold and smooth, it slid inside easily. He felt the eyeball loosening. With a burst of pain, it popped free and fell into the palm of Vincent's hand, cupped against his cheek.

'No! Please!' Stray cried.

A scattering of sparks and colour, he tried to blink his eyes but the left one couldn't close. For a moment, he thought it was blinded, then the world came back into focus. The most incredible thing: he was looking out from the gloved hand with his left eye, while his right eye was in place. The two pictures didn't match. His brain tried to merge them, but the left eye was sideways. A horrible vertigo passed through his spine with a spike of nausea. He screamed.

He closed his right eye and let the left eye orient itself. The world flipped around and straightened. Vincent lifted his gloved hand until the eyeball was staring directly into his own.

'Yes, Raymond, there you are. There's your soul. You can't really see a man's soul until his eye is extracted from the body. Everything else, all this, blood and skin and bone, trash, it gets in the way. Let me show you.'

He rotated the ball, slowly, sending waves of pain along the cord that still connected it to his brain, until Stray was able to see his own face, the disgusting hole and the optic nerve hanging out.

'See?' Vincent said. 'You've left that behind now. We just need to remove the other one.'

'Please…' He tried to speak but his words were lost in a spray of vomit.

'Oh, Jesus. Don't be sick on your eyeball, you'll spoil the view.' He let the eye dangle loosely down Stray's face and released it.

The world spun again. When it righted, he found himself staring into his own lap. Vincent removed the callipers.

'Eleanor,' Stray said. 'Please, help me.'

'She can't hear you,' Vincent said. 'Stop talking, you'll make yourself throw up again. I can't stand mess.'

'Eleanor… Eleanor… Can you hear me? Somewhere, faraway, inside. Do you remember Oslo? The snow. It was freezing cold. You were in love. It was wonderful.'

Vincent took hold of the right eye and opened the lids, forcing the mismatched left and right perspectives to clash together. Stray's brain whirled in agony. He screamed and found no release.

'Oslo,' Eleanor said.

She let go of his head and it dropped forwards.

'What are you doing?' Vincent shouted.

A roar like the sea silenced everything.

Epilogue

Eleanor followed the directions she'd been given through the hospital to her sister's room, but she couldn't go inside. Standing in the hall clutching some flowers and a card, she stared at the closed door. She felt nauseous. The door opened and she jumped back, but it was only a nurse coming out. She saw the edge of a hospital bed and a drip, before the door was closed.

'Is she alright?' Eleanor whispered.

'She's stable, but she's weak.' The nurse looked her up and down. 'Are you a relative?'

'Half-sister.'

'Well then, go inside if you like, but don't wake her.'

'I can't.' She looked at the door and shook her head. 'Could you put these flowers inside for me, please?'

'Why don't you do it yourself?'

'I… I can't.'

'It's alright, she's asleep. You won't disturb her.'

Eleanor pressed the flowers into the nurse's hands. 'Please, you do it. I'm in a rush. I have to run.'

'But…' The nurse looked confused and annoyed, but she took the flowers. 'Are you sure…?'

'Thanks.' Eleanor turned away and hurried along the corridor before the door might open again, disclosing a glimpse of Beth in her hospital bed, fixed with tubes and wires.

It was a relief to get outside into the fresh, cold wind. She headed into the city centre. Liverpool, her home. She had requested a transfer back to Merseyside Police, pending the results of an enquiry into what had happened at the estate. With the deaths of Daniel and Carmichael, and the injury to Krush, the process would drag on, but her version of events had been provisionally accepted, and Stray had explained everything to the investigators. He had won their admiration for his work de-hypnotizing the survivors of the tragedy, and helping them readjust to reality.

Eleanor bought a newspaper and two coffees downstairs then took the lift up to her new flat that overlooked the docks. The extra coffee was for Stray. He was staying in her spare room while he got himself back on his feet. He'd joined a Narcotics Anonymous group, and was looking for work. A vast landscape of cloud loomed through the floor-to-ceiling window along the landing of the top floor. She saw that the entrance to the flat was open. The newspaper fell apart in a cascade of pages.

Inside, everything seemed in place. The living room was neat, just like she'd left it. The kitchen was spotless. Nobody had used it all day. Her bedroom door was open. She went inside and saw immediately her laptop was missing. She had left it open on the desk.

'No…'

She ran to the spare room where Stray was staying. Empty. The new clothes and a few books she'd bought him were gone. He'd even taken the duvet.

'Oh shit. Raymond…'

She sat down on the bed and tried to think. Where would he be? He knew the paths of homelessness better than she could ever imagine. He'd be long gone by now. She froze – *had anything he ever said been true?*

The phone in the hall started to ring.

If you enjoyed this book, please let others know by leaving a quick review on Amazon. Also, if you spot anything untoward in the paperback, get in touch. We strive for the best quality and appreciate reader feedback.

editor@thebookfolks.com

www.thebookfolks.com

More fiction in this series

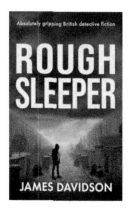

ROUGH SLEEPER
Book 2

Eleanor Rose rejoins the force when a serial killer dubbed
The Binman terrifies Liverpool. He is suffocating his
victims with a refuse sack and discarding their bodies like
trash. Her detective sister, Beth, is confined to hospital
with a serious knife wound and a bad case of insomnia.
Both are determined to catch the murderer. Will they
prevail or succumb to the madness gripping the city?

FREE with Kindle Unlimited and available in paperback!

Other titles of interest

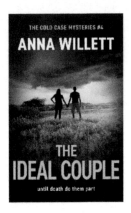

THE IDEAL COUPLE
by Anna Willett

Detective Veronika Pope heads to an old mining town in
Western Australia, tasked with the cold case of a couple
who went missing there some three years previously.
Everyone in the town seems to be hiding something and
she gets few leads. But the more she probes, the more
cracks appear, and if she can avoid falling into one, just
maybe she can get closure for the couple's family.

FREE with Kindle Unlimited and available in paperback!

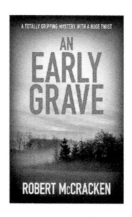

AN EARLY GRAVE
by Robert McCracken

A tough young Detective Inspector encounters a reclusive man who claims he holds the secret to a murder case. But he also has a dangerous agenda. Will DI Tara Grogan take the bait?

FREE with Kindle Unlimited and available in paperback!

Sign up to our mailing list to find out about new releases and special offers!

www.thebookfolks.com